To Tylieanen
Best Wishes
From Plunder To

Cheryl Susan Leonard
7/31/22

McBee Magic: Treasures of Plunder Bay
A Dægbrecan Publishing Book / December 2021

Published by Dægbrecan Publishing

Book design by Nicholas Edward
Cover design and internal artwork by Will Garrett

First Edition N

Library of Congress Control Number: 2021951753

Leonard, C. S.

ISBN 978-1-955810-12-8 (Hardback)

C. S. Leonard

McBee Magic

Treasures of Plunder Bay

Dægbrecan  Publishing

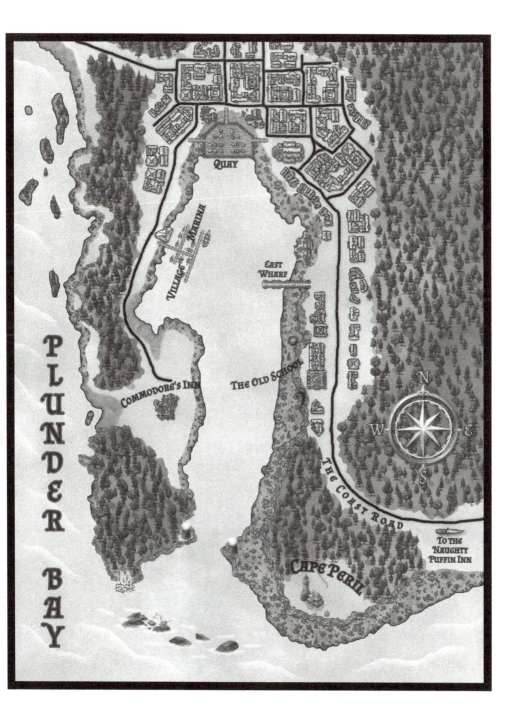

The Magical Languages of Britain, Ireland, France, and the Low Countries

N
nw · ne
W · E
sw · se
S

Norn

Norn & Scots Gaelic

Scots Gaelic

Scots Gaelic

Irish Gaelic

Manx

Old English

Welsh

Cornish

Frisian

Saxon

Frankish

Breton

Gaulish

Old French

Old High German

Occitan

Galician

Asturian

Basque

Gascon

Cisalpine

The Powers

Brewing

Enchanting

Creating

Finding

Realizing

Seeing

Protecting

Conjuring

McBee Magic

Treasures of Plunder Bay

Unwanted Treasure

The old salt-kissed cottage with its towering addition sat shrouded in icy morning fog. Inside its cozy kitchen, Miranda McBee lit the new moon candle and poured boiling water into each of three teapots on the sideboard. As Miss Mew circled between her ankles, she gazed out into the mist clinging to the rocky cliffs along her northern seaside home. She was intent on *seeing* what was happening a half a world away.

Beyond the mist, a two-masted schooner, flying a red banner, lay at anchor in a sunny white-sand cove. A lone figure stood on the quarterdeck scanning the horizon for any sign of other ships. For months, whispers had spread amongst the island bars and alleyways across the Spanish Main—a rumor of some great treasure that would soon be passing through. Those of dark intent kept constant watch, though they were not alone. The precise location and time of the crossing had been methodically charted by powerful forces beyond the imagination of any ordinary brigands. For some, this treasure could buy power and the freedom to dominate—for others, it could end a peaceful way of life.

It was no surprise when the watcher on the schooner saw the topsails of another ship on the horizon. The other ship sailed with a strong westerly wind and was closing fast. It was the warship *Stinger*, a thirty-six-gun frigate, well known in sea lore. As she trimmed her sails to slow, she opened every gunport. There she was, all dressed out for war with not another ship in her sight—for by now, the anchored schooner had vanished in a sudden, low fog bank that rolled in despite the sunny sky.

Then, quite suddenly, another ship appeared—sailing out into the open waters from between the islets to the north. She flew no flag but the banner of a crescent moon. She appeared to be a lightly armed merchant vessel with a swivel on her bow and sixteen gunports. Since her sails were full and she rode high in the water, it would have been no problem to bypass the slowing frigate. Whatever her captain's original intent in the cove, upon seeing the *Stinger*, the moon ship rapidly changed course to cut behind the threat and thus avoided a deadly broadside attack. Even so, the *Stinger* fired two of her portside cannons as she steered about, but the shots fell far in front of the moon ship's bow.

Once safely out of range, the moon ship began the slow task of turning in the wind, then closed back toward the *Stinger*, staying on its windward side, making it almost impossible for the frigate to position her guns for broadside shots at her adversary. As the wind died away to little more than a breeze, the two began a slow-motion dance for the better part of an hour, with the occasional cannon blast from the *Stinger*—as the moon ship strafed the calm, blue sea, firing occasionally from the swivel on her bow. The only real action beyond this feeble play fire on either ship came from aloft as seamen scurried up the rigging of both ships to look out in every direction, searching the waters for the ship they were really waiting in ambush for.

Precisely at high noon, the cloudless blue sky darkened and the water grew choppy, despite the lack of wind. The sails of the two sparring ships went completely slack, and both were lifeless in the water—totally becalmed by the elements. The choppy sea began to spin violently, and a waterspout spun up in their midst, sucking the fog on the water up with it and exposing the schooner. The waterspout grew taller and taller as it moved around the ships, drawing close to the schooner. With incredible energy, the spout sucked all the water out of the northern end of the cove into a great column of swirling water hundreds of feet tall.

The schooner dropped and lay motionless, listing on its port side on the sandy bottom. Those who watched from the other ships stared in fear and amazement at the size and power of the water funnel. Before any had the chance to consider the possibility of all that water crashing down on them, the funnel dropped inside of itself, creating a giant sea swell where it rushed over the exposed coral and starfish, lifting the schooner back to the surface. It occurred to both combatants that they had missed tragedy—they were soggy and adrift, going nowhere, but they were still intact!

As the water returned to the tropical cove and the surface calmed, other anomalies began. As if to foretell the next scene in their pirating adventure, black clouds closed in over the cove, blocking the sun and casting an ominous, dark shadow over the three ships. The crews of the moon ship and the *Stinger* looked on in awe, only to have this phenomenon outdone by an eruption of giant sea bubbles from the center of the cove. Suddenly, the promised treasure ship materialized in front of them, rising with the bubbles. A cheer went up aboard the *Stinger* as the crew hoisted a black flag, displaying her gruesome pirate insignia, and signaling their intent to take the treasure.

It was no matter that in that moment the sight was certainly not what they expected. Instead of one of the great ships, like a Spanish galleon or a British man-o'-war, the crews saw the rotting hull of an ancient cog that surely must have been sucked up from the bottom by the maelstrom. This was not the expected, prized cargo vessel—it was, in fact, a sorry sight. Inexplicable to all who looked on, there was no crew in sight. Water poured from every hole and crevice and the wood of the old boards looked incapable of floating.

If any of the visitors had known deeper sea history, they might have recognized her as the wreckage of the proud cog *Merry Gale*—a friendly trader that sailed among myriad shores from her berth in the Irish Sea for many years, but which went down in a storm over one hundred years ago.

Baffled, but still determined, the *Stinger* lowered a longboat crew of a dozen or so heavily armed ruffians. The ship let off a few shots in challenge to the moon ship, lest she or her crew try to lower their own longboat. The *Stinger's* men rowed hard and fast, laughing loudly, and shouting horrible threats at anyone who could hear them. Once near enough to the sorry-looking cog, they cast their grappling hooks. Every hook they threw found its mark on the old ship's rails, and just as quickly broke away with a chunk of rotted wood. After many tosses and countless curses, they decided to try another approach. They went back to their oars and rowed around and around the *Merry Gale*, peering up into holes and using harpoons to pry away patches of the hull.

At length, they determined there was no treasure to be

had in the barely floating ship, and they turned back toward the *Stinger* with another sinister thought in mind. The moon ship, lazily drifting behind them, would be a prize worth taking. She appeared a sturdy and nimble vessel, sparsely crewed and certainly outgunned. As a pirate rule of thumb, the higher riding and faster the ship, the more valuable the cargo—not mere barrels of rum and crates of dried crop, but precious metals and gems likely pillaged from Mughal traders from distant seas.

The thought of being taken by the *Stinger* was certainly on the minds of those aboard the moon ship. Until now, they had outsailed the frigate and just as they knew they were no match for her guns, they also knew they dare not be boarded by her crew. Since it was obvious no valuables were to be found aboard the wreck of the *Merry Gale*, the crew of the moon ship had no need to deploy their ancient bag of tricks to retrieve the treasure for themselves. Retreat seemed the smartest plan for now, but they were still completely at the mercy of the wind.

The captain of the *Stinger* shook a fist in frustration at the windless sky, and in response got a lightning flash and a loud rumble of thunder. It was at this point that the moon ship became the benefactor of a surprise wind squall. Her captain acted quickly, putting his master seamanship to the test. He let the moon ship's sails run loose with the wind to give the effect of out-of-control confusion. Seeing this, the captain of the *Stinger* believed a storm to be brewing and made great haste to furl and reef the ship's sails, securing them tightly. The pirate captain had no desire to become the next victim of this cursed cove.

When the *Stinger's* sails were secured, the moon ship's captain brought his ship immediately under trim and, with the help of a now moderate southerly wind, she was able to escape and be on her way back to her origin before the frigate could set full sail again and get up to speed after her. After witnessing bizarre natural calamities, absent treasures, and a ship that could seemingly command the winds, the *Stinger*, and her now nearly mutinous crew, slunk out of the harbor. The schooner had slipped away during the maneuverings between the moon ship and the *Stinger*. It was close to sunset when the cove was devoid of all but the still floating, pitiable cog.

At 7:07 p.m., in response to the report of a shipwreck, The Royal East Island Constabulary's patrol boat came upon the wreck of a battered sailing ship. In the deepening light of dusk, the cog—which bore faint letters near the prow that read *Merry Gale*—seemed to barely float above the waterline. The waves in the cove were strangely absent, despite the rough water in the sea beyond the ring of islets. The scene felt eerie to the patrol's crew, unnatural in many ways—and not a shark to be seen near the wreck, which would be expected under normal circumstances. Seeing the sorry condition of the rotting vessel and no survivors in the water, the officers cut their motors and drifted closely enough to carefully climb aboard the vessel.

As the cog was slowly sinking, the officers quickly searched the hold and other compartments, finding corals, gasping fish, and crustaceans in place of crew, cargo, or any modern instruments. They removed some ancient charts, the captain's log, and two small treasures they found packed in a bed of soft kelp in the *Merry Gale's* roundhouse, then hurried off the vessel as the water eddied around their calves. Before the sound of their engines died away completely, the *Merry Gale* slipped silently beneath the waves back to her resting place.

The Broom Falls

At precisely the same moment, Miranda's cell phone rang and the broom in the corner clamored to the kitchen floor. Startled, Miranda dropped a handful of teaspoons she was drying and said aloud to the empty kitchen, "Was that necessary? I already know Penelope is coming." Then she picked up the cell phone and answered yes to most of the odd questions she was being asked. Finally, she said, "I'm sorry, I didn't quite understand, inspector. Are you sure you have the right party? Where are you calling from?"

It wasn't the heavy accent of the caller that was confusing her as much as the message she thought she was hearing. Nevertheless, a few minutes later, the very private Miranda McBee was giving a total stranger directions to Cape Peril cottage—without a clear vision of where things were headed. After the call, Miranda plunked down at the table, leaving the cell phone precariously perched near the sink of dishwater. She stared into her empty teacup, then dumped the leaves onto her saucer and began sloshing them around.

Inspector Pablo Martinez of the Royal East Island Constabulary drove through a light, spring rain, complaining in Spanish to his English-speaking GPS. In time, the inspector groaned and surrendered to technology. This was, after all, his first real look at this strange northern land. It was not what he expected to see.

C. S. Leonard

The Coast Road and miniature fishing villages looked more like postcards or paintings one might see in a gallery, rather than a real place.

A remote, sea-swept corner of North America was the last place the inspector had ever thought he'd willingly find himself, but he was happy to be off that darned airplane and behind the wheel of a vehicle again—even this confounding rental. After more than an hour of driving, the inspector passed the first road signs to the place now known as Plunder Bay.

Beyond the turnoff to the village, the road rose more steeply through the highlands along the rocky coastline. The spring shower was just passing, but a fine mist still fell on his windshield. He slowed to watch for a narrow, unmarked, gravel lane to his right, but he was really thinking about other things. Only a case this important, involving tragedy and death, could have brought him so far from home, and at great personal expense. No one knew he was here. There would be no rewards for what he was doing, just the personal satisfaction of doing the right thing. Unless of course he was found out—then the price would be severe.

He reached a very high point where the road curved inland from the coast. Just as he decided he'd missed the lane, he had to hit his brakes hard to avoid a low-swinging tree branch. There it was—the driveway he'd been looking for. It was more forest floor than gravel, and it wound through a thick mass of evergreens and hardwoods out toward the cliffs.

He came to a clearing and through the misty sunshine the inspector saw Cape Peril lighthouse for the first time. It sat completely alone out on the point near the cliff, very much as he had imagined it would. Surprisingly, it was not the spooky old place of his recent nightmares. From this distance it looked more like a dollhouse cake decorated in white icing beside a spiraling candy cane. The light tower's red spiral matched the cottage's red metal roof. Inspector Martinez thought it looked a good deal bigger than the bungalow he had expected when he heard the word *cottage*.

Adding to the pleasantry of the landscape, the inspector saw a young woman—early twenties, with long, wavy, strawberry-blond hair unloading bags and boxes from her car. He parked, stepped out, and straightened his shoulders. As he approached, he tucked his hat under his left arm and extended his right hand. "Inspector Pablo Martinez of the Royal East Island Constabulary," he said. "You must be Miranda McBee?"

"Oh, no, I'm Penelope McBee," the young woman answered, surprised to see the kind-looking stranger in her driveway. She realized this official-looking man—very dark in his stark-white uniform—was from somewhere far from Plunder Bay. He had broad shoulders and a clean-shaven face. After shaking hands, she explained, "Miranda is my older sister. She lives here. I'm just in for the weekend."

"I see the two of you have already met," said a slender woman walking towards them. She was a few years older than her sister and had honey-blond hair that grazed the top of her shoulders in a wavy lob cut. Most striking were her intense grey eyes. She was supporting a large basket on her left arm. "I'm Miranda McBee," she said, giving her slightly taller kid sister a quick sideways hug around the shoulders with her free arm. "I thought since it was such a gorgeous spring day, the three of us could have our meeting out in the gazebo. The tea is ready, so just follow me, Inspector."

"A most excellent idea," agreed the inspector as he followed both women around the house and across the lawn to a weathered wooden gazebo overlooking the ocean. "I thought that after our conversation on the phone you might think me a lunatic."

"I'm sure the inspector isn't the lunatic here," said Penelope, zipping her jacket. "I think my sister is rushing spring a bit by making us take our tea in the gazebo."

The inspector shuddered a little in the bracing wind and tried to think of something positive to say. "What an astounding view this is." He stepped closer to the edge where he could see the white caps rolling in from the sea, breaking on the rocky beach below. Then feeling a bit lightheaded from the height, he stepped back and was happy to take a seat in the gazebo.

A colorful cloth had been spread on the small table where Miranda had placed a pot of her proprietary-blend tea and a plate of sweet cakes. After a few minutes, and a sip and nibble, the inspector began to feel quite comfortable. Seeing the refreshments hit their mark and their guest more relaxed, Miranda began, "I am quite intrigued by what you had to say on the phone, Inspector. Something about orphans in our family?"

Penelope wished she had been privy to what was going on before she had arrived—but coming home to surprises was nothing new. She'd been away for most of the past four years and had just finished the last semester of her last year at the university. But this was a bit much—orphans in the family, and an inspector from where—the islands? She played it cool and decided to press Miranda for details later.

Despite their obvious curiosity, Miranda and Penelope spent the next hour answering more questions than they asked. The inspector learned that the sisters had been raised in the city but had spent their summers with a great-aunt and -uncle who had lived at the lighthouse. The lighthouse and cottage had been built in 1730 by the family's most famous ancestor, Captain Benjamin McBee, who had come from Scotland. Although the captain had no children, he had plenty of relatives who had been willing to come and keep the light after he was lost in a sea battle with pirates in Plunder Bay.

The house had been in the McBee family for generations. The sisters had inherited the cottage and a small family business from their great-aunt and -uncle. They didn't move in, however, until four years ago when Penelope went off to the university and Miranda took up residence, alone. The lighthouse itself, being privately owned, was never commissioned, but continued to operate until a few decades ago when the government installed two very modern lights, one at each entrance to the bay.

"That's when the lighthouse went dark," Penelope added, gazing up at the structure.

"It could still be saving lives, because the harbor lights do little to keep craft off the deadly reef beyond the bay," said Miranda. "But what's important today is why you're here. Please, tell us your story."

Inspector Martinez felt quite optimistic about this visit and about the story he had to tell. It seemed to him this was the right place and the right time to deliver his request. He took a sip of tea, placed his elbows on the table, folded his hands with his index fingertips lightly pressed together, and began to make his case.

"Early last March, one of my patrols came across a shipwreck. It was a tragic sight. The ship was destroyed, and the crew and any adults aboard were lost. That left me in the care of two orphaned babies—twins, I think. They were the only survivors of the wreck, tucked safely inside the cabin, protected by a bed of kelp."

"How odd," exclaimed Penelope. "But ..."

At that moment, there was a frightful blast of cold air from behind them. It blew things on the table over and sent the wooden wind chimes into a frenzy. Miranda McBee looked at her sister, but Penelope was staring quizzically back toward the house. She looked as though she might be listening for something when the company was joined by a scraggly green parrot who flew into the gazebo and landed on a perch that was obviously his special place.

"Inspector Martinez, let me introduce Blue—the family parrot," said Miranda.

The inspector looked amused by the green bird named Blue.

Penelope explained further, "His full name is Blue Blazes and he's a very old bird who sailed with some very wicked seamen."

"Oh, I see. So does he maldecir ... that is, curse?"

"Not today, I hope," said Miranda.

They all three laughed and the inspector continued with his story, "Before you ask me how this might affect the McBees here at Cape Peril, let me give you the key piece of information. In the wreckage, we discovered some very old sea charts and the captain's log. This lighthouse was to be one of the destinations of that ship."

Miranda and Penelope both raised their eyebrows and looked sideways at one another. Blue let out with a sharp squawk.

"Now, I like a good mystery, but solving this has been most difficult—perhaps because the charts were old and from another century entirely. The names and locations on the chart matched nothing I could find on any map or the internet. I studied the coastline and while I couldn't find the modern-day locations for the old sea chart, I thought Plunder Bay looked similar to the markings on the map. I decided to contact your harbormaster here, a Mr. Jacques d'Eon."

The sisters nodded in unison. Jacques was a longtime friend.

"He was very helpful and explained the renaming of the village. He spoke very highly of the McBee family, their years of keeping the light, and their commitment to safe sailing and to this community. He said he had known you both since childhood and even mentioned you, Miranda, as being exceptional at ... um, what was the word? Ah yes, brewing." He said the last word slowly, rolling the 'r' slightly.

"Tea, not beer," Penelope quickly interjected, as if to protect the family name.

"It is my belief that these twins are McBees, and they belong here with you. In fact, I think I see a family resemblance," he quickly added, running his hand across the top of his cropped, black hair.

"Babies? Twins? Inspector, I think you must be mistaken," said a wide-eyed Penelope. "To the best of my knowledge, we don't have any missing children in our family. That's the kind of thing we'd know about."

"Well, it can't hurt to hear him out, since he's already traveled so far. Please, Inspector, go on with your story," said Miranda.

"To make your decision even harder," he continued, "I do not know the exact cause of the shipwreck that stranded them, but I suspect it was not an accident. They were aboard a very old ship, a cog—not seaworthy in the least. In fact, it sank before we could investigate it further. There had been some weather anomalies observed in the area and there was the lingering smell of gun powder in the air. Someone, somewhere, put these babies on this boat and left them there through a gun battle of some kind. We found no evidence of other ships and there's no telling how long they were adrift. In fact, the cog appeared to be far too old to be any known ship in our lovely marinas—at least not for the last several hundred years."

"A cog, how very odd," puzzled Miranda, as though this was some kind of revelation.

"Mutiny!" screeched the parrot, rising to full height on his perch.

"Shush, Blue," scolded Miranda.

"Mutiny! Bloody Mutiny!" the parrot screeched again.

"Because of the circumstances, I believe en mi corazón—in my heart—these children are in real danger. They need to be protected, as well as raised—you understand? Should you agree to take them, there will be the tricky matter of providing proper papers and the like. Do you think that's something you could manage?"

"I think ... it could be done. But this is something Penelope and I will have to talk about and there are many things to be considered. Still, I feel hopeful we can help you with this problem."

Shortly thereafter, the gathering broke up and the sisters walked the inspector back to his car, then returned to clear the things from the gazebo and talk.

"Miranda, how in the world can you consider taking on a responsibility like this? Remember, I'm not planning to stay long. There's all the work and obligation, to say nothing of what others would say—and then there's the cost. I know I promised to help you get the business on its feet, but this is much more than I bargained for. Now that I have my degree, I'm anxious to go somewhere and start a career. This task you're considering will last a lifetime."

"We'll manage," said Miranda. "I've been *seeing* something like this in our future. It doesn't surprise or frighten me. In many ways, I know the inspector is right. Whether these children are McBees or not, they need us."

No sooner had Miranda spoken these words than Blue ruffled his feathers and flew off, squawking his favorite old vulgarities, along with some they had never heard before.

"What are you going to do about him?" Penelope asked, watching the parrot fly up to the light tower.

"Him? What's the worst he can do, embarrass us in public?"

They looked up at the old bird perched on the handrail of the tower, faintly obscured by the reflection from the windows.

Even though Penelope scoured the internet, made numerous phone calls, and even called an old friend from school who grew up in the islands, she could find no such entity in the world as "The Royal East Island Constabulary." Ten days later, the McBee sisters met again with Inspector Martinez. This time, they were aboard an international ferry somewhere between New England and the Maritimes. His appearance had changed somewhat. He had touches of grey at his temples, and he seemed to have either grown or pasted on a very convincing mustache. He was wearing a worn-out grey cardigan instead of his smart, white uniform, and his shoulders looked stooped. It was as if his whole career had already taken place and he was settling in for retirement. Still, there was something very powerful and charming about his demeanor as he strolled the sunlit deck, pushing a double stroller, and smiling at onlookers.

The exchange of the babies was made shortly before the boat docked. "Have you made progress in getting documents for the children?" he whispered.

"Enough to get them into the country," answered Miranda.

With that, Inspector Martinez of the maybe not-so-real Royal East Island Constabulary bent down and kissed each baby on the top of their pink, bald heads. "I have done my best to cover my trail in the last weeks. You must do the same—and do not try to find me again," he said, winking at Penelope. Then, he joined the throng of disembarking passengers and disappeared.

Now under the protection of the barrenwort necklaces Miranda had woven and the car seats Penelope had rented, the baby girl and boy drifted off to sleep for the ride home. Their names and ages were as much of a mystery as their heritage, but like all babies, they were beautiful to those who had already decided to love them.

The Captain's Wrath

Both sisters were in high spirits as they pulled away from the ferry landing, but it was not to be a happy or peaceful homecoming. This may have been because, in the end, neither of the McBee sisters had discussed their decision to bring the twins to Cape Peril with anyone else. Believing, as Miranda often said, that it's easier to ask for forgiveness than permission.

The closer the McBee sisters got to home that day, the stranger things became. There was distant lightning in the northeast sky—most peculiar for that time of year. The wind was blowing hard, and there were whitecaps on the water. Sea spray and spurts of rain were coming down in a most uncoordinated way. When they stopped at the gas station in Plunder Bay, a filthy-looking seaman in dirty white knee-pants and a red bandana leered at them, leaning against the stucco of the station while scraping under his fingernails with the tip of a dagger. Miranda shouted over to him while pumping the gas, asking if he was on shore leave. In response he spit through black and yellow teeth onto the ground.

The shops on the quay were all closed. Seagulls were diving and swooping menacingly in and out of high perches. More than one hundred of them paraded down the sidewalk, pecking at the closed shop doors as they went, untying mooring lines on the jetties, and trying to carpet bomb the car when it forced them off the road and into the air. In the park, a huge crimson banner the sisters

18

had seen once in a painting waved in the breeze.

As both harbor beacons were shooting yellow beams in spasmodic bursts instead of red and green signal lights, the sisters spotted Jacques d'Eon—the young harbormaster—sitting on the ground beside his pickup truck. Both he and the truck were helplessly ensnared in a thick fishing net that had blown over them. Just beyond where he was entrapped, on the outside of the seawall, two ancient, rotted longboats appeared to be scanning the shoreline. The long oars of both boats moved of their own accord, with no rowers to be seen. Penelope thought it was just a trick of the wind and the water, but Miranda thought otherwise.

When they stopped at the village intersection with the Coast Road, they caught a glimpse of a grizzled seaman in a navy peacoat with one sleeve pinned up. He was watching them and clearly didn't want to be seen, as he ducked quickly behind a delivery truck parked near the intersection. But the reflection of their headlights against his long sword had given his presence away.

When they looked up at the old Plunder Bay School, they saw battlements around the top of the building and numerous cannons pointing down at them in place of the normal gutters. They turned right and drove up the Coast Road towards home, dodging fallen tree branches and loose rocks rolling down the hillside. As they turned the car into the lane at Cape Peril, several coconut carved heads in a bundle were hanging from the mailbox. Their mouths were all sewn shut, but their unblinking glassy eyes seemed to watch them pass.

Finally reaching the cottage, Miranda and Penelope had to stay in the car because the wind was blowing so hard from every direction the doors wouldn't open. By now, the twins were hungry and getting fussy. Penelope looked at Miranda and asked, "Can you cast a spell or something to make this stop?"

"Are you kidding? No one's going to be able to get this under control. We'll have to use old-fashioned ingenuity. Any ideas?"

"Let's back the SUV up against the back porch steps and pop the tailgate. We can crawl out through the back. I'll hand the twins out to you and we'll slip in through the kitchen," suggested Penelope.

"Sounds good. Maybe that way we can avoid getting hit by one of these boomeranging branches."

Miranda backed the car under the porch's long soffit and they managed to safely unload the twins. As they entered the kitchen, they found it wasn't much better inside the house than it had been outside. The life-sized portrait of their ancestor, the renowned Captain Benjamin McBee, that usually hung on the main stair landing, greeted them—propped against the refrigerator door. The tall burly figure with his thick red beard and piercing blue-grey eyes looked intimidating in his dark-blue jacket over a blousy white shirt, clan tartan sash, and light doeskin britches. It didn't help to alleviate the mood that the portraitist had him posing with a basket-hilted broadsword buckled around his waist and across the shoulder.

"Don't give me that hang-the-jib look," said Miranda to the portrait.

"I think we should throw you out in the rain," Penelope suggested.

At that moment, the kitchen windows swung out on their

hinges, and the rain came pelting in at the sisters. Miranda quickly returned the portrait to its proper place in the hall, then began fixing baby food. Penelope used towels to mop up the rainwater, and although the gale raged on—most of it stayed outside. Miss Mew and Seadog were nowhere to be seen and their bowls sat untouched, full of food. All night long, the thunder rolled in and crashed down around them. The joists and rafters of the old cottage moaned, and the walls rumbled.

Despite the raging weather conditions, the two newest members of the Cape Peril family slept very soundly through their first night, but there was no rest for their caregivers. When they awoke in the morning, the electric power was out and the storm still raged. Two days later, the rain and wind stopped suddenly, but thick fog settled in around the cottage. Miranda had to light candles on the breakfast table because the morning sun couldn't penetrate the fog. The baby girl, seemingly overnight, had grown a distinctive single strawberry-pink curl that looped delicately on her forehead. Likewise, the baby boy was showing the beginning of sandy-blond strands.

"It was nice of them to grow a little hair since arriving. I was afraid we wouldn't be able to tell them apart," said Miranda as she sat pureed fruit on the table while holding the baby girl.

Penelope sat down at the table, holding the baby boy, and struggled to get apricots and applesauce onto the spoon and into his mouth before he spit it back out. "I suppose fog is easier to *conjure* and maintain than a raging gale. I wonder what's next?"

Then it happened—a sound so eerily deep and penetrating it sent icy chills down everybody's spines. A few seconds after the first blast died away, they were hit by a second. Both sisters covered the babies' ears, Seadog howled, and the dishes rattled in the cupboard. One of Miranda's favorite teapots vibrated off the shelf and shattered on the floor.

"What in the world is that?!" exclaimed Penelope.

"I think it's the lighthouse foghorn! I've never heard it firsthand before, but I've heard about it. That thing will surely bring the Coast Guard down on us," replied Miranda.

"Great, we'll all be deaf when we're hauled off to jail for kidnapping!" said Penelope, looking in the direction of the hallway's main stair landing.

Soon thereafter, the electricity came back on. The fog continued, but the foghorn stopped. Miss Mew spent the rest of the day out of sight in her basket bed. Seadog lay very flat with his muzzle pressed down on his shaggy front paws, his eyes peering up warily at anyone who walked past him. Miranda and Penelope were on baby duty and took turns catching a little sleep when they could. The twins seemed very content in the newly discovered little pantry off the kitchen that had been converted into a nursery and gated playroom.

A few days later, Penelope decided to risk the fog and make a trip into Plunder Bay for necessities like baby food and diapers. She thought that getting out to the main road might be tricky, but it would probably be clear from there—she was wrong. The little village was encased in the same dense fog as Cape Peril cottage. The streetlights were on and all the boats were still in their moorings. The seagulls were out on their normal patrols, but flying and circling low, dropping down for a tasty morsel here and there before taking flight again. Compared to the previous Sunday, things seemed almost normal again, so Penelope tried to get on with her errands.

Coming out of the co-op, she ran into Jacques d'Eon. He smiled at her and stopped right in her path. It was obvious he wanted to talk.

"Bonjour Miss McBee."

"Hello Jacques." She returned his warm smile and noted his comically formal introduction, considering they were longtime childhood friends.

"Isn't this weather terrible? I've never seen fog that lasted so long, and just when the lobster season is ending, and the lobster pounds need to be filled."

Penelope looked worried as she responded, "Hmm, yes, I hope the weather will improve soon. We need to get the village ready for the tourist season, and after the poor sales we had last summer, we could lose more shops if it isn't a good season this year."

"Strange thing is," said Jacques, "I understand it's clear up the coast and below us."

"So maybe, with some luck, it will clear here today."

"It doesn't seem likely. When I checked the radar about an hour ago, it indicated we're in the clear now, so there's really no explanation for the fog."

Penelope watched his deep brown eyes scan the bay, unable to see the edges of the western cliffside or the tops of the eastern hills, and thought how handsome he looked. "You know, looking around today, there don't seem to be any unusual characters about. But when we came through during the storm the other night, I saw a couple of strangers who I've never seen before."

"Oh ... who? What strangers?" asked Jacques.

"The one that stood out the most was an older man wearing a peacoat with his sleeve pinned up where his arm was missing. He seemed quite menacing."

"Hmm, yes," said the harbormaster knowingly. "That's Old Tom. He's not really a stranger. He doesn't visit here very often, but at ... special times he has been known to show up. Having lived here my whole life, I've run into some very interesting characters, not to mention some weather conditions that are impossible to explain."

"I guess with Miranda and me just coming in for the summers to help my aunt and uncle with the shop on the quay, we missed a lot of the strange goings-on."

"I have to admit, this week has been one to remember!" said Jacques, shaking his head.

"I hope you weren't hurt during the storm the other night. I saw you tangled in a fishing net when we came through. Miranda and I should have stopped to help, but we had our hands full at that moment. I hope you can forgive us?"

"There was no real harm done. That old net seemed to blow out of nowhere, and after a few minutes, another gust of wind blew it away. I tried to find it later, but it had disappeared. This is the only harm I suffered in the storm ..." he pushed up his right shirt sleeve.

Penelope was horrified to see a hideous bruise that covered his forearm. It looked like a writhing purple snake with a grotesque head and forked tongue, spewing yellow bile out of its mouth. She gasped and nearly dropped her bag of supplies. "Oh Jacques, I'm so sorry. Is there anything I can do?"

"No, but I know if there is anything you or your sister

could do, you will. Perhaps this will fade like the nasty bruise it appears to be. If not, I'll live with the consequences. I had no right to discuss my friends' private business with that inspector from the islands, but I swear I didn't say anything bad about your family."

"I know you would never do that, Jacques. We've always been friends. It's quite all right, and the inspector was calling on very important business."

Jacques looked up with a hopeful smile, and he and Penelope locked eyes for a moment.

"Let me help you get all this loaded into your car." He took some of Penelope's bags and opened the tailgate. "I guess you have company at the lighthouse—very young company, I would say?"

"Umm ... yes, we have two children ... well, ... actually babies, staying with us," she stammered.

"Family?" he asked curiously. As far as he knew, the two sisters had no living family.

"Yes ...," she said hesitantly, not knowing yet what the story was going to be to explain the arrival of the twins.

"Will they be living with you?" asked Jacques, puzzled.

"Well ... maybe ..."

"I've been wondering what your plans are now that you've graduated from the university. Will you be staying on in the village permanently?" He was watching her carefully, hoping the answer was yes.

"Perhaps a while—I think. I was planning to stay for the summer to help with the shop on the quay like I always do and then head back to the city ... but now ... well, I think I'll be staying to help with the new arrivals ... for a while, anyway."

Jacques had a hard time keeping a huge smile from

spreading across his face. "I'm glad to hear it. Say, if you're going to be around for a while, you might want to come to the open house at the fire department next week. We're recruiting for volunteers, and I know you've had some emergency medical treatment training. It would be great to have you on the volunteer list. Personally, I really like being able to help out and volunteer my time."

After placing the last of the parcels into the car, she slipped into the driver's seat and fastened her seat belt. "Sure, why not? If I'm going to be staying, it would be great to get involved in the community."

"I'll be seeing more of you then," said Jacques, this time letting the smile have free reign to spread across his face.

Penelope started the engine and gave a little backhanded wave as a slight breeze caught her wavy strawberry-blond hair.

"Well, stay safe!" he called out as she drove away into the fog.

It was a slow and cautious drive back to Cape Peril cottage, and Penelope used the time to think. Jacques had asked her questions that she wasn't fully prepared to answer: *should she stay in Plunder Bay?* She had worked hard to get her business degree and was anxious to get off to the city where jobs were abundant and pay was high. Still, she loved her sister and she owed her a lot. Miranda had sold their parents' house to pay for her university education and moved alone to Cape Peril cottage. At the same age as she was now, twenty-two, Miranda had given up her life and her job to take up making a living with nothing more than an ancient recipe for seafood seasoning and her knowledge of rare herbs, spices, and tea blends. If she stayed in Plunder Bay, she could use her business degree to help Miranda build a thriving shop and internet sales enterprise.

Back at the cottage, she reported to her sister the conversation she'd had with Jacques and some of the questions that came up. She also reported some of the bad news. "The harbor is as fogged in as we are. The boats have not been able to go out all week to check their traps, and it's the last month of the lobster season. There's no activity at the shops on the quay and the village looks like a ghost town, not a tourist in sight. This weather is going to have serious ramifications for people, and that isn't fair. We need a plan to get this nonsense under control."

"I've got a gooseberry pie in the oven for tonight," Miranda answered on a seemingly unrelated subject, but Penelope knew baking and cooking were Miranda's form of brilliant problem solving.

After dinner, the twins were playing on a quilt in the pantry, which was open to the kitchen but blocked by a baby gate. They held the gate to pull themselves up, and sometimes tried to climb over it. Both had full heads of hair that seemed to have appeared over the course of a day. The baby girl still had her pink, strawberry curl that fell daintily onto her forehead, but the rest of her hair was a soft, sandy blond. The baby boy's hair was also decidedly sandy blond.

"Have you noticed how thoughtful the little boy is?" asked Miranda, watching the twins play on the quilt. "And for as quiet as he is, his sister is quite vocal." She was prattling on, talking to him as though he must understand every word she was saying. Wooden clothespins and pan lids were their favorite toys for the moment.

Treasures of Plunder Bay

Seadog had eaten his dinner and fallen asleep with his nose in his empty bowl, just in case someone decided to refill it. Miss Mew sat on her haunches staring up at Blue, who was glaring down at her. All in all, it was a very tranquil scene in the cottage kitchen. Miranda served hot tea and homemade gooseberry pie, and she had made room on the table for a big, heavy book.

From the time Miranda and Penelope were children, visiting Cape Peril cottage and lighthouse each summer, Miranda had taken a keen interest in learning the history and legends of the village and the families that had lived there for many generations. The cottage library was full of books about the history of Plunder Bay. Miranda had become an expert on the McBee family history and everything having to do with the folklore and myths surrounding the McBees and the others who were a part of their lives.

"I've seen that book before," said Penelope. "Are we going to research a solution to this situation?"

"Well, I've already done some research, but I wanted your take too. Here, have a slice of pie and get comfortable."

Penelope refilled her teacup with Miranda's tea blend, *Sip of Sunshine*.

Miranda began, "This is the history of the McBee Clan, going back hundreds of years."

"We're fortunate to have our family history recorded. What a fascinating old book."

"The McBees were a small clan who usually worked for larger clans or noblemen in the Scottish Highlands. The men herded cattle when they weren't fighting in endless, stupid wars. The women stayed close to home to tend the farms and raise the children."

"So back then they were basically farmers, not sailors ... interesting."

"Here's where it gets really interesting," said Miranda. "According to our family history, the McBees' female ancestors had a special gift. They were very much in demand as dairymaids because they were good with the cows, but especially because they were renowned for making excellent cheese and butter. The upshot of their *brewing Power* allowed them to raise their children in the barns with the cattle, sometimes keeping the birth of sons a secret."

"Considering the number of men that died in battle, they had good reason," proclaimed Penelope.

"Exactly. Case in point, Captain Benjamin's father was recruited into the ranks of the pipers at a very young age. The pipers' role was to signal tactical movements to the troops. It's said that the bloodcurdling sound and swirl of the bagpipes boosted morale amongst the troops and intimidated the enemy. They were the bravest of souls and often the first to fall in battle."

"But Captain Benjamin didn't follow in his father's footsteps?" asked Penelope.

"According to the book, our captain was protected by his parents, who kept him hidden for quite a long while— warm and well-fed in the dairy barns—away from danger. When he was fifteen, after his father died in battle during a Jacobite rising, his mother arranged for a Danish sea captain, bound for Sankt Thomas in the Dansk Vestindien, to take him aboard his ship as a cabin boy and teach him the trade."

"Oh—so here is where the sea comes into the picture."

"I guess her motherly instincts told her that he would be

safer at sea than living in the Scottish Highlands. The family history goes on to explain how young Benjamin moved up through the ranks and at a young age, became the skipper of his own merchant ship, and went on to become a wealthy trader."

"And the rest we know from our great-aunt and -uncle's stories," said Penelope.

"Yes, and as you can see, the McBee *protection Power* runs deep in our family, and has made it easier to come up with the two things we need most right now."

"Names and birthdates," added Penelope.

"Exactly!" said Miranda. "The twins are of course both water signs and would have been born on the first day of the new moon last year, that would make it ... a year before last March third, which works out perfectly for Pisces."

"I don't believe it—you did their charts. Astrology! Really Miranda, it would have been more accurate if you had just counted their teeth."

"And of course, they must be McBees. Otherwise, there's no way we can claim their guardianship."

"Well, last March I was still at the university, head buried in business administration coursework. You can't blame them on me. I have witnesses," protested Penelope, only half joking.

"Of course not. They will be the offspring of ... our long-lost brother ... *Aaron.*"

"But we don't have a brother, and everyone knows it."

"That's because he's lost, more specifically lost at sea in a boating accident ... or better still, a shipwreck. I'll find something in the news."

At that, the old green parrot gave a loud guffaw, alighted from his perch, and left his droppings on the clan history book.

"Stick around, Blue, there's more family history to come," chided Miranda, wiping off the book. "Somewhere in this house is a small oil portrait of a man dressed in McBee plaid kilts and holding a bagpipe. Do you remember it?"

"Yes, I remember seeing it, but I don't know where it is now. I believe his name was Peter Magnus McBee, right?" said Penelope. "Auntie showed it to me once or twice."

"Yes, and according to this book, his wife was Cassandra Celeste, and they had a son named Benjamin."

"Our Captain Benjamin McBee?" asked Penelope.

As if in response, the great book suddenly flipped open, and the parrot flew back down and landed on the page documenting the family tree. After what seemed like an exceptionally long while, the old bird uttered one word, "Aye," and left the room by flying through the open kitchen door and up the stairwell to the light tower.

It was decided then, the children were named for the captain's parents, who had protected him and kept him safe. Once the names and birthdates were decided, Miranda went about jumping through hoops and taking advantage of legal loopholes to ultimately acquire a questionable document from a merchant marine captain, stating that the twins had been born aboard a ship with Canadian registry. With the occasional mention of Aaron—a much older brother who neither sister had ever met—Cassandra Celeste McBee and her twin brother Peter Magnus McBee were warmly accepted into the community without question by most, but not all, of Plunder Bay's residents.

Criss-Cross-Applesauce

Growing up at Cape Peril lighthouse was different from life at other cottages around Plunder Bay, but neither of the twins knew that. If there was anything unusual about Peter and Cassandra, their aunts encouraged it.

When the twins and their toys outgrew the kitchen pantry, the search was on for the aunts to find the missing playroom. They remembered playing there when they were little and had visited their great-aunt and -uncle at the cottage. Penelope remembered it being downstairs. Miranda thought it was upstairs. She said you had to push through a wall to find it, while Penelope insisted you had to crawl through a tunnel to get there. Both sisters agreed that if the playroom existed anywhere but their imaginations, it was circular with a large round window and a bright-blue rug. Logic told them that the most likely place to find such a room would be in the lighthouse tower, and they made many trips around the outside looking for the window. They found only a few peepholes visible from outside, but nothing like the window they remembered.

Both had nearly given up, until late one night Miranda thought she saw a light at the bottom of the side wall in her bedroom closet. She got Penelope out of bed and the two of them pushed and pushed against the closet wall until it finally opened into the very room they had been looking for.

"I told you we had to push through a wall to get in," said Miranda.

"There's another way too, I'm certain," Penelope argued. "But either way, someone left the light on, and by the looks of things it will need some cleaning before the kids can use it."

No sooner had the twins been moved into the playroom than the little pantry was made a storage area, and eventually it vanished completely. It wasn't discovered again until nearly two years later when Miranda was looking for a capiz-shell serving tray.

So it was that Peter and Cassandra McBee had a playroom all their own, with a large window onto the world and a soft blue rug. It was a playroom tailored and designed to enhance their unique talents. In time, Cassandra did find another way in and out by climbing into any of the cottage's window seats and crawling through. Everything in the playroom was just their size, for the time being—a tiny table with two chairs, an easel, a bookshelf, an old-fashioned kitchen playset, and a faded, blue and pink polka-dot rocking horse named Pokey. Across from each other in the round room were two humpbacked sea chests that Aunt Penelope painted with their names.

From the big, round window, Peter and Cassandra could look out on familiar surroundings or exotic jungle animals. All they had to do was say, "Window, show me ..." and it appeared. Between their imaginations and the special attributes of the playroom, sometimes they were aboard ships sailing into distant ports, or watching out of the windows of moving trains. Life in the playroom was a never-ending stream of pleasant tales and sometimes rather scary stories.

Like a well-ordered ship, life at Cape Peril cottage was run by bell instead of clock. One bell jingle was wake up, two jingles were breakfast, three called for lunch, four for playtime, five for toy pick up, six for dinner, seven for bath time, and eight meant bedtime. Behavior, when out of hand, was also managed by bell—a tinkling, little silver bell that appeared in thin air, usually when the aunts were out of sight or when the twins were alone in the playroom. Peter and Cassandra soon learned one jingle of *that* bell meant stop what you were doing. Two called to make things right, whether cleaning up a mess or hugging away your sibling's tears. At the third, dreaded ringing of the silver bell, the offender would quite involuntarily be seated on a chair until the little bell disappeared.

Penelope, who had stayed longer than she originally intended, was settling into village life and had joined the volunteer fire and rescue department. She told herself this enabled her to keep watch for any unusual visitors or events in the village, which it did—and it also meant she got to see Jacques on a regular basis. She put her business degree to good use by officially incorporating their little family business and adding an e-commerce component. Miranda and Penelope were now the proud owners and operators of the *McBee Maritime Spice & Tea Trading Company, LLC*. They received orders through the company website and sold their merchandise as before, from their little shop on the quay. *M.M.S.T. Seafood Seasoning* was still the best seller, but the tea blends Miranda produced were becoming popular. During the summers, their shop on the quay was a beehive of activity with tourists seeking specialty items, the regulars shopping for their favorites, and friends dropping in just to chat and visit.

Winters were long and cold at Cape Peril. When the big sandbox in the back yard mysteriously converted to an ice pond, Cassandra and Peter learned to skate, and Christmas was always white at the cottage. In time, the aunts ventured out to the park where the kids could swing and slide and spin under the watchful gaze of Captain Benjamin McBee's statue. There were driftwood fires on the beach below the lighthouse and, of course, wonderful picnics in the old gazebo. Blue and Seadog almost always went along on these outings, while Miss Mew chose to guard her cozy kitchen.

Forever mindful of Inspector Martinez's warning—that the twins were likely in danger due to the suspicious circumstances involving their discovery—the adult McBees kept a close watch. The woven barrenwort chains Miranda made to protect them as babies now hung on their bedposts, and always aware of unseen forces, the sisters provided a constant supply of spells, brews, and amulets to keep them safe. Miranda never failed to heed the whispered warnings in the wind, or the kitchen table messages written in sunlight that came through the wavy-glass windowpanes of the old cottage. As though in response to their roles as a protectors, Miranda and Penelope's *Powers* began to grow stronger and more acute. It was almost perfect, until it wasn't.

When Peter and Cassandra were five, they started school at the grade-school annex—kindergarten through the sixth grade. It was a dreary metal building down by the fish plant. The kindergarten teacher was Mrs. Lucinda

Matthews, and the aunts already knew her from her occasional visits to their shop and other dealings around the village. She was one of those people who always talked to adults about children like the children weren't in the room. Aunt Penelope was worried about the twins starting school. "How will we keep them safe, Miranda?"

"They're going to have to leave the cottage at some point."

"We could homeschool them until they're a little older, to avoid having Mrs. Matthews as their teacher. She and her husband are known to be snobbish and have a malicious streak towards those they consider to be different. The twins might be told anything about themselves, or where they come from, by a teacher with a grudge or a mean moral compass."

However, Cassandra was excited to start school. Her friend Gabrielle would be in the same class, and the two had played together often since Gabrielle's mother, Juliet d'Eon, opened the Mariner's Muffin Shop and Bakery next door to the aunts' shop on the quay. Peter, on the other hand, did not want to go to school for any reason and thought he could learn much more from their library at home.

The first day of school, there were only six boys in the class and Peter didn't know any of them. Cassandra seemed to know everyone already. That first afternoon waiting for the bus, some of the bigger boys were playing bump and crash with backpacks and Peter got scolded by the bus driver along with the others, despite only having been crashed into by accident. From day one, Peter tried hard to talk his aunts into sending Cassandra to school and letting him stay home, but that didn't work.

Peter learned to sit near the window and imagine he was

outside in the harbor looking in on the chaos, noisy kids, and demanding teacher. That way, he'd be able to take in all there was to learn from the bay, the sea, the shore, and everything else that was useful without getting bogged down too much by the commotion or Mrs. Matthews's tone.

The worst part of the day, and the thing that Peter hated most, was when everyone had to sit in a semicircle on the floor where their names were taped to the rug. "Criss-cross-applesauce," Mrs. Matthews would say, and that meant everyone was to go sit down on the floor and cross their legs. Sometimes she had to say criss-cross-applesauce several times, then she would turn the classroom lights off and on two or three times while she growled, "Criss-cross-applesauce!" As soon as her victims were trapped in place, she would keep them sitting there for what seemed like hours. Sometimes she showed them things or read to them while they were seated, but when trapped in place, Peter's brain went back outside, and anything the teacher said was just a blur to him.

In time, Peter and Cassandra learned that Mrs. Matthews encouraged and rewarded the children for tattling about anything and everything, even when they were in the wrong. The twins refused to play at this game with Mrs. Matthews and even declined the special role of "Hall Monitor" when Mrs. Matthews assigned it first to Peter, and later to Cassandra. Peter watched as the teacher's attitude toward his sister turned very ugly and she began being as mean to Cassie as she was to him. It was even worse when one of the parents was in the class as part of the parent volunteer program, because then Mrs. Matthews would show off and find fault with anything

Peter and Cassandra did. It was embarrassing to have everyone in town know you'd had your name added to the yellow—or worse—red, stoplight list on the blackboard.

"Cassie, how can you stand it?" asked Peter one afternoon.

"Mrs. Matthews is mean, but I like seeing my friends," Cassie responded.

Cassandra and Gabrielle got scolded a lot for talking. Mrs. Matthews called them Chatter and Gabby, causing the kids in the class to laugh and taunt them with the same names. One day, Cassandra had to sit on the floor during free time because Mrs. Matthews said she was telling lies.

"You ought to be ashamed of yourself! You lack proper parenting and haven't been taught how to behave."

"B–but I was only telling Gabrielle about what I can see out of my window in the playroom at home. There are whales and ships and sometimes even horses on grassy fields. I really like whales and horses ...," she said with tears in her eyes.

"You did NOT see anything of the sort, little Chatty. And don't go around telling Gabby or the other children any of your lies."

Cassandra hung her head and cried most of the day, which bothered Peter enough to bring it up at the dinner table that night.

"Lying is a pretty serious accusation for a five-year-old," said Aunt Penelope. "Cassie, what did you say?"

Instead of answering, Cassandra's head dropped and her eyes filled with tears again.

"I think she told the girls about the things the playroom window shows us."

"That's it!" said Aunt Penelope. "I'm going to school

tomorrow to give that woman a piece of my mind!"

"And tell Mrs. Matthews what?" replied Miranda, her usual grey eyes flashing green with anger at the injustice of it all.

Peter spent the whole next day at school watching to see if Aunt Penelope showed up. As it turned out, it didn't matter, because Mrs. Matthews wasn't there. As the aunts later found out, her house had experienced a weird power surge the night before that blew out every electrical appliance she owned.

After the first eight weeks, Mrs. Matthews scheduled the standard parent-teacher conference with Miranda and Penelope McBee. They met one day after school as the twins played in a nearby classroom. While the McBee sisters didn't have to sit cross-legged on the floor, they were placed on kindergartener-sized chairs at the snack table while Mrs. Matthews sat in her teacher's chair and talked down to them. Neither had expected to be told that Cassandra and Peter were the most brilliant, creative, or talented students she had ever taught—but neither did they expect, or ever forget, what she actually said to them that dreadful day.

"I'm an educator who believes in being open and direct with parents—or in your case, *legal guardians*, I suppose. I have seen Peter and Cassandra growing up around your shop and they seemed normal enough. Of course, I knew they were being raised up there alone, cut off from the world in that odd old house, but I had no idea of their behavioral problems until they were shown this year at school."

Hiding the wave of shock that went through her like a lightning bolt, Miranda said, "Oh, please go on, Lucinda.

I'm very interested in what you have to say."

Penelope, feeling like she had just been kicked in the stomach, watched Miranda cross her arms and lean back in her little chair. She knew it wasn't an accident that Miranda called the teacher by her first name. Penelope could think of a few other names she'd liked to have called her.

"Well, let's start with Peter. In a word, I would say that he is antisocial. He's absolutely vicious with the other children and he has no friends, Miranda. The other children in the class, even Cody who is twice his size, are afraid of him. When I correct his behavior, he ignores me like he's not even in the room. That's disruptive to the entire class. Worst of all, he shows no remorse for his behavior."

"And what about Cassandra?" Miranda asked.

"Well ... Cassandra, on the other hand, cares about nothing *but* being social. She's disruptive to the class, never stops talking, and she tells terrible fibs to impress the other children. It would be my guess that you have let them watch movies or listen to stories that are inappropriate for children their age. My three children are not allowed to watch or read anything that isn't on the KYCI List—that's the 'Keep Your Children Innocent' list—in case you don't know. Perhaps if you were their actual parents, you would have been more careful in their upbringing and taught them proper values."

At this point, Penelope, who was reeling with shock, found her voice. Sounding very calm and controlled—even though she was furious—she asked, "What about Cassandra and Peter's learning ability, their school progress—are there any test scores?"

"Oh ... they do well enough," Mrs. Matthews said, without really answering the question. "But under the circumstances, I cannot imagine they will do well in the long term. I'm recommending they undergo behavioral testing."

Penelope tried to follow with more questions about the twins' academic status, but Mrs. Matthews cut her off. "For the sake of the children, I think they need a stable home life. I'm sure that would be the best answer. So, just to give you a heads-up—I have asked family protective services to pay you a visit and investigate the home situation."

Miranda McBee stood up, ending the conference. "We will certainly consider everything that you have said here this afternoon. Is there anything else?"

"No, but I do hope we can resolve this problem before we get any further into the school year," replied Lucinda Matthews. She was feeling very pleased with herself.

The McBee sisters drove home to Cape Peril cottage in stunned silence. The aunts were livid with rage, but the backseat passengers were listening, so they kept their feelings to themselves. When the children were in bed, the two sisters lit candles and settled in with mugs of *Stress-Be-Gone* tea. Penelope started with a question she thought her sister could answer, "What happened today? Why does she hate our children? For that matter, I would say she hates the whole McBee family—what nonsense she spoke! All that about behavioral testing, and protective services, and that stupid 'Keep Your Children Innocent' list—more like 'Keep Your Children Ignorant' list. Miranda, what do you think—what's behind this?"

"What makes you think Lucinda Briggs Matthews

doesn't like our children, or us?" Miranda chuckled. "Just because she said our kids were misfits, our house was weird, and we might be child abductors—doesn't mean she doesn't like us."

Then, in a more serious tone, she continued. "But seriously, it runs deep, dangerously so. Lucinda's ancestors were wreckers who hold a very dark place in the village history, and to this day her brother is quite a scoundrel. I'm not sure of her motives, but they *are* malicious, I'm sure."

"Should we pull the children out of school, and what are we going to do when the authorities come to check us out?"

"I've got some ideas, and I don't give a fig about the authorities. We'll wait a little longer to see how things evolve, and about school ... well, a waxing moon is never a good time for life-changing decisions."

For the next few days, things at school were about the same for Peter and Cassandra. At home, they were getting very special treatment. The aunts felt pressured to make some important decisions. However, as things turned out it wasn't necessary for the adults to get involved. The twins, with the help of their friends, resolved matters on their own—in a most peculiar way.

The first Monday in November, Mrs. Matthews and her students were having a particularly bad day. They had started the day on the floor, with a long lecture from the teacher about how displeased she was with the whole class. Cassandra's neck got stiff trying to look up at the hair in her teacher's nose, but she knew better than to look away. Later, Mrs. Matthews took up several of their color-by-number sheets and threw them in the trash because they were messy. Peter got caught drawing a picture of a ship when he was supposed to be practicing his letters, and for a while he had to stand in the corner. Fortunately, he could see out of the window during his punishment. Free play got canceled for the rest of the week, and Paige threw up after lunch. They didn't get to go to music because the fourth grade had program rehearsal, and for some reason Gabrielle pulled both Caitlyns' hair.

"That's ENOUGH!" bellowed Mrs. Matthews. "CRISS-CROSS-APPLESAUCE!" There was something in her voice that sent her students scurrying to the floor at her first command. She turned out the classroom lights and announced that they would stay in their places, in the dark, until bus time. Everyone sat, their legs crossed, in perfect silence that seemed to last forever. Mrs. Matthews stood over them looking very angry, her hands on her hips.

It was actually Gabrielle who started all the trouble when she said, "Mrs. Matthews, why don't you sit down?"

"I'm fine. I need to stand right here and watch all of you."

"No, I mean why don't you ever sit down here on the floor with us and cross your legs?" said Gabrielle. "It really hurts after a long time."

"That's enough, Gabrielle. Be quiet or you will sit again tomorrow."

At that threat, Gabrielle uncrossed her legs and got up on her knees. Peter, Virginia, Madelyn, Josh, Cassandra, and one of the Caitlyns did the same.

"Criss-cross-applesauce!" said Mrs. Matthews, and much to her surprise, the kindergarteners repeated her words back to her.

"Criss-cross-applesauce," said the children. "Criss-cross-applesauce. Criss-cross-applesauce."

"I said CRISS-CROSS-APPLESAUCE, CLASS!"

screamed the frustrated teacher.

"Criss-cross-applesauce. Criss-cross-applesauce. Criss-cross-applesauce. Criss-cross-applesauce." The students were now chanting, some were clapping their hands in rhythm, and all were giggling, delighted with their new game. Everyone got up on their knees and the chanting got louder. One of them stood all the way up—it might have been Cassandra or Peter—but no one ever knew for sure, and soon everyone was standing. The chant got louder and lost its playful tone.

"Criss-cross-applesauce! Criss-cross-applesauce! Criss-cross-applesauce!" went the chant, as a dozen of the kindergarteners held hands and circled around the startled teacher.

Had another adult walked into the room at that moment, they would have seen Mrs. Matthews's surprised look turn to panic, and then to horror—but nobody came. Nobody came, and the rhythmic chanting went on until, as if pushed down hard by the shoulders, Mrs. Matthews sank to the floor. Her bony legs crossed involuntarily, and though she struggled to uncross them and stand back up, she was frozen in place—speechless. The chanting stopped and most of the children doubled over around her in gales of laughter. Peter, who could tell time and knew the buses were due at any moment, grabbed Cassandra by the hand and they went to get their coats. As the bus numbers were called, the kindergarten class left in small groups, many still laughing.

After the buses left, Mrs. Simpson, the fourth-grade teacher, found Mrs. Matthews. Several people tried to help her up and find out what had happened, but Lucinda Matthews could only babble incoherently, and so the ambulance was called. The muscle-relaxer medications her doctor prescribed finally loosened up her body, but they completely muddled her mind. She never could tell the story the same way twice after she was released from the behavioral testing and treatment center where she'd been sent to recover. Although Peter and Cassandra were never actually pronounced guilty for the criss-cross-applesauce incident, some in the school thought Peter and Cassandra McBee had instigated it.

As Lucinda Matthews had threatened, a Ms. Dubby from family protective services scheduled a meeting to inspect life at Cape Peril cottage. She arrived early one morning and looked very official in a business suit, her dark hair pulled up into a tight bun as she carried a briefcase and a camera. A smiling Penelope gave her a tour of the old cottage with its shiny lemon-waxed hardwood floors and gabled window seats.

"What a charming old house, bigger on the inside than it looks from the outside," their guest remarked when her tour ended in the kitchen. "I understand it has been in the McBee family for many generations?"

"Yes, with Peter and Cassandra the latest generation to live here," Miranda said as she set out freshly baked *fig* scones and poured them each a cup of her *Persuasion* tea.

"Now, what I need to see is the documentation for the children—birth certificates, legal guardianship, proof of citizenship, that sort of thing. We have not found much in the official records, and that of course has raised questions at the school."

"Ahh, yes," said Miranda, pouring Ms. Dubby a second cup of tea and sliding a manila folder across the sunlit kitchen table.

As Ms. Dubby opened the folder, a look of utter surprise and then befuddlement crossed her face. Her eyes blinked and she put on her reading glasses. She took them off again as if to see more clearly. She looked up at Miranda through a haze and when their eyes met, Miranda said softly, "These are the records you are looking for."

"Yes, yes. These are the records I am looking for," repeated Ms. Dubby, closing the folder and finishing her Persuasion tea and fig scone.

Mrs. Matthews did not return to finish her year with her kindergarten class until the last two weeks of school in June. It was worked out that Peter and Cassandra would finish their work before she came back, and they got an early start on summer vacation that year. During the next six school years, Lucinda Matthews did not speak to either of them, nor did she ever once look them in the eyes. It may have been an uneasy truce between Lucinda Matthews and the McBees, but not so for Gabrielle. During her years at the elementary school, she was known to stop by the kindergarten room from time to time, stick her head in the door, and call out criss-cross-applesauce, then run away in giggles.

Cassandra and Peter's lives were divided between home and school. Home was good—school was just something they had to do. That was because there was no excitement or enchantment in their early education—that was yet to come. To make up for how boring school was, Cassandra and Peter spent long hours in their playroom, which mysteriously grew with them. Peter went from building blocks to building model ships. Cassandra liked board games, but Peter never wanted to play until they figured out how to make the game boards life-sized. Then they could actually hop from space to space—slides and ladders, mole holes, and huge bug parts often filled the room. Foxes chased hounds, and flying saucers sometimes buzzed above their heads. Seadog joined them in the action, but the playroom was too rough-and-tumble for Miss Mew. Blue liked to come and perch. He seemed to enjoy watching the games, but left when balls or other flying objects were involved. He remembered all too well the game called "knock the parrot off the perch" that involved badminton rackets.

For Peter and Cassandra McBee, and their schoolmates, everything during those early years was a waiting game—they waited for summer, they waited for holidays, they waited for dinner, or playtime, or Saturday mornings. It never occurred to them that things were speeding up and soon there wouldn't be enough time to just enjoy waiting.

Shop On The Quay

It was a morning of soft sea breezes and bright July sun, and the quay was alive with locals and tourists. They were exploring the dozen or so old fishing shanties on the wharf that had been turned into brightly painted shops with waving banners and doors thrown open.

Peter was helping his aunts pack shipping boxes while Cassandra helped her friend Gabrielle set up the little café tables outside the muffin shop, swooshing the gulls away as they worked. Peter was not thrilled with all the commotion, especially the tourists who not only shopped on the quay but wandered through the whole village asking a million questions. Their favorite subjects seemed to be the magnificent old lighthouse that stood on the cliffs to the east of the village and the waterfall that careened down from the jutting rocks that formed the west side of the harbor.

When asked if they could visit the lighthouse or take a boat under the waterfall, someone from the village always explained that the lighthouse was privately owned and there was no road out to it. The waterfall created dangerous eddies where it fell into the sea and was off limits to any vessels, but there were some excellent little pamphlets in the bookshop that explained the entire history of the village and why it was referred to as both a harbor and a bay.

Aunt Miranda's best friend, Reynelda Tweaks, was the first to arrive in the shop that morning. She was a tall, thin

48

lady with piles of platinum curls and big tinted eyeglasses which made it impossible to guess her age. She said hello to Peter, then launched into a serious discussion with Miranda, "I don't see things getting any better. Word is that the Ministry of Education has made their decision, and they're going to close Plunder Bay School and send our students to Cape Crown. I suppose they have to fill up the expensive, new addition they're building."

"First our school, next it will be the bank and the post office, I suppose."

"That's not the worst of it, Miranda. I understand that the contents of the school—artifacts, antiques, and all are to be auctioned off before the end of summer and the building itself is to be demolished!"

"That's terrible! What about the theater and library wing? That's the oldest building in Plunder Bay. It dates way back—surely they don't intend to take a wrecking ball to it!"

Just at that point in the conversation, the two friends were joined by Adam Boggins, the science teacher and unofficial principal. "Ladies, I just came from the school," he whispered breathlessly while pushing his thick glasses back up the bridge of his narrow nose. "Mrs. Matthews and the other women from the Cape Crown Historic Society are at the school now making a list of things. It seems they have arranged to have their choice of items from the school before the rest are put up for auction."

"Blast their skinny, snooty hides if they'll touch anything in my kitchen!" said Maggie O'Day, joining the others. "There are pots and pans in that kitchen that belonged to my four times great-grandmother, part of her dowry before the wreckers set her ship onto the reef. People died retrieving those things from the sea, and I'll go down in a bloody fight before anything from Plunder Bay ends up in Cape Crown, and that includes our kids!"

"We have a society of our own that is not without some influence and *Powers*," said Miss Tweaks. "I suggest an emergency meeting of the Shipwreck Society tonight, at the old school library."

All present agreed and rushed out to pass the word.

While the Shipwreck Society, comprised of many of the adults from Plunder Bay, were having their meeting about the future of the high school and forcing the kids from Plunder Bay to relocate to Cape Crown, Cassandra was having a sleepover with Gabrielle, and Peter was fishing on the wharf between the shops.

"Do you and your mom like living here with your uncle Jacques?" Cassandra asked her friend.

"We'd like to have our own house someday, but my mom doesn't really make enough money at the muffin shop for us to have our own house. So, my uncle Jacques offered us his house. He's a great guy and basically the only 'dad' I've known."

"Where is your real dad?"

"In the Navy, or maybe it's the Merchant Marines, I'm not sure. He left before I was born and my mother doesn't talk about him. How about your parents?"

"Dead, I guess. They went down in a shipwreck, my aunts think, but they don't really know that much about it."

"Well, I've got my mom and uncle Jacques, and you have your two really cool aunts. I think we're kind of lucky."

"Wouldn't it be fun if someday we could be real sisters?"

"Yeah, and live in the same house—that would be a

blast!"

"But either way, I'm glad we live here in Plunder Bay, on the water—even if we do have to get on a bus and go inland to school with a bunch of strange kids."

"Yeah, unless they come up with something at the meeting tonight, that's exactly where we're going to be this fall," Gabrielle lamented.

The meeting in the library was crowded and noisy. The members of the Shipwreck Society were Plunder Bay residents whose ancestors helped to establish the village many generations ago. All of them were descended from seafaring folk of one sort or another. They'd grown up in Plunder Bay and had graduated from Plunder Bay School. The school, the old library, and the theater were iconic elements of the community, especially to this particular group of residents.

Barrister Brown had been invited to offer some free legal advice, and he started by asking Miss Tweaks and Mr. Boggins about the items of historical value in the school and who might be able to make a legal claim to them. Among the treasures listed were oil paintings, first edition books, trunks of salvaged, delicate, period clothing the theater used, and old hand-drawn maps and charts, some of them very large, that the harbormaster said were priceless.

"Those pewter plates on the wall in the cafeteria came from the wreck of the *Bristol Queen* in 1690. I'll not see those black-hearted brigands from Cape Crown lay onto so much as a tin spoon. There will be nothing left in my kitchen when they come to auction it off or steal it outright. I'll pitch it back where we found it!" shouted Maggie

O'Day, and a loud "Huzzah!" filled the room.

"Mr. Brown," interrupted Juliet d'Eon, "I think what Ms. O'Day and the others are trying to say is that the treasures in the school belong to the village of Plunder Bay. Most of them were recovered from shipwrecks off the reef. The local people brought them here so we could all share in our history, which at times has been a very dark affair."

Charlotte Cloutier added, "And—it isn't just things that were saved from the sea. Most of the folks here come from ancestors who were also rescued from those same wrecks or that settled here starting with nothing."

Barrister Brown cleared his throat and suggested drafting a letter to the Ministry of Education, threatening to sue for the appraised value of lost items. "The threat of a good lawsuit has won more battles than most people know, and it could serve as a bargaining chip with the Ministry," he explained. Then he checked his watch, mumbled about another obligation, and exited the library for calmer seas.

Mr. Boggins looked especially grim when the discussion was focused on losing the antiquities at the school. He had beads of sweat across his forehead and kept tapping his foot on the floor nervously.

"Poor Mr. Boggins," Juliet whispered to her brother. "He's terrified this gang will go over and loot the school tonight. I wonder if he's second-guessing his decision to come back here to teach for so little pay and give up what he would have been earning as a brilliant physicist. I wonder why he did it?"

"Don't forget, Juliet, he's a Boggins, and he'll steer his own course like the rest of his lot—some of them onto rocks of their own making. My money's on old Maggie. She said what most of us are only thinking. This crowd will follow her," said Jacques, looking in Maggie O'Day's direction.

After a lot of shouted words and threats that would not have been proper for children to hear, Reynelda Tweaks stood up, threw one end of her floor-length scarf over her shoulder, and walked to the center of the floor, directly under the big library clock. The room immediately hushed and even the air seemed to stand still. All eyes were focused on the remarkable figure before them. Miss Tweaks began her simple address to the members of the Plunder Bay Shipwreck Society, "All of you have been my students at one time or another. We have studied, and learned, and grown together in this special place. All of you have gifts and *Powers*, and all of you know what they are and how to use them. Follow your *Power*, not your anger, and believe me—we can solve this problem."

As soon as she finished speaking, the old clock that hovered under the domed, glass ceiling chimed twice, echoing off the walls of the bookshelves. The effect was immediate. To her former students, that meant class was over, and they filed out of the library in contemplative, quiet order.

Mr. Boggins was still unsettled, and that night he and his oldest son George rolled out their sleeping bags in the school basement, where they could keep an eye on things—especially the old wing. This was the first of many nights they would spend there. They weren't taking any chances.

Meanwhile, Peter who had been fishing on the wharf, was about to have an adventure that left him puzzled for many months. It started when a bushy-haired guy in shorts and hiking boots came up behind him and asked if he was catching anything. Assuming he was just some pesky tourist, Peter told him, "No, wrong bait."

"You're from around here, right?" the stranger asked.

"Yeah."

"Ever walk eastbound, along the beach?"

"Sure, why?" said Peter, reeling in his line.

"Found something interesting up there this morning under a big blue rock that's kind of shaped like an elephant head, but I made a couple trips back and now I can't find the rock."

"What'd you find?" asked Peter, smiling to himself because he knew exactly which blue rock the man was talking about, and he knew why it wasn't there.

"Not sure, exactly. Some kind of old coin, I guess, but if I show it to you, you can't tell anybody 'cause there might be more of them out there."

"That's okay," said Peter. "I don't know anything about old coins, and I've got to get home."

"Just take a look," said the stranger. He pulled a gold coin from his pocket, flipped it high into the air, and caught it.

Peter knew exactly what it was when it was handed to him, and despite his claim, he knew quite a lot about old coins. He also knew quite a lot about shipwrecks and Spanish treasure, and from all that he could see in the dimming daylight, this coin was a real doubloon. This tourist guy had probably gotten hold of one of the phony treasure maps that were for sale to gullible visitors, which gave him the treasure-hunt idea, but his being in possession of an authentic doubloon piqued Peter's curiosity.

"Might be worth something. Not sure," said Peter, handing the coin back and wondering if this guy could really be that dumb.

"Since you're from around here and you know the beach, maybe you could help me find the rock again. If we find any more of these, we could split them."

"It's getting late, and I've got chores to do at home ... but maybe we could take a look."

As the two strolled up the deserted beach, Peter was feeling a little guilty and a lot cautious. He knew perfectly well that they were not going to find the big blue rock. The tide had been out for at least two hours, and the rock the stranger was referring to was only blue when it was wet; when dry, it was as grey as every other rock along the shore. After a long walk in silence, the stranger asked questions that immediately put Peter on his guard.

"You're that McBee kid from up at the lighthouse?" When Peter made no reply, he continued, "And you have a twin sister, the girl with a pink streak in her hair, right? Where is she tonight?"

Creepy! thought Peter. He wasn't about to tell him where Cassandra was. "She's at home with our three vicious-breed dogs."

Peter realized immediately that this guy was no tourist. He knew about the lighthouse and he knew about the McBees. Gold doubloon or not, this was more of an adventure than Peter had bargained for. He stopped and looked casually around to see if there was anyone else in sight—of course there was not, and as he tried to think of a plan, he watched his unwanted companion pull a knife from his pocket and switch it open. Peter knew a hard ten minute run up the beach would put him directly below the lighthouse, and even in the dark he was sure he could find and climb the familiar path up the rocky cliffside. Unfortunately, his adversary, anticipating a probable footrace, moved to block him. "So where's the rock, Peter?"

"Why, bonny Bobby Briggs, any rock in particular you're lookin' for?" came an unexpected greeting from an old seaman in a peacoat with the left sleeve pinned up.

"Who the deuce are you and how do you know my name?" said the younger man with the knife.

"Why, we've shared a pint or two up at your place, The Puffin. Thought for sure you'd recollect yer Old Tom. I stroll this beach 'most every night. Say, that's a fine-lookin' tooth picker you've got there—new, isn't it? I likes the old ones better," said the man in the peacoat, pulling a wicked-looking, large, straight blade from behind his back. "Now this here's what I calls a knife! More than makes up for my lost left arm. Would you like a closer look, Bobby?"

"Settle down, old fellow. Me and the boy were just going for a stroll on the beach. The only reason I took my knife out was to scrape the sand out of my boot tread. I wasn't going to hurt him."

"Dang sure you weren't. And you'd be the better man for me thinkin' that about you."

While the two men were close enough to slice each other, Peter increased the distance between himself and them.

"You scurry along home now, Peter, tides a-risin'. You don't have to run, 'cause we're gunna stroll back up the beach the other way. Right, Bobby Boy?"

"I'm not going anywhere with you," protested the man in shorts. But the old sailor, blade still in hand, put his good right arm around the other man's shoulders, and by the time Peter stopped to look back, both were out of sight.

C. S. Leonard

Peter decided it would not be a good idea to discuss this incident with the aunts, who would think he had been foolish. When he and Cassandra were alone in the playroom, he told her all about it, and the two pondered the meaning of what had happened and the significance of the blue rock.

A few days later, during a busy mid morning on the quay, Peter, Cassandra, and Gabrielle were sitting outside the muffin shop when Ben Kurtz, a lobsterman who worked construction during the offseason, reported there was a work stoppage on the new addition to the Cape Crown High School.

"Found some trouble with the workmen's timesheets, and realizing what it would do to their overtime pay, the guys walked off the job. It will slow the Cape Crown clowns down, but it's not enough to stop them unless the weather gets bad," reported Ben.

"Looks like we're going to have to do things Maggie's way," said the man next to him. He took a sip of coffee and bit into a chocolate muffin.

Even the kids, who had not been in the meeting at the library, knew how angry everyone was about the high school closing, and they knew about Ms. O'Day's threat to pitch the antiquities back into the bay before letting them be auctioned off and taken by strangers. They also understood that Miss Tweaks had told her former students to go out and use their *Powers* to solve the problem.

"Yeah, Maggie's one tough gal. You know, one of her ancestors was first mate on a whaler out of Boston. The captain was a weasel and down around the Horn they had a mutiny on board. Old O'Day single-handedly put down

the mutineers without spilling a drop of blood—or rum—
and slapped the lot in irons. On the way home they came
across a herd of sperm whales, so O'Day turned them
loose. They made it home with the barrels full and a fair
share for all. The investors got richer, and the ship was
safe. Mutiny over."

"What happened to the weaselly captain?" asked
someone in the crowd.

"Don't know, as he was never heard from again."

Everybody laughed, including Cassandra and Peter who
had grown up with just these kinds of stories and loved
them.

"I've got news, too," said Penelope, coming out of the
shop. She read aloud from the newspaper: "Citizens of
Soulac found cracks in the structure of the Cape Crown
Bridge. The authorities closed the structure immediately
to protect the public. Highway engineers say the bridge
will have to be replaced and foresee it being out of service
for a year at least, weather permitting."

"How's that going to work for the school buses from
Soulac?" asked Gabrielle's mother, Juliet. They'll have to
go through Plunder Bay to get to Cape Crown, and that's a
long hard ride even in good weather."

Everyone had a theory about what might happen, and
the jovial tone of things could not have been more different
than the previous week's meeting.

Seeing the large gathering of friendly people she knew,
Ursula Boggins came out of the Bay Collectibles by
Boggins shop, bouncing a baby boy on her left hip and
holding her three-year-old daughter, Alexis, by the hand.
She was a sweet lady who always looked like she didn't
have enough time to sleep or comb her hair. "If anyone

knows someone who might be interested in buying a $600 quilt, I've got one for sale in my shop. It's the for the annual charity fundraiser, and I don't see any way we're going to be able to find a buyer."

"I thought you were going to put it in the big quilt show and competition that the Cape Crown Museum Fund holds every August."

"Not this year," said Ursula. "They had to cancel it. Seems like the people who usually enter aren't done *creating*, so there aren't enough entries. Everyone is so busy, and the weather's been nice. Guess no one wants to sit inside quilting."

Miss Tweaks whispered to Miranda, "I see a pattern emerging. How about you?"

"I have to give you credit, Reynelda. It looks like you were right that night in the library when you told us to follow our *Powers*, not our anger."

"*Seeing, finding, realizing, protecting, enchanting, creating* ... sounds very familiar. Maybe you should *brew* them some of your specialty tea and *conjure* up some nasty weather."

"I don't think the Ministry of Education would drink any tea I *brewed,* and *conjuring* any kind of weather is beyond my gifts, but you might give it a try," said Miranda.

"We have to hope this works. If the school closes, it's not just the kids and the village that lose—a lot of people are going to be out of a job—Maggie O'Day for sure. No wonder she's so upset."

"And what about you, Reynelda?"

"I won't be going to Cape Crown, Miranda, even if they offer me a job. I thought I'd let you know, but I haven't said a word to anyone else yet. What would they do with a kooky old librarian and drama teacher like me, anyway?"

Treasures of Plunder Bay

Cassandra was listening to this and had some idea what they were talking about when they referenced *Powers*, but she didn't fully understand. After her years of torture at the grade-school annex, she was so looking forward to going to school at Plunder Bay—and even though her brother wouldn't admit it—she was sure he felt the same. If anything was going to happen to save the school, she hoped it happened soon.

Cassandra kicked Peter under the table to signal him privately. "Peter, we need to pack that box of tea for Aunt Miranda so that she can ship it out this afternoon."

"Oh, right. I almost forgot she asked us to do that," replied Peter.

"Want some help?" asked Gabrielle.

"No, that's okay. It will only take a minute, and your mom looks like she needs the help here," said Cassie.

As Cassandra and Peter headed into the aunts' shop, Peter asked, "So what's up?"

"I think we need to get to the playroom and do what we can to save the Plunder Bay School."

"What makes you think we can do anything to save it?" asked Peter.

"I'm not sure we can. But you and I have seen that when we work together toward a common goal, it usually turns out the way we want."

"You mean combining our *Powers* to achieve the outcome?"

"Precisely," said Cassie.

"And the effect is magnified when we're in the playroom for some reason," added Peter.

That night after dinner, Peter and Cassandra McBee

headed to the playroom like they had done many evenings. They were joined by Seadog and Blue, who took up their favorite spots. The twins didn't take long to get down to business. They'd learned from years of playing together that they could make things happen by joining hands and simultaneously imagining the desired outcome. It was even more effective when others joined them, like the day they chanted criss-cross-applesauce and Mrs. Matthews sat down on the floor. They didn't fully know what was behind their ability, but hoped they'd be learning more about the magic that seemed to come to them naturally. They were beginning to realize, from overheard conversations and things they'd seen, that there was a lot more to it than what they understood.

As they stood together, they asked of the round window in the playroom, "Show us Plunder Bay School." The big, glass, double front doors appeared in the window.

Peter spoke next, "Show us the school on the first day of classes."

The twins held hands tightly and imagined the school open for business. In the window, activity picked up in front of the glass doors. Kids were unloading from buses and a steady stream of students were entering with their backpacks, gym bags, and musical instrument cases. They saw Miss Tweaks—wearing her first-day-of-school scarf— slow down upon entering and look back as though she heard a noise or felt someone watching her, then step through to the lobby.

"Well," said Cassie, "let's hope that worked."

"We'll know soon enough, I guess," replied Peter.

"Why shiver-me-timbers!" squawked Blue loudly.

The next morning, Peter was awakened by the continuous

ringing of someone's cell phone instead of the breakfast bell. It had barely stopped, when it started again. Cassandra was already at the kitchen table when Peter came down and Aunt Penelope was giving Aunt Miranda questions to ask whomever it was she was talking to on the phone.

"What's happening?" asked Peter, heaping a plate with pancakes.

"Mr. Boggins is waiting for the Ministry of Education to call him back and let him know if he needs to get Plunder Bay School ready to open. He told the aunts he's had several calls from Soulac saying they will be coming here to school," explained Cassie, giving Peter a knowing look.

It seemed the crisis was averted, and Plunder Bay School would be open for at least one more year. The students, who had gone to grade school in Soulac, would be joining them. After all the hype, hot tempers, call to action, and general hoopla, Peter was rather disappointed that there had been no explosions or floods, that Cape Crown Museum didn't disappear forever in a dense fog, or Mrs. Matthews and the Annex didn't get washed out to sea in a tidal wave. In the end, it was leadership, and the members of the Shipwreck Society coming together to do what they did best that turned a bad situation around—at least for now.

The Old School

T he old Plunder Bay School was opened for business that September by magic or luck. When Peter and Cassandra compared their schedules, they had no classes together and were in different homerooms. The two saw each other only between classes as one of them was going up and the other coming down the main stairs. Navigating across the span of the school and making it on time to back-to-back classes was crazy. Geography was on the third floor, math on the first, and depending on the day, either art on the second or PE in the basement of the main building. By the end of the first week of school, Peter was sure he'd seen everyone he knew and even the new kids from Soulac; most of them had cousins in Plunder Bay, so they were not really strangers.

The only unpleasant encounter Peter had that first week was with a boy named Walker Matthews and his buddies, who had come to the old school from the gated community of Bearing Cross. They thought they were big stuff, and looked down their noses at anyone who didn't live in their neighborhood. On Thursday, halfway down the stairs to the main hall, Walker grabbed Peter roughly by the arm and said, "Hey, Bud, where are the tennis courts at this dump?"

Peter was sure there were no tennis courts at the school, but he wasn't about to give Walker Matthews and his buddies the satisfaction of knowing that. The only thing like tennis courts Peter knew of was the net he had seen crumpled up in a dark, damp corner of the gym. "The tennis courts you're looking for are on the west end of the gym, right beside the pool. Don't know how you missed them," Peter shot back with the least little smirk.

Walker tilted his head sideways and gave Peter a long quizzical look, then said, "Oh yeah, I know where that is. Thanks, Bud."

Due to the last-minute influx of new students from Soulac, schedules were a mess. Some classrooms had more students than desks, while other classes were nearly empty. Sometimes, two whole classes would show up at the same room at the same time, and poor Mr. Boggins was running in circles. All the teachers were trying to help as much as they could. Everything but lunch was mass confusion.

Peter made his first new friend that week in Mr. Morgan's class. Mr. Morgan, the geography teacher, was a young guy who liked to joke around with his students. His pick the first week was a new kid who sat next to Peter, a boy named William VanSmithe, III. William had just moved to Plunder Bay from across the country with his parents who were marine biologists. He was a good student who was self-assured without being arrogant. He was already a favorite of the girls, who were seen checking him out and whispering giddily when he passed them in the hallway. This, along with his impressive name, made him the focus of Mr. Morgan's less-than-charitable sense of humor. During that first week, he made it a habit to pronounce William's name with a kind of corny upper-class English accent. By the end of the week, Mr. Morgan asked William jokingly if he had a middle name that sounded as royal as the rest of his name.

Cool as you like, William replied, "Damit."

This caught everyone by surprise, and the class laughed out loud.

"No, seriously, it's spelled 'D-A-M-I-T', my mother's family surname. And what can I say, my parents have a weird sense of humor."

Peter could see William's easy manner and matter-of-fact statement take the wind out of Mr. Morgan's sails.

Mr. Morgan took it well and had to laugh, then in a slightly more respectful tone of voice asked, "Have you considered just going by Will?"

"Yeah, sounds good to me—sure beats a lot of other things I've been called."

On their way out of the classroom, Will turned to Peter and said, "Before you ask me, the answer is no, 'Damit' is not really my middle name. It's actually something worse that I didn't need Mr. Morgan or anyone else getting hold of. I could just see someone coming up with a stupid nickname that I'd have to live with as long as I'm here. And I actually like being called Will."

Peter shrugged his shoulders and said, "Nice move though, and I don't like my middle name either."

Cassandra and Peter sat with the same group every day at lunch. Peter and Will got there first from language class and tried to save seats for Cassandra and Gabrielle. Most of the rest of the group were kids from their old school—Cody, Virginia, the two Caitlyns, Paige, Jason, and Daniel. Lunch was the best part of the school day. Not only was the food good—it was funny! Ms. O'Day usually included something that sounded crazy on the menu, and everyone always hurried to get their trays and find out what it was. So far, they had been treated to spiderweb soup with wart cookies, mystic stew with marvel bread, and today was lighthouse salad.

"Has anyone been to the library yet?" asked Paige.

"Our teachers told us that the schedules have to get straightened out before we can get in," answered Virginia.

"What's so great about the library?" asked Madelyn, who had just joined their group. I keep hearing what a terrific place it is."

"It may be a while before you get to see it," said Peter. "Mr. Morgan said today that he heard all the room assignments and student schedules have been done over. We're probably going to have to change homerooms."

Gabrielle spoke up, twisting a long black curl around her index finger. "I wish, I wish, I wish, we could get into one of Miss Tweaks's classes, but she only teaches library and theater, and that's just for the upper grades. You have to pass some kind of test she gives to even get into those."

Cody groaned loudly. "That leaves me out. If there's anything I hate worse than going to school, it's taking tests."

Friday afternoon, when Cassandra got on the bus, there was something she was very anxious to show Peter. She sat down in the seat right behind him because Cody had already plunked down in the seat next to Peter. The bus was filling up fast and everyone was anxious to be first out of the parking lot, but their driver was standing outside talking with Mr. Boggins. The buses at Plunder Bay always backed into their places and waited side-by-side before pulling out. It was the same today—but out of the blue, Cody jumped up and shouted, "Whoa!" He crashed down the aisle, toward the front of the bus, stumbling over feet and backpacks. He jumped into the driver's seat, found the emergency brake, and gave it a hard yank. He leaned back in the seat, panting. "That was close!" The whole bus burst into gales of riotous laughter. Cody, confused, looked around and realized the buses on the right and left sides were pulling forward.

"What's going on?!" said Mr. Knoll, their bus driver.

"I ... I ... th–thought," stammered Cody, his face bright red with embarrassment. "Well, I guess I put on the brake." He hung his head and went back to his seat beside Peter. The whole bus exploded with applause and jeers when Cody got off at his house, and for once he didn't have anything smart to say back.

Cassandra moved into the seat with Peter and handed him something from her backpack. It was an ordinary-looking seashell, and Peter looked puzzled.

"Put it up to your ear and listen!" she said.

The shell had the usual roar of the sea, just like any other shell Peter had ever listened to. "So what?" he asked.

"Didn't you hear anything, like someone talking? I found it in the scrap material box in the art room today. When I put it up to my ear, I was sure I could hear someone talking. It sounded like Miss Tweaks."

"Maybe she was in the art room."

"No, she was in the theater with her drama students. Maybe I just imagined it. I'll ask her on Monday if I get a chance."

In homeroom on Monday morning, Mr. Morgan handed out new schedules to most of the students in the class. Peter, Will, and Cody didn't receive one.

"If you didn't get a new schedule, just report to the library first period—that will be your new homeroom," explained Mr. Morgan.

"Finally, I get to see the famous library," said Will. He raised his hand. "How do we get to the library, Mr. Morgan?"

"Never mind," said Peter, "I know how to get there."

It was a hike to get to the theater and library wing through the crowded, noisy halls, with kids trying to figure out and follow their new schedules. The class bell rang before the three boys left the main building, so technically they were already late. They pushed their way through the crowd, hardly stopping to breathe, until Peter stopped in front of two heavy fire doors that separated the main building from the theater and library wing.

Once inside, it was like they had entered another world; this part of the old school was built of thickly cut stone, and the floors were wide, waxed, hardwood planks. The air in the dimly lit hallway was cool and fresh, and there was absolutely no noise, not a sound to be heard. It felt like they had entered a fortress, and it looked a little like a fortress too. They followed brass lantern wall sconces, converted at some point from natural gas to electric, toward the library. As they started down the long passageway, they passed a pair of outside doors on their right with a heavy chain and open lock hanging from the handles. Opposite these doors, on their left, were the closed doors to the theater with a marquee advertising the name and date of the next performance. The doors were guarded by two shining suits of armor with their lances crossed.

"I guess they're serious about not letting you in without a ticket," said Cody.

Beyond, the corridor ended with two bathrooms and a turn to the left, which the boys followed. In front of them loomed two massive, carved wooden doors, and above the doors was a placard with gothic lettering announcing the library. The three approached the massive doors slowly, and with a little trepidation—forgetting they were already late. On their left, just outside the library doors, they saw a dark, narrow stairway leading down. The boys could see a small landing, faintly illuminated, but beyond that there was only inky darkness.

"Let's go," said Peter, pushing open one of the heavy library doors.

They stopped and stared, wide-eyed at the room they had walked into. The library ceiling was very high, made of heavy timbered beams, radiating circularly out of a tall pinnacle above the center of the room, with skylights between them that let in an extraordinary amount of light from the pale blue, cumulus-clouded sky outside.

"Wow!" said Cody, turning in circles as he looked upwards.

The room had dark woodwork, long oak library tables that looked ancient, and upholstered straight-backed chairs. On one side was a high desk, and behind it were card files and cabinets with all kinds of artsy stuff, and a tiny clock with a sad face. Tall, dark, walnut bookshelves, some with ladders, fanned outward from the center of the domed ceiling, everywhere the eye could see, with more bookshelves beyond. The flat ends of the bookshelves displayed old-looking oil paintings of ships, intricate wooden ship models, bronze statues on stands, marble busts, antique brass ship instruments, and more. Each had its own small bronze lamp to illuminate the display and a brass descriptor plate.

Taking it in, it hit Peter that this place was more than a library; it was a museum—more precisely, a maritime museum, and it was way better than any museum he had ever seen. High above the room, Peter saw the magnificent library clock for the first time. It appeared to be floating, or perhaps hanging, from some invisible hook; he couldn't take his eyes off of it. The three boys stood in stunned silence.

Will broke the mood. "I know we're late, but where is everybody?" The room was absolutely silent and there was no one else in sight.

"We're over here," called a familiar voice. It was a smiling Miss Tweaks. She motioned them to follow her into the bookshelves. Peter gave the clock a last look and then followed Miss Tweaks, Will, and Cody single file.

As they got deeper into the stacks, it seemed like the space grew, the bookshelves seemed longer and taller the farther they went. Miss Tweaks, unphased, glided down the expanse, rounded a right at the end of their first bookshelf, hosting a portrait of Samuel de Champlain, then took a left down another long bookshelf, then a right. The stacks seemed like an intricate maze—Peter was glad they had Miss Tweaks for a guide, at least on their first trip through.

Finally, they came out into a rounded bay in the back of the library with stained glass windows reaching upward, displaying tempestuous seafaring scenes. Morning sun streamed from the ceiling onto a group of students, mostly girls, all talking excitedly. Peter was amazed that they had not heard a sound until they left the bookshelves. Cassandra, Gabrielle, and Virginia shared a high-backed setee. Others sat in deep leather-clad wingback chairs, and some of the students were sitting on the floor, leaning against the furniture. Everyone seemed delighted to be there, but Peter kept looking back at the bookshelves, wondering how he could ever find his way out again.

"I think we're all here now," said Miss Tweaks, looking over the group of students. "Let's get started. I don't know if you understand or not, but due to scheduling problems, I've agreed to take a homeroom this year, so here we are. All of you will spend your mornings with me, then go to lunch and your other classes. We'll just call our mornings history class and language or reading—I'll figure it out and it will make poor Mr. Boggins's life so much easier. We can't, of course, take the library for all of our classes because other teachers need to use it too, so I've decided we will create our own classroom."

Gabrielle winked at Cassie, Will raised his eyebrows, and Peter looked pensive.

Miss Tweaks continued, "There's a wonderful room behind the stage that no one else is using. In the past we used it as a makeup and dressing room for our plays. It's also where the actors wait before going up the steps and onto the stage. I don't remember it ever being used as a classroom in my time here, and the furniture is very old, so treat it with respect, please. The room access is just outside the library. We will have to do some deep cleaning and move a few things in the room, but that will make it our special place. So, if no one has any questions, we'll get started. Follow me."

As the students wound their way through the maze of bookshelves, Peter watched each turn closely, left at the shelf of big, thick books, right at the newer-looking books, right again halfway down the shelves of very old books with the rolling ladder. Then they followed Miss Tweaks through the main section of the library, under the great old clock, past the front desk, and through the high doors out into the hallway.

"Watch your step," she said, holding up her long dress as the line of students turned right down the dark, musty-smelling stairs, toward the basement. The stairwell was damp and slippery. Cassandra thought it smelled like the old wet bathing suit she'd left wrapped in a towel under her bed once. Halfway down the steps was a landing and a door to the right. Miss Tweaks opened the door, and the students filed into their new classroom.

Entering the room, they could see it didn't have windows, but when Miss Tweaks flipped on the light switch, instead of overhead fluorescent lights, brightly lit windows appeared, showing the blue sky and park-like setting that surrounded the school. There were boxes piled on desks, chairs piled on desks, boxes piled on boxes piled on chairs. The center of the room had been cleared so all the clutter was pushed against the walls. The cleaning and moving began in earnest and lasted all morning, to the delight of the students who were missing real classroom work.

By lunchtime, it began to look like a normal room, albeit with much more charm and character than a regular classroom. The antique desks' wooden tops gleamed with fresh wax, a colorful, patterned, Turkish area rug had been rolled out in the front of the room where Miss Tweaks's big mahogany desk was placed, and atop that was a cobalt-blue glass bottle containing a dozen or so posey flower pens and an assortment of scented candles casting flame-flickering light around the books on her desk. In a tall, orange and white Ming vase to the left side of her desk were several very old-looking papyrus scrolls tied with leather rawhide strips. On the wall behind Miss Tweaks's desk was a huge sea map that didn't resemble anything Peter had seen before; where there should have been country names, there were realms. Ancient sailing vessels and pirate ships floated across it, seemingly with minds of their own. Just to the right of the wall map were four steps that lead up to the back of the stage, as Cassandra soon discovered.

The students' desks were arranged in rows with a wide aisle down the center. An antique cheval mirror stood at the end of the aisle at the back of the room. The desks' wooden tops were slightly slanted and lifted to reveal storage space underneath. Madelyn explained that the little holes were for ink bottles. A few of the desks still contained an old textbook, feather quill, or tiny chalk board for working math problems. Cozy leather reading chairs, with plump, down-filled, throw pillows that matched the Turkish rug, were scattered around the periphery of the room. The musty moldiness that had risen from the dark hallway, for who knew how long, was gone.

At lunch, everyone saved a seat for Cody. He had worked hard all morning proving his superstrength by moving heavy furniture and carrying the biggest boxes all by himself. Gabrielle kept making a big deal about them being part of "Miss Tweaks's group," as she called it. "This is no ordinary homeroom," she said. "For one thing, it isn't homeroom at all, it's class for the entire morning, every day."

"I wondered about that too," said Virginia.

Cassie added, "And if we could have handpicked who we wanted to spend every morning with, it would have been the exact kids that are in this group."

Peter thought about what the girls were implying. He wasn't ready to jump to conclusions—that wasn't his way—but he had to admit the arrangement was unique, and even Miss Tweaks said she'd never had a homeroom before. Peter glanced at Will and Cody and the rest of the guys who were seated at one end of the table. Their conversation was very different. They were having a difference of opinion about today's lunch—fried planks and scupper sandwiches. When the bell rang, everyone scattered in different directions to their fourth-period classes.

When the silver bell rang the next morning, waking Peter to get ready for school, he found himself looking forward to the day ahead. For the first time ever, and he wasn't exactly sure why, he was excited to be going to school. He wouldn't admit it, but he couldn't wait to get into the new classroom. On his way, he stopped for a few minutes to talk with Bradley Boggins, whose locker was still next to his even though they were in different homerooms now. Cody passed them, and Peter motioned him on through the big metal fire doors leading to the theater and library wing. When Peter got to the class, all of the students but Cody were there. Peter stepped back out onto the landing at the entrance to their classroom and looked around for him.

Cassie noticed Peter looking for something from the landing and knew immediately there was a problem. Stepping out, she whispered to him, "What's wrong, Peter?"

"Cody's disappeared. I think he went down there," said Peter, pointing down the steps beyond the landing. "He's always got to do something dumb and get himself into trouble."

"Forget about it," Cassie said. "He deserves to get into trouble."

"Yeah," said Peter. But they both waited for him, worriedly staring down into the damp darkness from the landing outside the newly enchanted classroom door.

Miss Tweaks came out of the library and down the stairs, smiled at Peter and Cassandra, and said good morning. She walked past them and went straight into the room, and they heard her say, "We'll get started in a minute."

At the same moment, Peter and Cassandra heard someone running up the stairs, panting loudly. It was Cody. "Figures," said Peter. He started to call him a bonehead, but he stopped short when he got a look at Cody's face. He was sweaty and his eyes looked wild. He dropped down on his knees when he got to the landing, then put his hand over his heart.

"There's something down there," Cody said between gasps. "It almost got me."

"Probably the mold monster," Peter joked.

"Nothing human. It's big and furry, and made a loud squealing noise! It ran right at me and knocked me down and clawed me. See?" he said, showing them his badly scratched arms and torn jeans.

Miss Tweaks came to the door and asked, "Anything wrong?"

"I think Cody fell on the stairs," answered Peter.

"I'm okay, just ... umm—need to go to the washroom and clean up a bit. I don't need to go to the nurse or anything," said Cody, trying to sound calm.

"Go with him, Peter," said Miss Tweaks. As Peter and Cody stumbled up the stairs, Miss Tweaks pulled Cassandra aside and whispered, "Don't let him say anything to anyone about what happened down there. We don't want to give anyone a reason to close the school, and that might be all it would take."

When Peter and Cody were back from the restroom, Miss Tweaks started class by telling her students they could sit where they wanted because she already knew their names, and didn't need a seating chart. The five boys immediately grabbed the seats in the back of the classroom, while the seven girls jockeyed to sit with their friends.

"I know you all had a busy first week of school, and from what I have observed, you've all done well, used your gifts of *Power*, and distinguished yourselves." Miss Tweaks smiled at her students.

Gabrielle, who was sitting next to Cassandra, looked at her and whispered, "I told you this was a special class."

Miss Tweaks continued, calling each student by name: "Cody, I want to commend you for *protecting* your bus mates without thinking of your own safety when you thought the bus was drifting backwards out of control. Cassandra, you *found* my missing shell in the art room, thank you. It's very special, and I'd been looking for it for a long time. Please return it to me when you get a chance. Will, you *saw* the use of your middle name becoming a fiasco, and used quick thinking to divert a problem— proving you don't need a crystal ball, but you should consider getting one. Madelyn showed her considerable *creating* gifts in art class. Virginia and Daniel, your help in setting up the gym last week to make PE class bearable for the students this year clearly shows your *enchanting* ability. Caitlyn M., you used *brewing* to switch the raisins in the wart cookies with chocolate chips, much to everyone's delight, and Ms. O'Day didn't even notice that you did it; that's saying something! Jason, I'm not sure if you used *finding* or *realizing*—or maybe a little of both—when you tracked down extra desks for the new kids from Soulac who didn't have anywhere to sit in their homeroom class the first day of school. Caitlyn B. and Paige, great job working together and using *creating* to give the school's directional signs clear arrows so all the kids in the hallways could get from one end of the school to the other without being late for class! Gabrielle, in your unique way—just being Gabrielle—you used *realizing* to help make this class a reality. And Peter, you displayed small examples of all of the *Powers*. We'll have to see over time if that was just coincidence or if you have a special gift. I'm very proud of this class. All of you applied your gifts in terribly clever ways and demonstrated kindness in the process."

The class looked surprised at what Miss Tweaks said, and were pleased to be recognized. Each of them saw one another in a slightly new light, and they felt a little more connected after Miss Tweaks's observations of them.

"Having said that, I want to start by talking about the gifts everyone is born with. Using all of your gifts will make them your *Powers*, and all of you come from families who believe in this tradition. The *Powers* are *brewing, enchanting, creating, finding, realizing, seeing, and protecting.*"

As she spoke, the *Powers* appeared on the white board standing near her desk, floated from the left side to the right, then drifted around the room clockwise, ultimately landing on notepads sitting on each student's desk. This left the twelve students in silent awe.

Gabrielle raised her hand. "That's only seven. My mother told me there were eight *Powers*."

"She's right, and the eighth *Power* is *conjuring*, which can rarely be achieved until the other seven are mastered. Let me explain *conjuring*. Long ago there were magical realms, and those who had mastered all the *Powers* practiced *conjuring*."

Peter glanced at the wall map when he heard the mention of realms.

"The few great conjurers became sorcerers, and therefore the keepers of their realms. Over the next few weeks, we'll be discussing each of the *Powers* and how to master them. Let's spend some time now talking about our home realm, Plunder Bay."

Cassie looked fascinated and asked, "Plunder Bay is a what—a realm?"

"Indeed, Cassandra. Let me provide some background and history. It used to be named Boggins Bay, because in 1752 a peddler named Bartholomew Boggins struck a deal with the indigenous people to buy the harbor for the trinkets he carried. He built a trading post on this very spot. The theater and library wing are the former trading post and the oldest structure in Plunder Bay. In a few years, he grew rich from selling looted goods out of the shipwrecks off Cape Peril, along with the ill-gotten gains of pirates and smugglers. In a few years, brigands from all over the world knew of this place and nicknamed it Plunder Bay. It became a safe harbor for freebooters of all sorts who traded here or had repairs done in the shipyards of Soulac."

So much had happened that day in class that once they were home, Cassandra and Peter rushed through dinner to get to the playroom where they could compare notes. They emptied their backpacks out onto the little playroom table in the special room that over the years had grown along with them.

"Show me a magical realm," Peter commanded the window, and the Serengeti appeared.

"Do you believe the story Cody told us?" Cassie asked her brother.

"I think so. Cody's a big guy, and he obviously tangled with something that knocked him down and scratched him up."

"I'm certain Miss Tweaks knows what he saw down there, and she's worried the story will get out and cause trouble for the school."

"Keeping it quiet will be the tricky part. Will and I are going to take flashlights to school tomorrow, and the first chance we have to get away, we'll go down and take a look."

"I'm coming too," said Cassie resolutely.

Their first opportunity to check out the basement didn't come until two days later, when Miss Tweaks took several of the students to find books in the library. Peter, Will, and Cody had stayed behind in the classroom to unpack some boxes Miss Tweaks brought in. Gabrielle and Cassandra already had their books, so they were there too. After a lively discussion, Peter, Cassie, and Will headed down the stairs with their flashlights turned on. Gabrielle and Cody stood watch on the landing. Cassandra counted thirteen steps down to the basement level. Peter directed his light off the steps and shone it out in front of them through an open doorway and down a long passage. They were immediately met by three sets of glowing red eyes that almost instantly turned green from the reflection of the light. One creature scurried forward, and the other two turned and ran down the passageway in the opposite direction, dragging long hairless tails behind them.

"RUN!" screamed Cassie, but before she could get her legs to move, a huge furry creature ran right into her and knocked her down. Peter was slammed hard against the wall by Cassandra's fall, and Will jumped on the back of the thing and threw his arms around its neck. The two of them then went for a wild ride round and round amid shrieks and squeals of terror from the beast. Peter ran forward, beating the air with his flashlight. The two creatures that had run down the passage came scurrying back to join the fight.

Peter finally landed a solid hit with his flashlight, but a second later Will was on the floor scrambling on his hands and knees, trying to stand up, and groaning, "Ouch."

The adventuresome trio found themselves face-to-face with two of the beasts. In the beam of Peter's flashlight, they could clearly see two giant rats with powerful claws. Sitting on their haunches, they were nearly as tall as Cassandra. The third rat was behind them, cowering against the wall and blocking their way back up the stairs. Will felt around the floor for his flashlight. It had rolled behind some boxes, and in the process of retrieving it, he knocked one of the boxes over, spilling its dark contents onto the floor. The smell of rank sausages filled the passageway. In a flash, all three rats dashed forward, and each grabbed something from the spilled carton. Dragging whatever it was in their teeth, all three disappeared back down the passage.

Peter followed Will and Cassandra down the corridor and through the door. He closed it behind them and they ran up the thirteen steps, then pushed Gabrielle and Cody into the classroom and shut the door.

"Did you see it?" asked Cody. "The thing that attacked me?"

"Oh yeah!" said Will. "We saw it."

"Some huge rats—big and hungry—but just rats. We live in a fishing community. We've all seen rats before," said Peter, trying to keep Cody from getting too wound up.

"Just rats?" said Cody dejectedly. "Well, this school needs an exterminator right now!"

Then all five had a good laugh. They made a pact to keep the story to themselves, and to avoid the basement of the old wing.

The Smuggler's Bazaar

C assandra and Peter had hardly noticed that fall was everywhere around them. Things at school had occupied their minds completely. Now, they sat in the back seat of Aunt Penelope's roomy SUV and gazed out at the beauty of the colored leaves and the rocky coastline of their home. No one had said much about the trip they were taking until right before they all got on the road. The twins had heard about the Smuggler's Bazaar that was held every October in a village up the coast. The whole town would be closed for the three days of the Bazaar, and only invited guests could participate. To be invited as a vendor or a shopper, you had to be a member in good standing of a Shipwreck, Sailors, Smugglers, or Pirate Society. This meant that one of your ancestors had to be recorded in official historical records as one of these, though it didn't matter which.

The vendors and shoppers at the annual Bazaar came from all over the world to buy and sell relics from voyages and shipwrecks. The local shopkeepers, who had closed after the tourist season ended, rented out their store fronts to the Bazaar vendors for this big annual event. When a person bought any item, they had to keep it or bring it back to a future Bazaar to sell it. Those were the rules, and if you broke the rules, you were suspended from attending. That had apparently happened to Mr. Boggins; Cassandra overheard him saying his wife had accidentally sold a little bronze vase to a tourist, and it would be three years before he could go back.

After checking into a dingy little place called the Scottish Inn, it was time for everyone to get into their costumes. This was part of the fun, the aunts insisted, and everyone would be in disguise. Most people did not use their real names, so if you saw someone you knew, you had to pretend not to recognize them. Cassandra was more into the dressing up, but most of all she wanted to cover the pink streak in her light hair. It had been a constant problem for her—she was always having to explain that no, she didn't dye it. So, for the Bazaar, it would be pulled up and completely covered in a red bandana. After a great deal of discussion, it was decided that Peter's disguise could be an ancient, black leather, three-cornered hat, an eye patch, jeans rolled up to his knees, and a scarf around his waist. The aunts were decked out in long, hooded, tartan cloaks with insignia patches.

An elderly lady, dressed like a Massachusetts Pilgrim, smiled at the aunts like she knew them and asked, "Are the young ones of age?"

Miranda smiled back, handed her some documents, and the lady waved them through with a wish and a warning: "Have fun, but be careful."

Their first stop was a little cafe called the Creaky Spar. Aunt Penelope told them that should they get separated in the crowd, they were to meet back there, and not leave and go back to the Inn by themselves. During lunch, there was a lot of planning between the aunts about business matters—things they absolutely needed to do came first, then things they wanted to get done. Cassandra and Peter didn't hear a word, as both stared out the window of the little café in absolute amazement.

Treasures of Plunder Bay

There were dozens of shops, and tables of goods outside the shops. There were pushcarts, and people selling things out of packs on their backs. Some of the clothes were extreme, especially the Vikings, and there were a lot of bejeweled princess outfits and wizard robes. Many of the men wore plain, dark monks' robes, or sailors' uniforms, and there was no shortage of witch costumes. Peter and Cassandra were dying to get outside and have a closer look.

Instead, Peter got shanghaied by Aunt Miranda to visit a coin shop almost at the far end of the wharf. The shop was empty when the two of them arrived, but soon they were attended to by a serious-looking young man in thick glasses. Aunt Miranda produced a small leather pouch, poured the contents out into his hand, and asked the man if he had any idea what the coins were worth. The man seemed very interested, turning each of the half dozen or so coins over and over, then handing them back to her one at a time. He told them that if they wanted to sell any of the coins, his father would be in the shop tomorrow at ten o'clock to appraise them. Miranda smiled and left the shop quickly, leading Peter all the way through to the other end of the Bazaar and another coin shop.

This shop was also empty except for the proprietor, a stooped old gentleman with beady eyes who examined the contents of the leather pouch with a jeweler's eyepiece. Aunt Miranda dodged most of his questions, saying that the coins had been in her family for generations—she knew they were from various foreign lands, but she had no idea of their value. Rubbing his palms together and licking his lips, the old gentleman took a piece of paper from his pocket, scribbled a dollar amount, and handed it to Miranda. After looking at the amount, she snorted in disapproval, turned on her heel, grabbed Peter by the arm, and dashed back toward the Creaky Spar.

Aunt Penelope and Cassandra had better luck shopping. Cassandra had found a book for herself, and one as a present for Gabrielle on potions and charms. She confessed to her brother that the book she found for herself was *The Fine Art of Casting Spells and Hexes*.

After a whispered conversation between the aunts, Penelope announced, "Kids, if you promise to stick together, you can go out on your own. We have a lot of things to get done today and it won't be much fun for the two of you. Let's meet back here in about two hours. Don't spend all your money on junk, or let anyone talk you out of it either."

With that, Peter and Cassandra were off and down the wharf. Peter wanted to go on board some of the boats, especially a Chinese junk he had spotted. It turned out to be stocked with all kinds of old pots, kettles, and other cooking stuff.

"Oh well, it was the boat I wanted to see anyway," said Peter with disappointment.

"I've never seen so many people," said Cassie. "I wonder where they all came from."

"Look out there." Peter pointed beyond the harbor, where dozens of yachts and sailboats were moored. A constant line of dinghies and jet skis drove in and out.

"Wow, there must be a lot of money to be made selling stuff at these bazaars. Unless they belong to the shoppers who are rich enough to own yachts."

"Scrimshaw!" said Peter. He darted off to join a small crowd watching a man in an old-time sailor's uniform demonstrate how seafaring men on long whaling voyages occupied their time by shaving and etching designs on whalebone or whale teeth. He assured the crowd that he was working with birchwood. Then he showed some real antique scrimshaw, as the artist called it, and Peter spent more than he wanted to on a small scrimshaw humpback whale.

The lights were on in some of the shops and others had closed when the aunts met them in front of the café. The adults were over an hour late and burdened with packages. There was a group of musicians playing sea shanties on the street, and the restaurants were overflowing with lines of people waiting for tables. It was decided they would have dinner tonight at the Scottish Inn where they were staying and come back early in the morning.

"I have to look for costumes for Miss Tweaks," said Aunt Miranda as they started out the next day. "After that, I'm headed back to the bookstore to do some shopping for myself. What do the two of you want to do?" she asked.

"We saw a little cart called Broken Treasures," said Peter, who thought he was pretty good at fixing things. "And Cassie wants to go into the joke shop right next door, so I guess we'll start off in that direction."

"Don't forget, hot air balloons over the park at two o'clock! How about if we meet you there? It means that you are on your own for lunch," said Aunt Penelope.

It was a cool, crisp, sunny October morning with a strong sea breeze, and Cassandra and Peter wandered amongst the crowd and checked out the shops. The joke shop was easy to find and turned out to be more—much more—than rubber chickens and bobble heads. It was the coolest fireworks shop that the twins had ever seen, and they doubted the aunts would approve of anything they bought there. After looking around for a long time, Peter bought two little boxes of something called light whips, and Cassandra found a black light flashlight she thought was awesome.

They entered a little jewelry shop that Cassandra wanted to check out. Peter trailed along behind her. It wasn't crowded, so Cassandra took a lot of time looking at everything. She kept coming back to a tray of silver rings—some with stones, some without. Finally, she asked to see a little silver ring with a crescent moon on one side and a star on the other. In the center of the star was a small white stone. The clerk took it out of the case and Cassandra slipped it onto her pinky finger.

"Oh!" said the shopkeeper. "It's glowing! I've never seen it glow before. It must be your chemistry. All the pieces in this tray came from shipwrecks right here along the North Atlantic coast. This particular ring came from the wreck of the *Angelique*, a schooner that was carrying poor immigrants in the early 1800s. This ring probably was the treasured possession of some young girl whose heart was full of hopes and dreams for a better life. I think she would want you to have it, Miss, if you would treasure it as she did."

Cassandra pulled her brother aside, and holding her hand so he could see it, said, "It *is* glowing, isn't it, Peter?"

"Well, I don't know about glowing, but it does look brighter than it did before you put it on," he answered. "By the way, the *Angelique* that went down here wasn't a schooner, and it wasn't carrying immigrants. I think she pulled that story out of thin air."

Even so, it was obvious to Peter that Cassie liked the ring, but it cost more than she had to spend, so he gave her most of the money he had left. As they walked away, the shopkeeper called out after them, "They say if you want to keep it bright, just put it in a saucer of seawater under direct moonlight and it will glow forever."

Stepping out of the shop, Cassie muttered to Peter, "I wonder who 'they' is?"

"I don't know. She might have made that up too," replied Peter.

The twins wandered around the bazaar looking for the Broken Treasures cart Peter had spotted the day before near the Creaky Spar and again that morning outside the joke shop. Just when they decided to get something to drink and sit down for a while, Cassandra spotted a boy with a long, bleached, ponytail wig pushing the cart down a narrow alleyway.

"Wait!" she called out, and he stopped and looked back. "We've been looking everywhere for you."

"Me?" he said pointing to himself.

"Well, what you have in your cart," Cassie explained.

All in all, the contents of the cart were disappointing. There were some broken and splintered tools from old ships, a couple of rusty compasses, a cracked sextant, and some things made of pig iron with pieces missing. Finally, just when Cassandra was convinced Peter was ready to give up, he lifted a tarnished silver pocket watch out of the bin.

"It's been in the water; it might open if you're very careful."

"Where did it come from?" asked Peter.

The boy leafed through an old ledger. "It says here my grandfather bought it in 1985 from a lady who said an ancestor found it on the beach long ago, and she believed it was washed ashore from a shipwreck off Cape Peril. He thought it was made in Italy and he tried to fix it, but he couldn't. I guess that's how it ended up here with all this other junk."

"How much?" asked Peter, much to the surprise of the young vendor and his sister.

"Twenty. That's half price."

"How about ten?" said Peter, putting his money on the cart. The boy had the money in his hand before he said okay. Then, with a friendly wave and a broad smile, he pushed forward, leaving the twins alone in the narrow, deserted alley.

"Hello there, the McBee twins from up the East Shore!" Peter and Cassandra turned to see a gentleman in tweeds and bushy mustache approach them. He placed his hands gently on their shoulders. The biggest surprise might not have been that there was someone with them in the narrow alley, but that this person had broken the rules by calling them by their names. Before they had the chance to respond, the stranger continued, "I've been in your shop many times—couldn't get along without that marvelous seasoning. What's the use of living here if you can't enjoy your seafood?"

Whether or not they realized it, each was being gently guided toward the open door of a small shop on the far left, at the end of the alley.

"With all your shopping, you haven't had a chance to see what I've got to offer. Step in, I've got all the *Powers* covered."

The Cardboard sign above the door read, Dark Arts Emporium, and once inside, Peter and Cassandra believed the name was appropriate. The items for sale seemed to be divided into categories, and the first was *seeing*. In front of them were numerous crystal balls of various sizes and colors. There were also shallow mirror-bowls with pitchers, fortune-telling stones, and a wide assortment of tarot cards. There were several antique brass hourglasses, each with different colored sand. "The one with the red sand foretells of someone's death," explained the shopkeeper. There was a spyglass on a stand which, when looked through, could show the intent of any man's or woman's heart and desires. A hand-carved Ouija board caught Cassandra's eye, and seeing this, the shop owner whispered, "Buy it and you'll win the lottery for certain."

Peter and Cassandra tried not to look too interested, so the shopkeeper assumed that they wanted to look at something else. "*Brewing* is particularly interesting to many of my young customers. Come and see my selection of potions and ingredients, many of which are not to be found anywhere on this continent."

Cassandra and Peter wandered past a wall that was lined with shelves of small, colored-glass bottles and open containers of labeled jars with little scoops and scales to weigh the dried herbs and powders. Noticing his young customers were not that interested, he embellished. "In this flask is a potion I am particularly proud of. It's a reverse love potion—it will cause an immediate breakup among even the most ardent couple." Getting no reaction, he held up a second bottle with the claim that it was a sleeping potion used to put the recipient into a long nap of two or more weeks. Next, he held up a bottle of something he called pain pills, giving the twins a wink and explaining that they cause pain, instead of treating it.

While Cassandra pretended to be listening politely, Peter

had already wandered away and was looking at a box of shriveled monkey paws, tufts of hair in a basket labeled "Werewolves," and an assortment of dried spiders and bats in sealed plastic bags. There was also a copper caldron of what looked like rat tails and several kinds of shriveled ears.

"What do you do with these?" asked Peter.

"You use them to *conjure* the most fantastic monsters imaginable. When mixed with just the right potions, they spring to life, giving you great power to terrorize the faint of heart. A few strange creatures running around your school would certainly liven things up, I would bet."

"Not interested," said Peter. "We've already got too many of those."

Thinking that Peter was definitely a hard-sell customer, the gentleman turned his attention back to Cassandra. "No doubt you have been brainwashed about all that balance of good and evil, that a curse comes back threefold on its maker?"

Cassandra nodded.

"Well, that simply isn't true! Over here I have beginners' kits to create even the most advanced curses. Who are the people you don't like—people who have treated you badly, those you would love to get even with? A curse well done can last for generations."

"There's no one that I would want to curse for generations," replied Cassandra, trying to push Mrs. Matthews from her mind.

"I have no problem telling you I'm a master of the dark arts. If your interests are darker than the things here, I have others I would not dare to show you."

"Let's see the most evil thing of all the things you dare not show us," demanded Peter in a solemn tone.

Cassandra thought the shopkeeper's claim was a lie, because if he was truly a master of all the *Powers*, then he would qualify to be a sorcerer. He surely didn't look or act all that great and powerful—perhaps that was why Peter called him out. As if in answer to Peter's challenge, he reached behind the counter.

"Look at this," he said, unwrapping a disk-shaped object from a black velvet pouch. "It's the Spirit Wheel of Cardissa. Cardissa was a very powerful medieval sorcerer who could return life to the dead. It is done by placing the wheel like so, over the grave of the deceased." He placed the wheel on the table and spun the dragon arrow in the center. "Where it stops will determine not whether the body returns to the world of the living, but what form it will take upon its return. The outcome is unpredictable; there is no controlling it."

Peter and Cassandra were totally captured in the moment as they watched the pointer spin slowly around and around, until it stopped at one of the twelve strange symbols.

"So what would happen this time?" asked Peter.

"The body would have returned to life as a pretty young maid with exceptional musical ability, if I have read it correctly. That might have been worth a spin, but other symbols on the wheel speak of horrors too awful to imagine, and once set loose in the world, they cannot be called back. I came by this object quite by accident and of course I would never sell it, but I have been paid very well to use it a few times, with some interesting outcomes. Now, my young friends, what will it be? Perhaps the creatures, or the potions, or would you consider paying me to spin the wheel for someone you have lost?"

There was a long moment of silence when Peter and Cassandra could surmise each other's thoughts, then Peter broke the silence by announcing, "The price for what you offer is too high."

"But we haven't discussed any prices yet," said the shopkeeper in surprise.

More might have been said, but from out of nowhere, a small young woman with flaming red curls, in a dazzling blue cloak swept into the shop. She passed right between the owner and the twins, and in a cold, clear voice announced to the shopkeeper, "It's closing time. I'm sure you know exactly what I mean."

"Oh yes," said the shopkeeper dejectedly, as he walked over to the door and hung the "Closed" sign on the window of the Dark Arts Emporium.

She turned to the twins and said, "Leave here now. Believe nothing this man has told you. He has no *Powers* at all and collaborates with those who are very dangerous to your kind."

Peter and Cassandra were so happy to be back outside that they didn't even notice how late they were to meet their aunts for the hot-air balloon extravaganza. They headed in the direction of the magnificent lift off. In the bright sky above them, the twins saw the first of the magnificent balloons. They were the most graceful and glorious things either of them had ever seen, and their lifting caused a great deal of excitement among the rest of the crowd as well.

While her eyes were fixed on an awesome balloon of blue and gold, Cassandra felt someone step on her heel. A man had been following her so closely that when she stopped to gaze at the balloon, he ran smack into her. She turned to see who had collided with her and was unnerved by the sinister look of him. He was a tall man, wearing a brown monk's robe tied at the waist with a rope. The robe's hood was pulled down, covering most of his face. Cassandra stood motionless for a second, then shook off her surprise and discomfort at the idea that someone was following her so closely. She caught up with her brother, a few feet away, who was watching the balloons drift upward.

"That was weird," said Cassie.

"What are you talking about?" asked Peter.

"That man back there. He was following really close behind me, and when I stopped and turned around ... well it was really creepy."

"Guess I missed him," said Peter, as the sky above them was transformed into a kaleidoscope vision of hovering balloons rising above the harbor. As the last of the hot air balloons drifted out to sea, Peter and Cassandra caught up with their aunts, and the four hurried off to find a spot for dinner.

Because they beat the rush, the McBees didn't have to wait long for a table under the green canopy of The Trade Winds Queen, a barge being used as a dockside restaurant. The place was noisy and crowded, and they had to talk above the sound of the canopy whomping in the strong sea breeze. While they were waiting to order, Cassandra saw the man in the brown monk's robe. She caught her breath sharply and kicked her brother under the table as the hooded figure headed straight for their table. Much to her relief, at that moment he pushed back his hood, revealing a young man with short-cropped, light brown hair, soft brown eyes, and a shy smile. Cassandra dismissed her alarm and decided it couldn't have been the same eerie man that had been following her.

He introduced himself as Brother Josiah and asked if he might join them, since their one empty place at the table seemed to be the only vacant seat on the whole barge. There was a polite conversation with the young man about the weather and the large crowd at the Bazaar this year, but nothing personal was asked or told. When the twins began to showcase their purchases to the aunts, he focused very intently on his menu.

Cassandra couldn't wait to show off her ring and tell its story. Much to her surprise, both aunts were delighted, and said it was a very elegant little ring that probably had not been in the possession of a poor immigrant girl. Cassie said it reminded her of the moonstone ring Gabrielle always wore. Aunt Penelope said it was not a moonstone, but looked much more like a fire opal that had lost some of its trapped colors.

Peter's pocket watch met with much less excitement, especially since he couldn't get it open. Still, Peter had found something he liked, and he had gained the experience of bargaining down the price, which Aunt Miranda thought was an excellent bazaar experience. When Peter mentioned that the watch may have been made in Italy and could have gone down with a ship off of Cape Peril, his aunts paid the watch a little more attention. This also caught the young stranger's attention and he put down his menu. "May I have a look at your watch? Perhaps I can tell you something more about its history," said Brother Josiah politely.

"Sure," said Peter. Brother Josiah looked at it carefully and handled it very gently. Then, with just the right, soft touch, it opened smoothly in the palm of his hand.

"This watch was made by the Italian clockmaker Bernadeau Govi, during the seventeenth century. If you look closely, you can see the signature of the artisan, a backwards 'G' always found under the numeral 'VIII,' like a company logo. Govi made chronometers for the busy shipping trade and clocks for the rich and famous. Between 1650 and 1700, Govi was one of the richest and most powerful men in the city-states along the coast of what is now Italy. This is most likely a pocket or lapel watch that he made as a special gift to a brotherhood of monks he patronized. It is said he made them these timepieces to allow more time in their day for charitable works among the sick and needy. They were brave, artful fellows who used the gift of time wisely."

"Wow, that's amazing. How do you know so much about this kind of stuff?" asked Peter.

"In my studies I came across some journals written over several hundred years ago by the brothers of a small order, Il Confraternito de Ombre—the Brotherhood of Shadows. Since then, I have done as much research as I can to know about their history, and I come to these bazaars looking for any documents or artifacts that might give me more information. Someday, I hope to write a book about them."

"I'd like to read it," said Peter with a sincere smile.

"I'll give you the first autographed copy if you will do a favor for me in return?"

"Sure, if I can."

"Should you ever learn more about Govi or the watch, please let me know."

"How would I reach you?"

"I'll be around. My research is bringing me to these parts,

and I'm always at bazaars like this one."

The third and last day of the Bazaar, it was cold and stormy. The sidewalk vendors had packed up and were nowhere to be seen, many of the shops looked dark, and the streets were nearly empty. Cassandra and Peter were so intent on seeing anything they had missed, that they didn't notice how the weather had changed to a damp misty fog. At noon, they ran all the way to the Creaky Spar where their aunts were waiting for them in a corner booth. Aunt Penelope said if everyone was done shopping and they had seen all they wanted to see, they could get an early start for home after lunch.

"By this evening, the anchored boats and yachts will be gone, the streets will be completely empty, and only a few of the restaurants will remain open," explained Aunt Miranda. "And now for my favorite find of the Bazaar!"

"You'll love what she found for us," said Aunt Penelope, rolling her eyes.

"I've bought each of us a very special whistle. They originated in Ireland and were used by shepherds there many years ago. They are said to be enchanted. Each has its own tune, and they can only be heard from a distance. The sound carries on the wind and you can't hear a thing if you blow it in here."

"Why do we need whistles?" asked Cassandra.

"They're for an emergency. You know, like if we need to reach one another, or send out a call for help," explained Aunt Miranda.

"Or we could get the twins their own cell phones," said Aunt Penelope.

Miranda shook her head. "Cell phones aren't one

hundred percent reliable and besides, they can be a terrible distraction, not to mention expensive!"

"Got it," said Peter. "We'll communicate via big dog whistles."

While the aunts were talking, Cassandra had been sitting quietly looking around the dim cafe. Peter could see by the look on her face that something she saw was puzzling her.

"What is it?" he whispered.

"Look around at the people in here. Notice anything?"

Across the room, Peter saw both of the coin dealers—having lunch together. He was sure they were looking over at the McBee booth until they saw him looking at them and turned away. "So much for unbiased coin appraisals," he thought to himself. By the door, he spotted the couple from the joke shop and the little fellow from the Chinese Junk.

"Look, there's Brother Josiah, talking to the lady who sold me my ring. Doesn't that seem like a strange coincidence?" said Cassie.

"Yeah it does. And there's that kid from Broken Treasures with someone who I can't see from here," said Peter.

"It's some big guy with a red beard and a hat like yours," said Cassie.

"Look, over there is the woman in the blue cloak who came to the Dark Arts Emporium and told us to leave," said Peter, forgetting the aunts were right there and could overhear them.

"What are you two talking about?" asked Aunt Penelope.

"Oh, we were just noticing that this place is full of the people we saw while we were shopping. It seems an odd coincidence," Cassie answered.

"You two didn't get into any trouble while you were here,

did you?" asked Penelope, honing in on the bit about being told to leave the shop.

"Nothing they didn't handle well. I had my doubts about exposing the two of you to all of this, but you seem to have handled it in stride," said Miranda, much to the surprise of Peter and Cassandra.

She knows about the evil emporium, were the unspoken words that passed between Cassandra and her brother, but at that the topic was dropped.

The McBees headed back to Cape Peril, and the effect of the three-day adventure on Peter and Cassandra was intense. Both were exploding with questions that neither could quite put into words. There were so many things they wanted to ask their aunts, but it was Aunt Miranda who opened the information gates. "So, did the two of you have a good time? Was it what you expected?"

"It wasn't like anything I expected," said Cassie.

"How about you, Peter? Were you surprised by anything you came across?"

"Well ... I thought the Bazaar was going to be all about shipwrecks—but there was a lot to do with magic."

"I guess we should have warned you," said Aunt Miranda. "Anytime you're around people who know the sea, magic is not far off. After all, mermaids and sea monsters are as much a part of nautical history as sailcloth and schooners. I believe everyone has some magical ability, but people who live by the sea are especially gifted. They know things and are sensitive to what goes on in their world. It's how they survived for generations at sea. You two have seen so much magic growing up at the lighthouse that you take it as ordinary and routine."

Treasures of Plunder Bay

"Like the house itself—it's magical, isn't it?" asked Cassie.

"Exactly," said Aunt Penelope. "There are so many things you know but cannot discuss because some people don't believe in magic, or worse yet, they fear it."

"And those would be outliers?" asked Peter.

"You have learned a lot in the past few days," responded Aunt Miranda.

The Winds Of Change

W ithin a few weeks of the Bazaar, things at school started to get stranger by the moment. Will and Peter had managed to convince the others that Cody's giant rats were normal sized, but it hadn't been easy. Will had his own theory about the rats, but he kept it to himself, hoping word of them would soon die down. Rats weren't the only complication. Miss Tweaks's afternoon drama classes had started rehearsal for *A Midsummer Night's Dream*, scheduled to be performed right before the school winter break.

Miss Tweaks's homeroom students arrived one day to find their whole classroom and the back of the stage filled with huge pots full of dirt. Over the next few days, she had Peter and some of the others build tall wooden frames to support tiny green sprouts they planted in the big pots. Within a few days, fast-growing, green vines began to trail up the wooden frameworks. By Monday of the following week, the classroom looked and smelled like a jungle. Miss Tweaks loved watering the vines with a special plant-food mixture she had gotten from Aunt Miranda, and the plants grew and grew. Miss Tweaks called them her dream vines. They reached out of the pots and entwined their arms around each other in big green hugs. It was fascinating to watch, but more than a little weird.

Then there was the matter of the scarf. Miss Tweaks called it her Twilight Scarf.

101

"Look at it," she said, holding it up for the students to see. "I found it while going through some old trunks, looking for costumes for the new play. I don't know where it came from. Isn't it beautiful?"

The scarf was murky blue—almost black—and silky soft with sequin insets that shimmered and twinkled like small yellow stars in the evening sky.

"Feel how soft and luxurious it is!" she said, walking around the room with it so the students could touch it.

"It is really soft. I can't tell if it's made from silk or velvet," said Madelyn as she ran her hand across the top of the scarf.

Miss Tweaks wrapped it around her neck and tossed the two ends over her shoulders. It was so long, one end trailed the floor behind her. She walked down the aisle to the back of the classroom to examine herself in the old cheval mirror that was almost buried now in dream vines.

"Ahh, it's beautiful!" she said, her image delighting her.

The girls generally thought it was a little over the top, but complimented her on it, and the boys acknowledged it was really different than anything they had seen. After that, she wore the scarf every day while she was teaching.

Their lessons were focused on recognizing and enhancing their *Powers*.

"It's a simple concept, really, if you look at it from a practical perspective," she explained. "You must determine what it is that you do best ... what comes most naturally to you."

"For me that's eating!" said Cody. The class laughed at this.

"That's good Cody! So, you like food. You know what tastes good. You enjoy the *experience* of food. Your *Power* may very well lie in *brewing* amazing dishes or *realizing* the management of a great restaurant. We already know you have tendencies to *protect*, we saw that the first week of school. Maybe you will combine your *Powers* and become a nutritionist!"

Madelyn spoke up, "I thought *Powers* were something you had to work hard to obtain and keep."

"The strongest *Powers* are the ones that we have naturally," explained Miss Tweaks. "Every one of us is good at certain things. No one thing is better or worse than the other. Some of you have exceptionally successful fishermen in your families, they use the gift of *finding*. Those who can craft, build, and fix things are strong in the *Power, creating*—we all know people who amaze us with what they can achieve."

"So is making movies, writing books, and acting in plays the *Power, enchanting*?" asked Gabrielle.

"Yes, those are excellent examples of *enchanting*," replied Miss Tweaks.

"What's an example of *seeing*?" asked Daniel.

"That's a good question, Daniel. Have you ever played Chess or Checkers with someone who was hard to beat? They win because they can picture the outcome of different scenarios based on the placement of the chess pieces or checkers. They're able to look at the game board as a whole ... they see the big picture, so-to-speak."

"But how does that equate to the real world?" asked Paige.

"Well, we often see the *Power* of *seeing* at work in running a business, being a marketing specialist, or in the field of strategy and project management."

"My uncle's a city planner and volunteers on the Park

Planning Board. Does that mean he has *seeing Powers*?" asked Virginia.

"If he's good at it, then yes!" said Miss Tweaks. "Here's the thing ... you need to discover your *Powers* and then set yourselves up to be able to practice your *Powers*. If you can do what you do best, every day, you will be successful!"

"And if we are successful, we'll be happy," exclaimed Caitlyn M.

"That's right. And why is being successful and happy so important?" asked Miss Tweaks.

The class was thoughtful and the room was so quiet you could hear the dream vines growing.

"I think I have it," said Cassie. "When people can do what they do best, and feel successful and happy, they're able to help others."

"Exactly! Understanding and using our *Powers* makes our village, and ultimately the world, a better place. I saw this recently when the village came together to keep Plunder Bay School open. Putting anger and frustration aside, and doing what we all do best, resulted in a positive outcome for many people ... including all of you, I hope."

"But what happens when we aren't able to do what we do best, and put our *Powers* to use? I mean that's the real world too," said Peter.

"Sadly, you are right, Peter. When people are trapped in situations or jobs where they can't do what they love, or are forced to do what they aren't good or talented at doing, they hurt. Hurt leads to many negative outcomes and we can find ourselves in a very dark world. Which leads us to today's homework!"

There was a collective groan across the students in the classroom.

"I want each of you to go home this evening and find a quiet place to contemplate. If you have one, light a purple candle, and for the best results, hold a labradorite, moonstone, or amethyst crystal in the palm of your left hand. I like to add a drop of essence of jasmine oil to my candle—but that's strictly optional. Ask yourself, while you are contemplating in your quiet place, 'What would I do now, or tomorrow, if there were no constraints on my time or my movements'. In other words, if you could do anything you wanted to do—what would it be? Then, I want you to write down which of the *Powers* are involved with doing the thing you would love to do, if you could! Don't worry, you won't have to share this with the class ... unless you want to."

That evening, after dinner, the twins compared notes on their homework assignment and shared their exploration of their *Powers* with the aunts.

"I'm glad Miss Tweaks has started you on discovering and purposefully using your *Powers*," said Aunt Miranda. "Our *Powers* are enhanced by the sea, and the many generations of ancestors who understood and followed this wisdom."

"Has she mentioned the realms of the ancient world, and how they come into the picture?" asked Aunt Penelope.

"We've just touched on it," said Peter, "nothing in much detail yet."

"Well soon you will learn that your own *Powers* are strongest when you combine them with spells and enchantments using the languages spoken by our ancestors," said Aunt Miranda.

For the kids from Plunder Bay and the rest of the

Maritimes, this was mostly Old French, Gascon, Old English, Welsh, Cornish, Irish Gaelic, Manx, Scots Gaelic, and a little Norn. For kids from other realms across the sea, the languages would be completely different.

A few days later while doing research in the school library, Cassandra found a book of maps that showed the history of languages spoken across the British Isles and France going back one thousand years.

"Look at this," she said to Peter, pointing to a particular page in the book.

"Looks like someone else was researching this information. Maybe a student from the past?"

"Can you make out the writing in the margin, next to this map from the fifteenth century?" asked Cassie.

"Well, my Scots Gaelic is less than proficient, but it looks like it's talking about hexes. Something to do with a hex being more powerful when spoken in the ancient language of the person you are cursing," said Peter.

Hearing the twins whispering while deeply engrossed in a big map book got the attention of several of their classmates who were nearby.

"What did you find in there?" asked Jason.

"Basically, how to cast a hex with double the intensity," replied Cassandra.

"Ooo ... what's the trick to doing that?" asked Gabrielle with a gleam in her eye.

"Say it in their ancestor's ancient language versus your own," replied Peter.

"That's dark magic," said Virginia.

"Well, I don't plan to do any hexes," said Cody, "so I can forget about learning other people's ancestors' ancient languages. I'm having a hard enough time learning my own ancestors' language. Heck, I wasn't that great with plain old English to begin with."

Madelyn, ever practical, added, "But, if you knew who your most dangerous enemy was, you could focus on learning a few key spells in that enemy's language. It could be a powerful weapon if you ever needed one."

Will chimed in, "What if you both have the same ancient language?"

"That's a good question," said Cassie.

"We have so much to learn ... and I want to know it all!" said Gabrielle.

The kids headed back to the classroom to pack up their things in anticipation of the lunch bell. When they got back to the room, lugging their books on genealogy, etymology, and phonology, they found Miss Tweaks behaving strangely. She was looking at herself in the mirror and having a conversation with her reflection. The drama students said that Miss Tweaks liked to live inside whatever theatrical play she was working on. They said she got a little strange like this every year, because she was a true artist of the theater. That was the way the drama students talked. Cassandra wasn't sure that Miss Tweaks was saying lines from the play, and Peter thought she'd gone completely mad.

A November gale was blowing on the Monday afternoon that a stranger came through the main doors of the school building. Cassandra and Peter were standing alone outside the cafeteria when the stranger lost hold of the door handle. Both doors blew open, crashing back against the outside walls. A mass of leaves blew into the main hall, and in the flurry the twins saw a fellow in a parka with a wool scarf wrapped around his neck.

"Help me out here!" he snapped.

Peter and Cassandra rushed forward and tugged on the doors with all their strength and weight. Finally, the doors closed and latched.

"Where's the main office?" the man demanded, stomping his wet loafers, and unwrapping his scarf. "I'm here to see Adam Boggins."

The twins pointed toward the office door and hurried off down the hall, leaving the unpleasant stranger to his own devices.

"Wonder what his problem is?" asked Peter.

"Maybe it's another one of Mr. Boggins's unemployed relatives coming to live with him," conjectured Cassandra.

Glen Amadan was not another relative come to torment Mr. Boggins; it was much worse than that. By the next day at school, the rumor was circulating that Mr. Amadan had come to take Mr. Boggins's job. They said he had been sent by the Ministry of Education to be the new principal of Plunder Bay School. Right away, he moved into Mr. Boggins's little office behind the secretary's desk. Paige said she had seen him nosing around the restrooms while the classes were in session, and Jason had seen him inspecting the gym. The last period on Friday, Mr. Amadan called an unexpected assembly in the old theater for the whole school. The velvet curtains on the stage were closed behind him, and he was standing in front of a low podium. Peter knew how high the podium was, as he had moved it around several times. He also knew that Mr. Amadan was standing with his knees bent to make himself look less gangly as he introduced himself.

At one point, Mr. Boggins, who was sitting in the front row with his physics students, got up to offer him a microphone. It must have had a short, because when he finally found the switch to turn it on, it made a loud squealing sound and sparks flew. For a second, Mr. Amadan looked frightened, and he dropped the mic. Then he went on to prove he didn't need a microphone. As expected, the gangly, balding, middle-aged stranger announced he was the new principal—a full-time, permanent principal.

"I've been called in by the Ministry of Education because they have had several complaints from students' families about confusion with class scheduling, and squalid conditions at the school—including the presence of rats. I'm inclined to agree that there are serious problems here. The school could certainly be cleaner, and more importantly, I've found several serious code violations."

He let them know that he had ordered a full inspection of the building by the authorities, and he intended to immediately deal with some serious issues like poor discipline and a lack of student supervision.

"Students' unacceptable behavior will be corrected right here and now! We'll be implementing a strict dress code—starting with no jeans. In the morning, all students will go from their buses to homeroom. You may stop at your lockers, but there will be no lingering or socializing in the halls."

With those words, the new principal slapped his sweaty palm down on the podium, making a loud splat that sounded a lot like a wet fart.

"L-O-L," whispered Gabrielle, trying to contain her giggles.

Treasures of Plunder Bay

"Students will sit with their next period class in the cafeteria, seats will be assigned, and you will stay in them. There will be teachers on duty, in the lunchroom, at all times. Your fourth-period teacher will dismiss you from the cafeteria and take you straight to their classroom." He slapped his sweaty hand down again—making the same unfortunate sound.

"In the evenings, you will remain in your seventh-period class until your bus is announced. You may stop at your locker, then go directly to your bus. Above all, you will treat all adults on staff with respect and maturity."

"That's stupid," whispered Cody. "My locker's up on the third floor. I'll miss my bus."

"Most importantly, under no circumstances will you *Plunder Bay* students form groups to taunt or threaten the Soulac or Bearing Cross students. That STOPS right now!" he almost shouted, as another *PFFTT* sounded from the podium.

Several students turned and looked at Walker Matthews and his pals. They had wide grins on their faces and were obviously enjoying this attack on the Plunder Bay kids.

With that, someone backstage parted the curtains slightly, and the sweet smell of *A Midsummer Night's Dream* filled the theater. The curtains closed back quickly, but not in time. A long green vine had escaped, and two of its tentacles reached out and bobbed and bounced in rhythm with what was being said, over the top of Mr. Amadan's black combover. As he continued his tirade, riotous laughter filled the theater. Then from somewhere in the back, a voice called out to the dancing vine, "Squeeze him!" The whole auditorium broke out in hysterical fits of laughter.

110

Will looked at Peter. "That was Mr. Morgan. I'd recognize his voice anywhere."

"Awesome!" said Peter, laughing so hard he could barely speak.

The laughter continued, overpowering the thumps on the podium, until someone in the back must have called buses, and the theater emptied out completely. There was reportedly some pushing and shoving in the main hall that afternoon, and Caitlyn B. said the Bearing Cross boys got the worst of it. Trash cans were upset, and a locker door was broken off.

At Cape Peril cottage it was a weekend of nonstop phone calls. Plunder Bay parents called to tell the aunts they were certain Mr. Amadan had been sent to make sure the school was closed forever. Code violations sounded serious enough, but this new principal had deliberately started a war between the village kids and the students from Bearing Cross. In less than a week, he had incited violence and destruction of property to a place they loved. He had also endangered everyone in the school—not bad for four days on the job.

Fortunately, an unexpected ice storm closed the school on Monday, giving everyone a three-day weekend to cool off. Unfortunately, it had also delayed this year's start of lobster season. On Tuesday, Miss Tweaks wasn't her usual wacky self. In fact, the whole school was quiet, like the calm before a storm. In gym, Coach organized teams and let everybody play basketball. His strategy was to mix up the students from Plunder Bay with those from Bearing Cross and let them blow off steam on the courts.

Mr. Amadan was in the cafeteria every day at early lunch; it was the first chance most of the students had to see him up close.

"So I guess we're all going to wear pleated khaki pants or skirts—or can we wear other colors too?" asked Caitlyn M.

"This is the only pair of dress pants I own," said Paige, one of five children in the Boggins's family.

"I'll be wearing jeans, no matter what," pronounced Gabrielle. "He can send me home, *if he dares*."

Virginia laughed and said, "No worries, girls. He'll never make that rule stick. Mrs. Lee, the algebra teacher, says there will be a hundred arguments with parents any time he tries to make his case. She said this kind of thing happened at the last school where she taught."

"I wonder if he knows how much it costs to buy new clothes?" said Cody, sliding down to the girls' end of the table.

The new principal showed up in the library early the following Tuesday morning. The students were certain that Miss Tweaks had not come in yet, but she appeared suddenly from behind the bookshelves soon after he arrived. They met in the center of the big room right under the clock.

"Miss Tweaks, you were not at any of my faculty meetings last week. I suppose you know I am the new principal, Glenn Amadan?"

"Oh yes," she said. "Most unfortunate."

"Missing my meetings or my being the new principal?"

"No, your name—A-ma-dan. That's an unfortunate name ... for someone who speaks Gaelic, but you don't, so I guess it doesn't matter. But Glenn, now that's a perfectly lovely name ... means valley."

With a look of utter confusion, he said, "I came over yesterday morning to observe your homeroom, but I couldn't find it. How do I get there?"

"That depends on which way you are coming from."

"Never mind. Go on with your class and we can talk in my office at 3:15 p.m. Please be there and be on time."

Peter thought that if Mr. Amadan was coming from the basement, he could be eaten by giant rats, or if he was coming from the theater, he could be strangled by deadly vines. They needed to formulate a plan to keep him from finding their special classroom. Will ran down to the bottom of the stairs at the basement level and took out the light bulb. He reported that at least some of the musty stench had returned. Daniel closed the door from the classroom to the back of the stage, and dragged two pots of vines in front of it. Peter and Jason ran around to the other side and moved the backdrop on the stage; this hid the door from that side. Cody was out of breath when he arrived with the finishing touch—a little metal sign that read, "Audiovisual Equipment Closet." He said he had a devil of a time unscrewing it from the third-floor audiovisual closet door. Once firmly in place on the outside of their classroom door, all five stood on the landing to admire their work.

"This won't fool him for long," said Will. "Even he can't be that stupid."

If their new principal intended to go in search of their classroom the next morning, his plans changed. As the buses were pulling in, two white sedans, a grey minivan, and one red truck parked in the visitors' lot at Plunder Bay School. Both sedans had government plates, and one of them was marked "Ministry of Education." The grey minivan had a "Department of Health" decal on the door, and the red truck had "Fire Marshall" painted on the sides and back tailgate. They arrived together because they had all met at the Naughty Puffin Inn for breakfast that morning to go over their plans. All but the fire marshal intended to be there the rest of the week.

Mr. Amadan was delighted by their arrival, and he took his six guests on an extensive tour of the building. After touring and going through the problems that needed investigated, they ate lunch in the cafeteria at a large round table set with tall glasses and white linen napkins. If any of the guests were offended by mystic stew and mud pies, it didn't seem to hurt their appetites. The new principal jabbered on, smiling and talking with his hands. It was obvious to the students who were watching that everything was going his way.

The health inspector—a jovial, portly, old fellow—decided to begin his work in the kitchen with coffee and an extra round of mudpies. Of course, that put him under the power of the remarkable Maggie O'Day. Halfway through their second cup of coffee, the health inspector confided in Maggie his obsession with anything ghostly or supernatural. He wanted to know if the rumors he had heard were true, and if there was any chance that the old school was haunted.

Maggie seized the opportunity to share some blood-chilling tales about events and unearthly sightings in the school over the last 90 years. She recounted in detail about the three Irish workers, buried alive when building the west wall, who were likely to show up when food was being served. Of course, there was a smuggler murdered in the old wing, who sometimes appeared in a bloody shirt with the dagger that killed him still protruding from his torso. She was only halfway through the gruesome story of

Bartholomew Boggins's ghost, searching for his gold bars, when he begged her to stop. The Inspector of Health was so shaken by the stories that he asked Maggie to accompany him on his inspections. He hurried through his report and turned it in by late afternoon, insisting he must get home before dark.

The young fire marshall was another story. He was from Soulac, had graduated from Plunder Bay School six years before, and had been a member of the elite drama group. Like the health inspector, he did not work for the Ministry of Education, and he had no reason to find problems at the school. He went about his job methodically, checking the smoke detectors, fire escape plans, hydrants, and fire exits. When he came across the door marked "Audiovisual Equipment Closet," he checked to make sure it was not locked, then walked away, and chuckled heartily to himself. Next, the fire marshall inspected the electrical and heating systems. Finally, he went to the theater and stood for a long time, remembering his high school sweetheart and his first kiss. He slid a copy of his report under Principal Amadan's door before that evening.

The two auditors from the Budget Office were loaded up with all the files they needed. They went straight to their task, and an hour after lunch they were deep into stacks of the school's financial records. Before they left for the day, both assured the principal that they had found serious problems and the possibility of missing money.

There were also two building engineers from the Ministry. Their job was to inspect the structural safety of the old school. After examining pages of blueprints they went outside to scrutinize the roof and foundation. The next morning they put on safety helmets and coveralls.

Treasures of Plunder Bay

With flashlights and clipboards, they set out to walk or crawl through every nook and cranny, and it was only logical that they would begin with the older wing.

If Miss Tweaks noticed the little metal sign on their homeroom door, she never mentioned it. That morning, her students coaxed her to give them free reading time in the library. Perhaps because she was busy in the theater, or because her students insisted—they were all very much into the books they were reading—she agreed, and led them up and into the back bay of the library. Cassandra and Gabrielle settled on floor cushions with their books. Peter took his book to a cozy armchair beside the pedestal with the handcrafted model of the ship called the *Angelique*. When they were all seated, books in hand, she pulled her tinted glasses from atop her curly pile of hair, put them on, and in a soft, sweet voice said, "May you all thoroughly escape into your adventures!"

Shortly thereafter, the taller of the two engineers began his inspection in the library. As he checked for creaking floor beams or signs of rot in the wide board flooring, he heard strange sounds coming from behind the bookshelves. At first, he thought he heard a jungle cat—no, it sounded more like the revving of an airplane engine. As he wandered closer to the sounds, a wooden spear went whizzing past his head. He stopped, looking to retrieve the evidence, but when he removed a book, he saw only a wild boar running for its life on the other side. He stepped back quickly and shook his head in disbelief. Carelessly, he wandered farther into the maze of books. At one point, he was astounded by the strong smell of lilacs and the buzz of bees. When he looked at his feet, he saw he was standing in a field of grass. Further on, he heard air bubbles escaping from a big armchair containing only an open copy of *Twenty Thousand Leagues Under the Sea.* He was wandering in a daze, trying to find a way out and only going in circles, coming back to the same place where he had removed the book. Feeling a sudden chill, he looked down to see soupy green swamp water rising around his ankles as something scaly slithered past.

"Help!" he heard himself say in a weak little voice.

After what seemed like hours, the engineer crawled out from between the shelves on his hands and knees. He moved stealthily past the front desk, looking back over his shoulder. When he reached the doors, he stood up and escaped into the hall outside. He leaned against the wall, hardly noticing that his shirt was soaked, his boots were covered with green slime, and he had lost his clipboard.

His intention was to report his experience to the office, but at that moment his companion, the short and stocky engineer emerged from the basement. His coveralls were shredded, and he had scratches on his face and arms. There was a terrible-looking red mark, like a rope burn, around his neck, and strands of dream vine were still clinging to his back and ankles.

Neither man asked any questions about the other's condition, and without saying a word they made a mad dash out of the building to their car. On their long ride back to the regional capitol they did not discuss the events of the morning, they didn't tell their bosses, they didn't even tell their wives. The next morning, the secretary got a call from the department saying that the engineers were each working on their final reports at home and would be mailing them to the school sometime after the holidays.

Principal Amadan's last great hope of completing his

assignment and closing the school permanently before the holidays fell to the two auditors. They had been working diligently for three solid days. At this point, they were deep into the accounts of the theater department, where they had found irregularities. As they rifled through spreadsheets they became aware that the school had borrowed money from the theater accounts on several occasions to pay bills. To them, that meant that money that should have come to the school from the Ministry, to cover legitimate expenses, had been mishandled.

New spreadsheets were started. At the closing of the day they compared their figures and discovered that yes, there was money missing. The funds had been misdirected, or mishandled, or perhaps even stolen—by the Ministry—not the school! It appeared they had been shorting the money allotted to Plunder Bay School for most of the last twenty years. It was a scandal of criminal proportion.

They would have to turn in their own bosses, and spend weeks in court testifying. The thought of that was too much to bear. Both ladies closed their account books and put them away neatly. They packed their laptops carefully, and told the secretary good night. On the way home, both decided to immediately quit their jobs with the Ministry before they got dragged into this big mess. After all, they concluded, there were lots of jobs for good accountants in the business sector, and the pay was better.

Nothing had gone as Mr. Amadan had carefully planned, and without giving a reason, the frustrated principal canceled the school play. Out of spite, he declared there would be no more sports games with other schools for the rest of the year and no more after-school practices. He canceled all clubs and club meetings. Then, to really end any extracurricular activity, he dismantled the band. After that, he basically disappeared. He remained the principal, with full authority, but stayed in his office all the time—if he came to the school at all.

Four days into the holiday break, Cassandra and Peter went for a morning walk in the woods. The branches on the pine trees bent low with ivory frosting, and the snow crunched under their boots. They ended their walk by pushing and dragging the Yule log in across the porch. It was part of an ash tree that had fallen last winter. It had been cut and trimmed in the summer and had waited here ever since. Getting it into the keeping room fireplace was a major operation involving Peter's runner sled. Once in place, they decorated the log with holly and ivy branches. That night after dousing the log with wassail and sprinkling it with wheat flour, they started the fire with a remnant of last year's log. The kindling burst quickly into flame, and the big log smoldered, just as it was supposed to do.

Every evening for the rest of the holiday, the family would gather in the keeping room and add fresh dry wood and bark for the glowing log to kindle, and someone would remove the fireguard, toss herbs on the fire, and say a little verse to bless the house. The aunts suggested that Peter and Cassandra should select an herb and give the first blessing of the season. Cassandra worked hard to *realize* her blessing. She studied the herb books in the conservatory and wanted to burn frankincense resin, but settled for rosemary because her first choice was probably the only thing not growing or preserved in Aunt Miranda's stash of exotic plants. As she tossed her herbs onto the fire that night, she said:

"Herb of the Winter Sun,
Protect and purify this home.
May health and safety here reside,
All year until the next Yuletide."

She told Peter later that she had felt very magical at that moment.

Peter, in fact, forgot all about his part in the Yuletide blessing until a few minutes before it was time for him to do it. He ran outside and grabbed a handful of pine needles. When he threw them on the fire, they crackled and filled the room with smoke. On top of that choking fiasco, he remembered he was supposed to say something, so he blurted out:

"Let all this smoke go up the flue,
And send your evil back to you."

His blessing didn't make much sense and the rhyme was pure accident, but a moment later the occupants of the keeping room heard a loud swoosh of wind that seemed to rush in from every corner of the old cottage. It joined with the smoke in the keeping room, forming a whirling black funnel that lingered a moment in the room, then with an ear-splitting suction noise, vanished up the chimney, nearly taking Blue with it. Everyone in the room but Blue and Miranda rushed outside to see if the chimney was on fire. Miranda and Blue knew better. Peter had unknowingly undone a curse that none of them knew they were under.

When the old bird stopped cursing, Aunt Miranda said to him, "Putting a curse like that on Cape Peril cottage was a *conjuring*, done by dark forces. Trouble has been following Plunder Bay since we got back from the Smuggler's Bazaar. I hope we haven't put Cassandra and Peter in harm's way. Neither of them is schooled enough to deal with this kind of danger."

"Storm's a coming! Storm's a coming!" squawked the wise old parrot.

Phantoms, Demons, and Wraiths

January came to the village of Plunder Bay with a vengeance. Huge waves crashed against the harbor seawall and pounded the rocky shoreline. Many of the storms came out of the northeast and were accompanied by snow and sleet. The local fishing fleet was safely moored in the harbor, but the captains of the big tankers heading down the coast kept watch for the great Cape Peril light, knowing that decommissioned as it was, it would still warn them if conditions were too rough to continue on their course. The greater danger that January, however, arrived in a couple of black vans. Only those who kept the night watch knew about the arrival of these nocturnal visitors to the bay.

Since the holidays, each of the adults at Cape Peril cottage took precautions in their own way. Aunt Penelope bought a radio scanner and tuned it to the police frequency. As a fire-rescue volunteer, she had approval to monitor police activity. Aunt Miranda added cloves of garlic to the potpourri baskets around the cottage. Peter got the job of sprinkling salt on the door stoops. Aunt Miranda had Peter and Cassandra bring down their Irish shepherd's whistles and test them outside in the wind—there was some doubt as to whether or not they worked. Peter thought he could hear Cassandra's whistle playing a quick little jig. Although she listened very carefully, Cassandra could not hear Peter's. Aunt Miranda said that she could hear both of their calls, so carrying their shepherd's whistles became a new rule.

Because it gave her a sense of confidence, Cassandra now wore her little silver ring all the time, on her right pinky finger. Peter had cleaned up his Govi watch and decided to carry it on strands of dream vines he had braided for his whistle. Aunt Penelope instructed the twins that if there was ever any immediate danger, they were to go to the playroom and stay there. Both Peter and Cassandra thought precautionary measures at home were overdone, and worst of all, it had been decided that the aunts would drive them to school and pick them up every day.

Things at school were also peculiar. Cody came to homeroom one morning certain that he had seen a shadowy stranger standing in the dark at the bottom of the back stairs.

"There was somebody down there, I swear it. I couldn't exactly see him, but I could hear him making a hissing noise," Cody announced at lunch.

A few days later, Caitlyn B. said there had been two phantom figures in long black capes shut up in the office with Mr. Amadan. She couldn't exactly explain what she meant by phantoms, but she said they seemed unreal. Next, it was Gabrielle who got spooked by two demonic-looking beings who lurked outside the second-floor washroom and whispered to each other. Daily, more students reported seeing strangers in the shadows and dim places of the school, but no one actually got a good look at any of them. Mr. Boggins could often be seen wandering through the building muttering to himself, and Miss Tweaks seemed nervous and agitated. In truth, everyone at the school was jittery with a sense of some dark, eerie presence.

Treasures of Plunder Bay

Even Ms. O'Day was not her usual cheerful self. More than once she had the odd sensation of someone tugging at the key ring she kept looped through her apron ties. She sensed that things in her kitchen had been moved or tampered with. Several days in a row, while she was serving lunch, she had the chilling sensation of someone behind her in her kitchen, watching the students as they went through the lunch line. More than once, Peter and Cassandra saw her turn quickly to look behind her. On one occasion she had turned around completely and beat the air with a spatula.

"Hey, Peter, don't laugh, but have you ever had the feeling that someone was watching you?" said Will, on their way to geography after lunch one day.

"Yeah, I've had that feeling a lot lately. Is there any place in the building where you feel it really strongly?"

"Up on the third floor. I hate being up there when nobody else is around. Cody's locker and mine are down at the far end in the corner. I can hear what sounds like a whispering conversation. I know that Cody hears it too, but after word of the rats got out, he won't say anything."

"I notice no one ever asks to be excused to go to the restroom in the middle of class anymore. I think everybody's freaked out," said Peter.

"You're right about that. In music last week the teacher asked for volunteers to go get some stands from the basement and nobody would go. Maybe we should talk to somebody about this—maybe the teachers would be more likely to do something if they knew about it."

"It's hard to report something that no one has really seen. Maybe we should just go after whatever it is if we get close," said Peter.

"Yeah, like then we'd have proof, and if we didn't get hold of anyone or anything, we could pretend like the two of us were just horsing around."

"That could work—then we wouldn't look like idiots."

It was a bold plan, and one that they didn't have to wait long to execute.

The Plunder Bay students arrived one morning in late January to find chains and padlocks on the theater doors, and no sign of the suits of armor. There was a sign on the marquee that read, "Theater Closed for Repairs." Miss Tweaks had her homeroom meet in the library that day. Peter and Cassandra loved being in the library, but things there began to change as well. One day as Cassandra was winding her way through the bookshelf maze, she thought the shelf with the big old books looked emptier. A few days later, all the books belonging in that section were gone. Peter saw that the little clock with the sad face was missing from behind the front desk, and the model of the *Angelique* was gone. His favorite painting, the grey schooner with the crimson banner, had vanished too.

First chance he had, Peter caught Miss Tweaks alone. "There's a lot of stuff missing from the library, and it sounds bizarre, but we think the school is full of whispering phantoms that no one can see. Maybe they are stealing stuff from the school?"

"I know ... I know ... it's so frustrating dealing with things that can't be seen. They're always underfoot, and when I bump into one of them, they always wait for *me* to say, I'm sorry. But remember, Peter, things that disappear from here have a strange way of making their way back."

On their way to lunch a couple of days later, some of the

older girls who'd been in the library were telling Madelyn, Cassandra, and Gabrielle about the substitute teacher in their social studies class.

"She must be over six feet tall, and she wears these crazy open-toed pumps with straps that lace up her ankles, showing her purple toenails."

"I know who you're talking about," said Madelyn. "When she was here subbing for algebra last week, she had a purse she said was made of real snakeskin."

The boys were lagging behind, and just as the girls came to the doors leading out of the old wing, Cassandra stopped and stared into the corner on her right. Gabrielle had stopped too, and the other girls went on without noticing they had lost some of their audience.

"What is it?" Peter asked her, as Cody and Will caught up with them.

Cassandra was facing the corner behind the door and pointing where the two walls met, about a meter away. "I'm not sure, but I think someone is standing there. Can you see them, Gabrielle?"

Before Gabrielle could answer, Will gave Peter a flying tackle and the two of them went bumping and crashing against the wall.

"Ouch, that hurt," said Cody.

"What hurt?" demanded Peter, catching his breath and regaining his balance.

"One of you stepped on my foot."

"No, we didn't," said Will. "We weren't even near you."

"Yeah, you did," insisted Cody, trying to hop on his one good foot.

"What's this?" said Cassie, stooping to pick up a round fuzzy ball from the floor.

"It looks like dryer lint or a black cotton ball," offered Gabrielle, "but look at your hands, Cassandra. They're all dirty."

"Look at the two of you." Cody laughed, and pointed at Peter and Will. "You've got black stuff all over your hands, and you've rubbed it on your faces. It's like parts of you are missing."

"It must have come from this thing," said Cassie, examining the black ball of fuzz she held in her hand.

"Drop it in here," said Gabrielle, handing over a plastic sandwich bag from her backpack.

"C'mon, we're late for lunch," said Cody, limping past them.

Will was staring at his hands in amazement. "They're disappearing." Then he looked at Peter, who was missing half his face, and they all looked to Cassandra.

"Let's hope it washes off," said Peter, and all four darted back down the hall to the bathrooms outside the library.

"Still got the fuzz ball?" Will whispered to Cassie when they finally sat down with their lunch trays.

"It's in my locker," she said, then they all quickly changed the subject.

While talking on the phone that night, Gabrielle told Cassandra that Paige Boggins said her father had run into something lurking in the hallway behind the gym, early the day before. "When he demanded, 'Who's there!' the thing just disappeared. Her dad calls them wraiths."

After the call with Gabrielle, Cassandra and Peter headed to the playroom to examine the soft black ball, still wrapped in plastic.

"Whatever they are, we at least know how they do it. It

must have dropped this when Will and I crashed into it."

"Yeah, that was a lucky accident."

"It wasn't an accident. Will and I had that planned. We decided last week that if we could get close to one, we'd make a grab to see if it was real."

"Then was it one of those things, that hisses and whispers, that stepped on Cody?"

"It ran over Cody trying to get away from us, but I'm sure I saw its pointy white teeth."

"So, what are they, and why are they in our school?" asked Cassie.

"I don't know, but if the aunts find out, they'll keep us home—so I'm not going to say anything, are you?"

"Peter, you know the aunts will find out, if they don't know already."

As it turned out, the hissing whisperers were not very good at hiding their presence. Even if they couldn't be seen, in time everyone knew they were there. After a month, the shadowy whisperers were the topic wherever people met. The burning question was—why were they there?

Gabrielle's uncle, the harbormaster, believed that they had come to help the Ministry close the school. Mr. Boggins and Ms. O'Day felt sure they had come to rob the place of valuable artifacts, especially any magical conduits. Miss Tweaks told the aunts she was certain they had been sent to destroy the spells that had protected the old school and its students for more than one hundred years. The secretary was overheard telling the coach that there was money missing from the school, and she wondered if Adam Boggins was behind it because he roamed the school day and night for no apparent reason. Some of the students even believed the whisperers had come to protect Walker Matthews and his troublemaking friends.

If Miss Tweaks had asked Ms. O'Day, she would have learned that food and other items were missing from the kitchen, too. First was a small pair of sugar tongs, then a carved wooden rooster that just flew away. She was telling this to Peter and Cassandra one afternoon when they were hanging out with her in the kitchen. The buses had been gone for several minutes, and Aunt Penelope had still not arrived to pick them up. The hallways were deserted, and Peter and Cassandra were relieved when they discovered Ms. O'Day was still there. She seemed as happy to see them as they were to find her.

"Time to pack things and take them out of here," she said, scurrying around the kitchen, loading her treasures into a big canvas bag she always carried. "I've had my fill of those demons—or whatever they are—hanging around in my kitchen all night. I hope that rhubarb pie they gobbled down last night gives them hives. They can't even open a little carton of milk without spilling it. The pewter is going to take some effort, but if the two of you will help me ..."

As she removed the heavy, antique-pewter platters from the wall, Cassandra wrapped them in meat-packing paper, and Peter slid them into double garbage bags for added padding.

"My mother had a little poem. A lesson she always recited about just this kind of thing. It went like this, 'No matter your wealth or power or fame, gains and losses work out the same, as the story goes, the old gull knows, what the Sea gives up, she'll soon reclaim.'"

She had just picked up the bag when Mr. Amadan appeared. "Working hard or hardly working, Ms. O'Day?"

"Have to work late all the time now that your creepy friends come in here at night, leave me a mess, and steal things."

"I have no idea what you're talking about," said the principal.

"Sure you do. Trust me, folks around Plunder Bay are not as stupid as you'd like to think. Everybody knows your buddies are creeping around the school day and night looking for things to steal."

"I came to discuss some problems I have with your lunch menus. If you children—the McBee twins, right?—would just wait out in the hall, this will only take a moment."

"No, they won't. I'm ready to go home and so are these kids," said Maggie. She grabbed her coat, gathered up her bags, and pushed Peter and Cassandra along in front of her.

"I'm warning you, Ms. O'Day." Glen Amadan stepped in front of the exit, blocking their departure. "Do not try my patience or I'll ..."

"Or you'll what?" Maggie put her coat and bags down and stepped toward the principal.

Principal Amadan backed slowly out of the kitchen, without taking his eyes off of the big, angry lady in front of him. When he backed into someone behind him, he turned to confront them, but seeing absolutely no one there, he immediately apologized to the empty space and hustled away from the doorway and went around the corner.

"GET OUT OF MY GALLEY, YOU EVIL THING!" roared Maggie O'Day at the empty space left by the principal's hasty departure. She grabbed the kitchen push broom and positioned herself for battle.

Suddenly, Cassandra was being pulled backward by an unseen force, holding her by both arms. Maggie grabbed the broom by its bristle end and swung it's handle in the air like a broadsword. Afraid of hitting Cassandra, she shifted to poking the handle into the air above the captive's head.

"Water!" shouted Cassandra.

Peter dove for the sink and came up with the sprayer. He pulled the trigger, and no one was spared a shower, but Cassandra was loose by the time they had wiped the water out of their eyes. Nothing could be seen except a sooty puddle of water on the floor.

Mr. Amadan was back, now that the danger appeared to be averted, and looked at the sooty puddle and then up at the others. "Oh my, I simply don't know what to make of this. I'm afraid you and I have frightened these poor children out of their wits. You know, children, I think the world of our Ms. O'Day. She's an excellent cook and so creative, but she gets too excited. We'll just keep this little incident among ourselves, and I'm sure there's something I could do for all of you in return."

"You can start right now," said Maggie. "Carry this bag out to the trunk of my car and then mop up your mess."

"All right," said the principal, smiling sheepishly as he lugged out the bag with the pewter platters.

Maggie sent a text to Penelope that she was bringing the children home, and not to worry about coming to get them. On their way to Cape Peril cottage, they passed the McBee SUV coming down the Coast Road on the back of a tow truck. Peter noticed the front fender was dented and a tire was flat. Maggie O'Day took them right into the kitchen and told Miranda exactly what had happened. Aunt Penelope arrived in the middle of the story. She had called Jacques to give her a ride home and was much more upset over what had happened to the twins than over the minor car accident she had had coming to get them.

"Kids, head to the playroom and start your homework, please," said Miranda. She then brewed a pot of Cornflower Clarity tea and the three of them sat down with their heads together.

"How bad is it, Maggie? Is the school unsafe?" asked Penelope.

"It's not good. The school is overrun with sinister beings that lurk in the darkness, spy on everyone—even the kids, and steal everything they can carry out."

"What are they, exactly?" asked Miranda.

"Some have called them phantoms, others demons, Adam Boggins has decided to refer to them as wraiths, and the kids mostly call them the whisperers."

"Are they in league with someone on the inside—Principal Amadan?" asked Penelope.

"Well, he knows they are there and does nothing, but he seems afraid of them. Mr. Boggins is a nervous wreck, and Reynelda is acting stranger than usual."

"Oh no, what do you mean?" asked Miranda.

"Well ... you know she's always been a bit ditsy, but lately it's like she's been put under a spell—walks around with that darn scarf on all the time and acts like she's in a trance, mumbling to herself."

After loading Maggie up with tea samples and dried herbs, and thanking her for taking such good care of the twins, the aunts announced that Peter and Cassandra would not be returning to school until they could be sure of their safety. The aunts had never forgotten Inspector Pablo Martinez of the Royal East Island Constabulary and his warning that the twins were in danger and needed protecting. The question that nagged at the conscience of both aunts, was whether the danger had followed the twins to Plunder Bay. And, if that was the case, why now? This wasn't anything they could discuss with anyone—at least anyone of the here and now—but discuss it they did.

At eight bells, when the twins were ready for bed, Aunt Penelope called to them to come down to the kitchen for cocoa. Thinking they were in serious trouble, they took their seats at the kitchen table and were surprised by what Aunt Miranda had to say. "We were planning to keep you safely at home until things at the school were sorted out."

"We're worried about you and the other kids too," said Aunt Penelope.

"However," said Aunt Miranda, "we've been overruled. Secrecy forbids us from saying by whom, but the general consensus is that you've proven you can *protect* yourselves and others at the school, and you are needed there."

"And, thanks to my outstanding driving skills, you get to ride the bus again," said Aunt Penelope.

On their way up the stairs to bed, Cassandra stopped on the landing and looked at Peter. "Who are they talking about?" she asked.

"I don't know. I wondered that too, but it didn't seem like a good time to ask."

"Well, whoever it is, I'm glad they overruled keeping us locked up in the cottage."

"And I'm glad to be back riding the bus," said Peter. "I hate having to wait around to be picked up when we could be halfway home if we were on the bus."

And with that, the big portrait of Captain McBee shifted sideways ever so slightly on the wall above them.

Treasures of Plunder Bay

The next morning was more dreary than usual. Sleet pelted against the library windows. Halfway through class, Miss Tweaks called Peter and Cassandra aside. She handed Peter a set of keys on a blue ring. They were old keys of unusual shapes and sizes. She handed Cassandra something carefully wrapped in white tissue paper. It was not difficult to see that it was her Twilight Scarf.

"This needs to be put away now with the rest of the enchanted theater trappings. I've let it get too strong of a hold on me. One needs to know when too much of a good thing is ... well, please, would the two of you take this and go up the stairs from our classroom to the back of the stage? There is another identical room, opposite ours, on the other side; perhaps you already know where it is. Inside, you'll find several trunks of very special costumes, period clothing salvaged from shipwrecks. Please put this away for me in any one of them. Then use these keys to lock all the trunks, and don't forget to lock the room when you leave."

She might have added, "Be careful and don't be seen," but she didn't have to say the words; it was obvious by her manner. They wondered what prompted her to give up the scarf, had someone said something to her? Peter and Cassandra thought they remembered a locked door that led off the stage, but neither had ever seen it open, or been inside. Finding the door was child's play for Peter and Cassandra, who had grown up in Cape Peril cottage. Once through the door, they went down mirrored steps to a windowless room, the same size and shape as the little room they used for class.

Finding the right key to fit each trunk took longer than they thought it would. By the time they finished, locked the storeroom, and got back to join their classmates, the lunch bell had just rung. Peter put the keys in his pocket and tried to find Miss Tweaks at lunch, and later on, at bus time. Little did they know that no one—not even the invisible whisperers—had seen her slip out of the school right before lunch. That afternoon, Reynelda Tweaks was a woman on a mission.

Tea With Miss Tweaks

Before Reynelda Tweaks arrived, Penelope covered the table in a forest-green cloth. She chose brown candles and, because it was a new moon, she used cinnamon oil in the lamp. Miranda had a kettle boiling on the stove and the teapot was ready to brew her strongest black tea. She put slivers of ginger, chamomile, and peppermint in small dishes on the table, to be added to each cup. All these things were chosen to bring comfort and courage to the tea drinkers. From her earlier phone call, it sounded like Reynelda was desperately in need of both when she asked Miranda to assemble the charmed circle.

Reynelda was the first to arrive. Summer Blinken and her sister-in-law, Autumn, drove in next. They were both delightful, elderly ladies who looked and dressed enough alike to be sisters. They were the two most experienced members of the charmed circle, and masters of *creating*—known for their extraordinary prize-winning quilts. Their wisdom was always valued, and they could be depended upon to show in a magical emergency.

Summer shooed the curious gulls away with the elegant black cane she always carried. "It does come in handy for so many things, but these days I dare not try to walk without it."

"Summer does come before autumn, and that proves she is older, even if my poor Marty did die first," said the other, adjusting her black wool skirt to cover her pointy high-top shoes.

"That only proves you drove him to an early grave."

"He was eighty-nine and still pulling traps when he fell overboard. Your Arnold was just too mean to pass before his younger brother," protested Autumn, continuing their friendly, but long-lasting dispute over age and widowhood.

When the others—Juliet d'Eon, Charlotte Cloutier, Ursula Boggins, Candice Carpenter, Elizabeth VanSmithe, Caroline Moreau, and Lauren Blanchard—arrived, the tea was poured and pinches of the herbs were added to each cup. The twelve women joined hands, and thrice recited in unison:

"Give us clarity and courage from this cup,
Goodness and wisdom for all abound,
Strength in our numbers is what *we've* found,
Evildoers will gain no ground"

Reynelda sat silently for a long time drinking her tea, then she began, "I put away the last of my things from the theater. I am afraid my days at Plunder Bay School are numbered. I should have left when Mr. Amadan canceled the play, but I felt that my students still needed me— especially this year's seventh-grade class, the neophytes. This class is the largest and most magically gifted group of students I have ever worked with. My drama classes are *creating* and *enchanting,* but my seventh graders can actually make books come alive. The old library has not been visited by so many novel characters in all the years I've been teaching here. Just the other day, I had a wonderful chat with Alexander Graham Bell, and I had to hurry the whole crew of the *Nautilus* out so I could go home last month."

Treasures of Plunder Bay

"I've thought also that this group of kids has something special," said Juliet d'Eon, "ever since they were in kindergarten together."

Miss Tweaks looked sad. "I have practiced and taught the gentle magic arts all my life. I do not believe I have ever harmed the soul of anybody that had one. I love children and delight in helping them master their *Powers*. Until the last few weeks, I did not think I had an enemy in the world, but something is terribly wrong. I think someone has sent an evil force to destroy me. I fear they see me as more of a threat than I am."

"What do you mean, Reynelda?" asked Miranda.

"There is something going on, and dark forces are behind it. I believe the Twilight Scarf was planted for me to find and to cloud my head and judgement."

"Why? What's the reason?" prompted Candice Carpenter, Daniel's Mother.

"My *Powers* are not by far the strongest. I never achieved *conjuring* at all, and I'm certainly no sorceress. But someone thinks they have to have me out of the way to achieve their evil end."

"Tell us what you know, and we will try to figure out how we can deal with it together," said Summer Blinken authoritatively.

"I knew about the dark visitors when they first arrived, and so did Adam Boggins. He said he actually came face-to-face with one in the basement of the old wing, in the middle of the night."

Ursula spoke up, "My husband is sure they are only talented outliers trying to catalogue and steal magical artifacts and conduits from the school."

"Which would be a waste of time," added Autumn

138

knowingly.

"But you think it's much more than that?" queried Caroline Moreau, Jason's mother.

Miss Tweaks continued, "It's not just those that prowl the place all night—and perhaps they are just outliers, but there's another force, a much darker magic force. I can feel their presence everywhere, and sometimes I hear a deep rasping whisper, almost like they are struggling to breathe air."

At this point in her story, Miss Tweaks stopped and took another sip of tea, momentarily closing her eyes.

"The reason I know they are sent by a powerful force is because the spells that have protected us for over one hundred years are nearly spent."

Summer and Autumn locked worried eyes. "The protection spells are getting weaker?" they asked in unison.

"Yes," answered Miss Tweaks. "Weaker and weaker by the day. I've moved my classes to the library, and I keep the students close to me. It's like a shadow is closing in on the whole village."

"How can you tell?" asked Elizabeth VanSmithe, Will's mother, who was attending her first meeting.

"Well, after feeling their presence, the air is cold and rank with evil counterspells. I don't know what else to tell you, except that if they had the power to destroy me or my students, they would surely have done it by now ... but how much longer we can keep them at bay is unknown."

Miranda added, "The old books tell us that these kinds of entities may be the henchmen of a powerful conjurer or even a sorcerer. Who could they be working for and what are they after?"

"I've mastered *enchanting*, but my other *Powers* are

marginal at best. I'm stronger when I'm in the old wing of the school, especially the theater and library, and I've been doing my best to protect the students, but it's becoming nearly impossible," said Miss Tweaks.

"None of your *Powers* are weak, Reynelda," said Lauren Blanchard, Caitlyn B's oldest sister.

"And now we will add our *Powers* to help get this figured out," proclaimed Miranda.

Penelope spoke up, "It may not help the situation, but over the holidays, we discovered that Cape Peril cottage was under a curse. We uncovered it quite by accident, and rid ourselves of it in pretty much the same way. Actually, Peter did. I'm wondering if any of you have discovered something similar, or if not, perhaps you should go home and do some deep cleaning and serious house blessing."

Summer asked, "Reynelda, can you hold out until Saturday morning? We'll all meet in the old wing of the school and do some serious deep cleaning of our own."

Autumn added, "Right. They may be a match for any of us alone, but together our *Powers* are strong, and our intentions are pure."

"And don't forget, ladies, an evil curse can be sent back threefold upon its sender, so let's give these evildoers a Plunder Bay version of their own medicine!" exclaimed Charlotte.

"Well," said Reynelda, "I do feel better. I guess we will all have to hit the books. It may be time for an old enchantress like me to learn some new tricks."

The old parrot, who had been quietly observing the scene around the cottage kitchen table, suddenly made his presence known. "Rum all around!" he screeched.

The members of the charmed circle repeated their

opening spell in unison and left smiling, but all of them were deeply worried.

As the aunts cleared away the tea things and put the candles and tablecloth away, Penelope looked worriedly at Miranda. "You know, all of this started not long after we got home from the Smuggler's Bazaar."

"I know. I've been thinking about that too. It's the first time the twins were exposed to the outside world since we brought them home to Cape Peril lighthouse. They'd never been outside of Plunder Bay before the trip to the Bazaar."

"Do you think this is the danger Inspector Martinez warned of?"

"Maybe. But why? Why break down the protection spells at the school?"

"Maybe because the twins are more susceptible at the school than at the cottage?"

"Well, that's a good point. No evil can get to them here," said Miranda.

"But why steal all the magical conduits from the school?"

"It's like they are looking for something. Either that, or they think the school is left powerless if they take all the magic elements out."

"Or both!" concluded Penelope.

"The darker evil that Reynelda feels has me worried the most. She wouldn't have mentioned it if it wasn't serious," said Miranda.

When Reynelda left Cape Peril cottage she felt emboldened, and was determined to fight for her students and herself. She fixed a light supper and pulled out two books that she had recently checked out of the library. One had an excellent spell for protection and purification of enchanted places. She had worked a spell like this in the theater and library when she first came to Plunder Bay School many years ago. It seemed to her that now would be a very good time to renew or refresh the spells in those places. It was too bad that the spell had to be cast when the moon was done waning and therefore dark. The moon was in the correct phase only for tonight, but to do the spell meant that she had to be in the school alone with the whisperers about.

"Oh well, what's the worst that can happen? It should only take a few minutes, and someone else is sure to be around this evening," she said to herself.

Reynelda felt better when she saw Mr. Boggins's car parked in back of the building, and the light on in his classroom. Not feeling so alone, she opened the outside door that led directly into the hallway of the old wing. The theater doors were still chained so she headed toward the library. She had decided to cast the protection spell there first, then she would go through her classroom to the back of the stage to cast the protection spell in the theater.

It was really very simple—she went to each of the four main compass points of the library to set the spell in motion. On the east point she placed a pumice stone and a small folded fan. To the south, she positioned a smoky quartz and a burnt match, representing fire. At the west point, Miss Tweaks left a coral stone and seashell. And on the north end, she arranged an agate and a small bag of soil. That done, she went to the center of the library and lit a brown candle right beneath the glass domed ceiling. She spoke the words of her spell:

"All friendly earth,
Water, wind, and fire,
Cleanse and protect this place,
From all things evil and dire."

Leaving the candle to burn out and seal the spell, Miss Tweaks gathered her things and hurried down through her homeroom and up onto the stage. The theater was completely dark, so she turned on the footlights. She had just finished visiting the east and south compass points when an icy-cold chill slapped her across the face. At that moment, she knew she was not alone.

"What are you doing?" came a hollow, raspy voice that echoed through the empty theater. It was frightening that she could not see her questioner, but she had a job to do. She crossed the room to the western point, which was in front of the stage.

"Stop NOW, crone!" came the threatening disembodied voice.

It might not have been the best time for a fight with this invader, but this magical theater was most certainly the place Reynelda Tweaks would have chosen.

"You are not wanted here, evildoer!" Miss Tweaks called out. She placed her tokens in the orchestra pit in front of the stage just as a loud, hideous shrieking filled the room. She pushed her glasses on top of her head, gave something like an orchestra conductor's signal, and a phantom band broke into a spirited march, drowning out the horrible sound. As she moved toward her last point on the north wall, the rousing music broke down into a muddle of loud discords. She pulled her glasses down, and the band began playing a soft peaceful melody.

Treasures of Plunder Bay

The footlights on the stage flickered and the theater went black. She stood there for a moment in total darkness, and she could hear breathing not far away. Miss Tweaks took off her glasses, and bright spotlights came on. They moved with a slow, sweeping motion across the stage and seats and into the darkest corners of the room.

A minute later, the spotlights began to pop and explode one by one in a rain of broken glass that fell to the floor all around her. When all the lights had gone out, Miss Tweaks put her spectacles back atop her curly pile of hair, and the room was suddenly bathed in a spectrum of dazzling streams of colored search lights that came and went from every direction.

Having completed her task along the north wall, she headed for the center of the theater just as the rows of seats began to vibrate and shudder. There was an awful wrenching sound of three hundred theater seats being ripped loose from their anchor bolts. Some were already rising into the air and thrashing wildly, held down only by the other seats in the row, not yet pried free.

Seeing that she had left the last of her matches as a token to the east, Miss Tweaks waved her glasses to light a spiraling chandelier of candles that floated high above the theater in the center of the room. Loud whistles and wild applause broke out from the theater spectator gallery. Every seat was back in place, filled with lords and ladies, kings and peasants, soldiers and sailors, and pretty maids. Hamlet's father's ghost floated above the stage, and the cast of *Brigadoon* was onstage taking bows. The knights of Camelot in full armor stood around the walls, and gallant Musketeers made sweeping bows to the drama teacher. Miss Tweaks said her incantation:

C. S. Leonard

"All friendly earth,
Water, wind, and fire,
Cleanse and protect this place,
From all things evil and dire."

She calmly walked toward the theater's main entrance. With a wave of her glasses, the chains slipped off and the double doors leading into the hall swung wide. Miss Tweaks had cast her spells and made a spectacular exit. But far from feeling brazen, she was deeply shaken. She knew she had just faced a very dark source of evil.

Thursday morning, Miss Tweaks kept her students grouped closely together in the library bay. No one seemed to be much into their books. Perhaps they missed the soft ticking of the library clock, which—like so many other things—was missing. Below where it had hung was an empty pedestal with a burned-out brown candle. Seeing their teacher looking pale and tired, several students inquired if she felt all right. She brushed off their concerns by saying she had had a difficult night and would soon be herself again.

When class finally ended, Miss Tweaks walked with them to the cafeteria. Peter and the others could see her in the kitchen, drinking tea and reading from a large old book. Every so often, she would look up and say something under her breath, like she was trying to teach herself a poem or lines from a play. It was then that Peter remembered he still had her blue key ring in his pocket. He got up and walked over to the kitchen where she was sitting.

"I couldn't find you yesterday afternoon to give back your keys. I'm sorry."

"Oh, that's all right. You keep them, Peter. Just don't tell anyone you have them."

"But you're going to need them."

"I'm not so sure about that. I've never been any good with keys. Locking things up is just an inconvenience for me. In fact, I would be very surprised if I ever used keys again," she replied, thinking about how she cast the locked chains from the theater door the night before.

"Is anything the matter, Miss Tweaks?" asked Peter, feeling very worried about her.

"Peter, I scored a minor victory last night in the theater— but in so doing, I tangled with a powerful, dark-magic force, and I sense that the battle isn't over. I feel as though my time here at the school may be coming to an end."

"No, you have more strength than anyone here, and your students totally support you. What can we do to help?"

"Peter, if anything should happen to me, I want you, Cassandra, and the rest of the class to go on with your studies. You've learned a lot this year, and you're a talented group. Your aunts will be a great help to you. Always trust them. And Peter, I almost forgot, I brought you my grandfather's information on clocks. I hope you find it helpful."

"I'll come by the library later and get it," promised Peter, wondering if his teacher had noticed the library clock was missing and knowing this wasn't a good time to mention it.

"It's not in the library, it's ..."

Here, her voice just trailed away, and her eyes looked glassy. Peter could see Ms. O'Day a few meters away, still serving lunch. Across the crowded cafeteria, Cassandra and Gabrielle were looking over at him. He needed to get some help for Miss Tweaks, but he wasn't sure who to turn to. At that point, she spotted Mr. Boggins out in the hall. She jumped up, leaving her book and glasses on the table, and ran into the front hall, calling out his name.

The next thing Peter saw were two strangers in long black raincoats with their hoods pulled over their heads. They came up behind Miss Tweaks and each took her by an elbow. She was lifted off the floor, and Peter saw her feet still moving as though she were trying to run in the air. The two dark strangers swept her out through the front doors. Before the doors banged shut, Peter heard her calling, "HELP, Adam! Maggie, HELP!"

Peter, followed soon thereafter by Cassandra and Gabrielle, ran out of the cafeteria after them, calling, "STOP! Put her down! Let her go!"

They might have caught up with the kidnappers, except a third dark figure in the same long raincoat stepped out and put his arms out to stop them. Cassandra screamed at him to get away, and Gabrielle stomped her boot heel into the top of his foot. The tall stranger was hopping on one foot, moaning in pain as Peter jumped onto the hem of his black raincoat that was trailing on the floor.

"Go after them!" he yelled to the girls. "I'll hold this one off as long as I can!"

The girls darted out the doors just as the stranger turned and grabbed Peter by the front of his shirt and lifted him up into the air. His face was covered by the hood, but Peter could feel his hot breath, and caught the strong smell of garlic and a whiff of aftershave cologne.

"Master Peter McBee," he whispered. "We will meet again."

Treasures of Plunder Bay

"Put the boy down," said Mr. Boggins in a surprisingly calm voice.

"Perhaps you want to test your *Powers* right here and now, with one hundred students watching from the lunchroom," threatened Maggie O'Day—speaking softly but raising both of her ham-sized fists like a boxer.

"I don't think that will be necessary," said Mr. Boggins.

"Sooon," whispered the stranger, putting Peter down and rising to his full height. "Sooon."

The shadowy stranger rushed out the door into the icy rain, dark coat fluttering furiously in his wake like a swarm of black birds.

"Are you all right, Peter?" asked Mr. Boggins. "Don't mind that one, a nasty chap from out of town. They are just visiting—will be gone soon, just like he said." And with that, he pushed his glasses up his skinny, long nose and headed quickly down the hall.

Cassandra and Gabrielle came back through the doors at that point. Gabrielle was nearly hysterical, and Cassandra explained that Miss Tweaks had been taken away by the men in a black van. They tried to stop the van, but when the third creep came out, it tore through the lot and nearly ran them down before turning left onto the Coast Road. The seagulls were screeching wildly and flew behind them like they were trying to follow.

"Something terrible has happened to Miss Tweaks," sobbed Gabrielle, and Cassandra nodded in agreement.

Maggie O'Day put her big arms around all three children. "Kids, listen to me. Reynelda can take care of herself. I can't figure out why they would nab her like that in front of the whole school. It would take more than the likes of them to do Reynelda Tweaks any real harm. Don't cry, Gabrielle. Peter and Cassandra, use the phone in the kitchen and call your aunts right now and tell them everything that just happened. Gabrielle, use your cell and call your mother, and I'll call your Uncle Jacques. Those creeps will bring Reynelda right back when they find out how much trouble she can be. Now, I'm going to have a talk with Adam Boggins."

"Peter, while I was outside just now, I used my whistle," said Cassie. "Maybe the aunts heard it and they'll come after us. We can take Gabrielle and try to follow the black van."

Peter knew that several minutes had already been wasted, and he wondered how much of a head start the van would have on anyone trying to catch it. The whistle worked, and within five minutes, both aunts pulled up in the SUV. They had already texted Gabrielle's mom, and they signed all three children out of school. On their way out, Peter ran back to the cafeteria to get Miss Tweaks's book. With dismay, he discovered that Miss Tweaks's glasses were sitting on top of the book she had been reading.

As he met up with his aunts, Penelope gasped. "On no, Miranda. Reynelda doesn't have her glasses."

The aunts drove up along the Coast Road for several miles, then back around the village, searching for the black van that had taken Miss Tweaks. They drove past her house, and after dropping off Gabrielle, they turned toward home. As they passed the school, Reynelda's green cube car was still in the lot, and the black van was back in front of the school.

"Stop!" cried Peter. "I'll go in and find out if she's back."

"No, I will," said Aunt Penelope. Miranda, you get behind

the wheel, and you two stay in the car."

In a few minutes, Penelope walked out with Mr. Boggins. They parted, and she came back to the car alone and reported that no one had seen Reynelda since she had been taken away at lunch time. She went on to report that almost everyone in the cafeteria saw what happened, and the whole village was in an uproar.

"There was a police officer in the office talking with the secretary, and she claimed Miss Tweaks told the principal this morning that she was resigning from her job, then left willingly with two men. Maggie O'Day was in the office too, calling the secretary a boldfaced liar. And to top it off, Amadan is nowhere to be found," reported Penelope.

"Did Mr. Boggins tell the truth about what happened?" asked Peter.

"Adam is a funny person. He can't stand any kind of trouble. He said he knew there were strangers in the school, and he had made a bargain with them to make sure they didn't steal anything else. He insists he cannot imagine them a danger to anyone, especially Miss Tweaks."

"I don't think he was telling you all that he knows," said Peter. "In the first place, there is a lot of stuff missing from the school, like books and paintings, and even the library clock is gone now. After he made that creep put me down, he just walked away. He didn't even try to go out and rescue Miss Tweaks or see if Cassandra and Gabrielle were okay."

"Peter has a point," said Miranda. "It sounds like Adam Boggins is afraid of these people, or he would never let the first trinket be taken out of that school. He and Reynelda have been friends for years. I wonder why he did nothing to save her? He must know more about them."

"You two met with Miss Tweaks yesterday afternoon at the cottage. What did she say?" demanded Cassandra.

Miranda blinked back tears. "She said there was dark magic permeating the school and that it wasn't safe. The protection spells were weakening, and she was afraid for herself and the students."

"If it helps to know, she told me she scored a victory last night in the theater," said Peter.

"In all the years I have known Reynelda, I have never known her to be afraid of anything or anybody. She moved forward with the protection spells before we could help her," said Aunt Miranda.

"In doing so she's kept the school safe," replied Aunt Penelope.

"We have to find her!" Miranda wiped back another tear that had escaped down her cheek.

The Siege Of Cape Peril Lighthouse

Jacques d'Eon explained to the Coast Guard officer, "Sometimes the fishing boats coming back into the harbor late at night leave their bright lights on. They're not supposed to, but it helps if it's foggy."

"Well, we got a complaint that the old Cape Peril lighthouse was operating again, and I have to investigate it, you understand that?"

"Yes, of course, but people have been a little antsy around here lately. There have been some questionable characters around the village, and we have someone missing—a teacher from the school. I would guess you got this call from someone whose nerves are on edge."

"So what kind of a place is Plunder Bay? I've heard a lot of stories, and I guess you've lived here all your life?"

"Just a typical fishing village, nothing out of the ordinary, some tourist trade in the summer, that's about it."

"Many of the stories I've heard go way back. Like how this used to be a notorious pirate hideaway, and strange things have been happening here ever since. What I'm particularly interested in is the lighthouse. What do you know about it?"

Jacques felt the spot on his arm tingle where the ugly bruise he received years ago used to be. "I don't know all that much, but I understand it was privately built and owned. I don't think it was ever officially commissioned, but it stayed activated until sometime after the Second

152

World War. The young family that lives there now are friends of mine, two sisters with their niece and nephew. None of them would be running the light."

"What about the history of the place?"

"The local tourist brochures explain that the property has been passed down through the same family—originally from Scotland—for several generations, and the lighthouse dates to the 1700s. It was constructed by one of the property's ancestors because there were so many shipwrecks on the reefs beyond the harbor. He was lost in a sea battle here in the bay in 1755. There's a statue commemorating him in the park. Big fellow—would remind you a little of Henry the Eighth, but wearing an eighteenth-century Scottish tartan sash. I wouldn't have wanted to tangle with him back in the day."

"Since you know the McBee sisters, it won't be any problem if my crew and I go up and take a look around the cottage and lighthouse?" asked the Coast Guard officer, more as a statement than a question.

"I don't think that would be such a great idea. I hate to do anything to disturb the family, especially the children."

"If it would be reassuring for them, you're welcome to come along," said the officer, "unless you'd rather not, of course."

Two weeks had passed since Miss Tweaks's abduction, and there was no news about her. The whispering wraiths and their black raincoat buddies had disappeared from the school, and Miss Tweaks's dozen homeroom students had been split up and shuffled among other classes. The theater doors had been padlocked again, and the McBee twins were back to being driven to school by one aunt or the other.

On a snowy February afternoon as they neared home, Cassandra spotted a black van parked on the side of the road across from the lane to Cape Peril cottage. They passed it slowly, watching, and expecting anything, but because the van windows were tinted so dark, it was impossible to see if there was anyone inside. For a moment, Cassandra hoped there was more than one black van like the one that had nearly run her and Gabrielle down that awful day. At the same time, Peter was hoping that Miss Tweaks would be walking up the lane when they turned the corner. As it turned out, the hopes of both twins were not to be realized. Aunt Penelope sped up the lane, then hit the brakes hard. Cape Peril cottage was surrounded.

There were at least three military-looking jeeps, two police cars, and the harbormaster's green truck. Strangers in uniform were wandering around the grounds in the ankle-deep snow. Some were taking pictures, and most were staring up at the light tower. When Aunt Penelope stepped out of the vehicle, a Coast Guard officer and the harbormaster came over to greet her.

"Why are you here?" she asked a man in a Coast Guard uniform.

"My name is Captain McMullen, and you must be one of the Miss McBees?" said the officer. "We have received an inquiry about an unauthorized light coming from the lighthouse. We had hoped that you might give us the opportunity to have a look around—just routine."

"This is really not a good time," said Penelope. Her sister signaled her from the entrance hall window by tapping an imaginary wristwatch, then holding up both hands as a signal for ten minutes.

"Shouldn't be a problem unless you've got something to hide," said one of the police officers joining the group.

"Of course we don't have anything to hide! Let me at least get the children settled in the house and find my sister. I'll come back in a few moments and let you know."

"Looks like these kids are big enough to fend for themselves. We'll just follow you in," said the police officer.

As they approached the house, sweet and gentle Seadog was making a terrible racket, barking, and snarling, and throwing himself against the inside of the cottage door. It took a little while longer for Miranda to appear and, at the police officer's insistence, go lock up the "vicious animal." Finally, she opened the door, smiling and dusting flour from her rosy cheeks with the bib apron she wore over her jeans and sweater.

"What's going on?" she asked, addressing the half dozen men jockeying to come inside.

The Coast Guard officer stepped forward and introduced himself, smiling more broadly than he intended as he made a mental note that this thirty-something, with her blond hair and grey eyes—or were they blue?—was really cute. Very politely, he explained that this was just a routine event, answering a complaint about a disturbing bright light. Miranda invited him in but put out her hand to bar the others.

"I'm sure not all of you need to come in, but for those of you who do, please leave your boots outside. I have just finished vacuuming and mopping all my floors, and your shoes would ruin a whole afternoon's work. Peter and Cassandra, go straight to your *room* and stay there, please."

Captain McMullen and two of the younger coastguardsmen obediently took off their shoes and entered, followed by both police officers, who merely wiped their feet. Jacques and Penelope stayed outside by the car talking, while the four remaining men leaned on their vehicles, wiping snow from their faces and stomping their feet to stay warm.

Once inside, both policemen followed Cassandra and Peter up the main stairs. By the time they reached the landing with the portrait of Captain Benjamin McBee, the twins had rounded the corner at the top of the stairs and disappeared. That left the two of them to open and close bathroom doors, wander in and out of bedrooms, and peer into the neat closets. One opened the top drawer of Penelope's dresser only to have it slam shut on his fingers. The other tripped on a bathmat and bumped his head on the shower stall. They searched upstairs for at least ten minutes, but they did not see the children again nor did they find the missing teacher hiding out with her friends after burglarizing the school—which had been rumored by some of the Matthewses.

The officer and two coastguardsmen had been herded into the kitchen by Miranda, where Jacques and Penelope eventually joined them. Captain McMullen asked some questions about how long it had been since the light was operational and how long the sisters had lived there. He had heard of their seafood seasoning and seemed very interested in their shop on the quay.

After getting the niceties out of the way, Captain McMullen asked Miranda about accessing the light tower. She pointed to the red door beside the brick oven and explained that there was no electricity up there and the stairs were steep and slippery, to say nothing of the bitter cold. She suggested they bring in their boots and put them back on. They thankfully acquiesced, and that process was both embarrassing and lengthy.

"We'll be careful," said Captain McMullen. He turned to the harbormaster and asked if he wanted to accompany them.

"No, I think I'll stay down here where I belong. You should probably do the same."

As they tugged on the heavy red door, the hinges creaked, and before they started up, Blue left his kitchen perch and darted out ahead of them. The steps were narrow, winding, dark, and slippery—all the things they had been warned about. The younger man had a flashlight on his equipment belt, and before long he was leading the way.

By this time, the two policemen had come back down from the upstairs. They wandered through the keeping room and stopped short in Miranda's conservatory. They examined the herbs hanging from hooks in the ceiling to dry, they browsed through strange plants in little pots, and brushed away some sweet-smelling vines that tried to entangle them. Both were particularly interested in her copper cauldron. One scraped some residue from the bottom with his index finger. He held it to his nose, then touched his finger to his tongue to taste it.

"That might not be a good idea," said Penelope, joining them. "My sister uses herbs like these to make the teas we sell in our business. Some things here could even be considered mildly dangerous. Herbology is a science, and that goop you just tasted is concentrated whipple blossom. A little more and you'd have hiccups, probably until sometime next week. We can ask her to come in if you have questions."

Treasures of Plunder Bay

After a very long climb up the lighthouse stairs, Captain McMullen and his companion reached a landing and stepped inside a thick-walled round room decorated in cobwebs. Inside were two small windows, and with the growing darkness outside, the flashlight came in handy. They found a large globe suspended on a stand and a rustic, rectangular table covered with sea charts and some ancient nautical instruments. The paper was parchment, and brittle to the touch. To one side of the room a tattered hammock could be recognized. A dusty oil painting of a two masted schooner leaned against the wall, and Captain McMullen guessed intuitively it was Captain McBee's ship. Looking around, the only footprints to be found on the dusty floor were the ones they had made themselves. Captain McMullen, being a seaman at heart, loved the room. It had character and history—something about it was absolutely magical, and he felt a strange connection to the place.

Entry into the lighthouse tower room involved steps so narrow they were more like rungs of a ladder. The glass chamber had an astounding view far out over the ocean and, of course, there was a telescope.

Officer McMullen's companion was focused on the tower room's light. "Look at this lens, Captain!"

"Hmm, in all my years, I've never seen anything like it. It's not a Fresnel; it says on the plaque here it was made in Germany. I wonder how they got it over here back then, or for that matter, how they ever got it placed up here," said Officer McMullen.

"Wow, do you believe it runs off natural gas, not oil? It must have an amazing reach."

"I'd give a month's pay to see it shine. In its day, it

probably saved hundreds of ships and thousands of lives. This Captain McBee must have been an amazing fellow. Wish I had known him."

While Captain McMullen was entranced in the light tower, things in the playroom had gotten most uncomfortable. For the first time ever, the twins heard footsteps in a room above them. The playroom was smaller, the table and chairs had shrunk, and the window on the world was gone. It felt more like the playroom from years ago when they were very little. The usually cozy room was so cold they could see their breath, and they had no way of knowing what was happening or how long it would last.

Back on ground level, the crowd was clearing out. The police officers had left, the coastguardsmen had returned to their warm vehicles, and Jacques and Penelope had gotten a fire department call and had to leave. That left Miranda and the one young coastguardsman waiting in the kitchen, by the red door. It had not been an unpleasant wait for him, as she insisted he have a cup of her newest tea and try one of her still warm hot cross buns.

"Sorry for putting you through all this trouble, ma'am."

"Do you like being in the Coast Guard?" asked Miranda, to help kill the time.

"I like being under Captain McMullen. He's a great mentor, smart—reads all the time, and he loves the sea. He has this great sailboat of his own and invites us to go out with him sometimes."

"Glad to know you feel that way, Hedges," Captain McMullen said, coming down the last two steps and emerging into the warm kitchen. "Miss McBee, I cannot apologize enough for disturbing your household on this ridiculous invasion of your miraculous old lighthouse. I can only hope that it stands another one hundred years. It has been a pleasure I will long remember. I'm only sorry that my visit happened under such unpleasant circumstances."

He was comforted by the warm smile Miranda gave in response to his sincere apology. Her smoky-blue eyes twinkled with warmth and appreciation, and he had to fight off the improper urge to ask her out on a date.

Dinner was late, but the twins had filled up on hot cross buns before Aunt Penelope returned from her fire-rescue call—a fender bender that involved a black van. The driver was a stocky fellow staying at the Naughty Puffin Inn. Perhaps by coincidence—but maybe not—the call that had sent the Coast Guard to Cape Peril had come from there as well.

Aunt Miranda thanked them all for helping her get through the siege on the lighthouse. She even treated Seadog to a whole hamburger for stalling things until the place was in the proper state of rewind.

"What did they find up there?" asked Cassie.

"Exactly what they expected to find, especially after Jacques's well played history lesson. They found about eighty years' worth of dust and grime, and a not-so-perfect example of fast crosstemporing, especially if Captain McMullen stops to wonder why the view was so impressive through snow and dirty glass.

"Crosstemporing—what's that?" questioned Peter.

Miranda got up, made three laps around the kitchen table, and poured herself another cup of tea before she sat back down and thought about how to explain a force she was not sure she totally understood herself.

Aunt Penelope looked amused by her conundrum and picked up the explanation. "Crosstemporing is moving from where one is, into another place and time. It's a physical reality. You actually go between places and times. Once they went through the red door into the lighthouse, they had crosstempored to a time in the past."

"And similar, but different," explained Aunt Miranda, seeming to get her composure back, "is transplaning, which is going to another place or time—in your mind only. Transplaning is not a physical reality. Most of us do it unconsciously every day. *Enchanting* is one example of transplaning. If Reynelda were here she could tell you more about it. A vivid memory, a song, good book, or even a movie, can send you psychologically to another place and time."

"What about the light?" Cassandra asked. "It's on a lot this time of year. Won't there be more complaints from the village?"

"The light crosstempores far beyond this harbor. Outliers will not notice it or be able to prove it was shining," stated Aunt Miranda with a smile.

Peter, who was fascinated by time and clocks, and had been able to tell time since before he could read, found the concept of crosstemporing riveting. He wondered how crosstemporing would work with his Govi watch. Brother Josiah had said the monks could slow time. So many questions were running through his head.

The Substitute

The next day, Mr. Boggins did the morning announcements. He continued to twist the truth to reassure students and parents, stating that rumors of unusual visitors in the school were not true. He went on to say that one staff member had taken a long leave of absence—and a permanent substitute was assigned to teach her class. Miss Tweaks's students were glad to be back together again after having been shuffled around for two weeks. When they went through the big library doors that morning, they found their permanent substitute.

Madelyn exclaimed in a whisper, "It's the lady with the purple toenails."

At this, her classmates turned in unison to stare at the substitute's feet. There were no purple toenails to be seen, just polished black platform boots that laced all the way up to her knees—and that was quite a distance, because she was very tall. She was stylishly dressed in a black pencil skirt that came down to the top of her boots and had a slit over the left knee, a white-silk, button-down blouse, and a strange black-and-white-fur bolero jacket with black-leather trim around the cuffs and collar—which she had flipped up so that it encircled the back of her very long neck.

"What's she wearing, a Dalmatian?" asked Virginia.

"I think it's a snow leopard, and hopefully a fake one!" said Gabrielle.

"Pleeze zit down," she told them in a deep, raspy voice,

thick with an accent.

Peter looked up at the empty space where the library clock used to hover. Through the skylight was a starless night—even though it was daytime. The place felt cold and empty. Already he didn't like this intruder.

"My name iz Mademoiselle Sowbierre. I have only been in zis place a few months. I come from Paris and I am a journalist by trade. There, I was working for ze most popular glamor magazine on ze continent."

"She's a phony," whispered Gabrielle. "Listen to the way she talks with that fake French accent."

Cassandra believed her friend because Gabrielle, like many in the village, was fluent in French.

"I have not found any lesson plans or zeating charts left by your last teacher, and I don't like zis big room. It's freezing cold," she said. Then she looked around at the students, and for some reason turned to Gabrielle and said, "Jou are ze McBee girl?"

Everyone laughed, and the substitute looked confused.

"I'm Cassandra McBee, and this is my friend Gabrielle d'Eon," said Cassie.

"Well, tell me what jour last teacher did, what jou were studying wiz her," she pressed, without taking her gaze from Gabrielle.

There was complete silence from everyone until Will spoke up with a makeshift answer. "Mostly what we studied was history and reading."

"Oh, I zee, language arts—zat makes perfectly good sense. Being a writer myself, we will drill down on zose specific skills. I hope all will go well among us. And do jou always have class in here?"

"No," volunteered Gabrielle. "Sometimes we read in the

theater, but it's been chained up."

"Mr. Amadan told me jou have a classroom, where iz zat?"

"It wasn't a classroom. It was a kind of closet in the basement—very small, no windows," offered Cody.

"Oh, I zee. Well, we will make do for now. If jou don't have a book, go get one and spend ze rest of ze morning reading. I will have ze principal assign us a room."

"Do we have to sit out here at the tables, or can we spread out through the library?" asked Jason.

"Do whatever jou did wiz jour old teacher."

Once loose in the library, the class were back on home ground. They broke up into small groups and vanished among the stacks.

"I don't believe she worked for a magazine. Why would she want to be a substitute teacher in Plunder Bay? This is the middle of nowhere compared to the fashion center of Europe," said Caitlyn M.

"I know, that doesn't make any sense. And what did she say her name was, Sowbear?" asked Paige.

"She definitely thinks she's very glamorous. With that long, straight, blunt-cut platinum-dyed hair, and her runway model walk, she must think she's the real deal," added Gabrielle.

As the morning wore on, Mademoiselle roamed through the library, where she had added snug-fitting, red leather gloves to her outfit. It did not occur to the students that she was searching for them until she caught Cody by the arm on his way to the bathroom.

"Where have jou been all morning?" she snapped.

"Reading where I always sit, over there behind the credenza—that big cabinet thing."

"Go find ze others right now and have zem come out here."

Cody rounded up his classmates and passed the word they were supposed to go back up front. Students filtered in from every secret corner and secluded spot in the library and sat down at the long, antique oak tables. Mademoiselle Sowbierre stood with her leopard-fur arms folded across her chest, tapping her leather-boot toe on the hardwood floor. She was smiling in a maniacal "fooled me once, but never again" kind of way.

"I'll be keeping a much shorter leash on each of you from this point forward," she said menacingly in her deep voice, dropping her accent for a moment. "Stay right here where jou are until class iz over."

She dismissed them at eleven-thirty and followed them down the hall, past the theater and into the main part of the building where she veered off to Principal Amadan's office.

The topic at lunch amongst Miss Tweaks's students was not the substitute; it was the apparent absence of the whisperers, and if there was any word about Miss Tweaks. Her neighbors had been checking on her house, and one of them found a set of car keys and had taken her little green car home and put it in the garage. Mr. Boggins was not on anybody's good list after lying about the whisperers and Miss Tweaks. Even Paige had given up trying to defend her father. Almost all of the students now carried cell phones, set to do-not-disturb, and kept out of sight so they wouldn't be confiscated. Their parents felt better knowing the kids could call them immediately if strangers showed up at the school.

"Any kind of protection is a good idea," said Cassie,

wondering which would work better in a pinch—her shepherd's whistle, or Gabrielle's new cell phone. She hoped she never had to find out.

The next morning, the library was again freezing. Mademoiselle Sowbierre banged on the radiators with a meter stick and then a metal pry bar, used to prop open the library doors in hot weather. "I cannot tolerate zis awful cold. Where iz zat little room wiz no windows? It cannot be zis freezing." When nobody moved or said a word, she tried a new tactic. She pointed at Jason. "You. Lead us to the room," she said, forgetting her accent again.

Jason felt his body acting of its own accord. He looked apologetic as he involuntarily stood and started to lead the group to their old classroom behind the stage. Much to their chagrin, they all followed Jason and Mademoiselle Sowbierre out of the library and down the half-flight of stairs.

At the landing, they found the door to their classroom still identified with the "Audiovisual Equipment Closet" sign. The room, however, was different than it had been when they last occupied it. When Mademoiselle Sowbierre flipped on the light switch, the windows did not appear. Instead, they saw a dingy white drop ceiling and fluorescent lights that hummed loudly. The furniture was the same, but it looked dirty, scraped up, and worn out. The beautiful Turkish area rug had a hole in it that wasn't there before. All of Miss Tweaks's personal items were missing, including her cobalt-blue bottle of posey flower pens and her scented candles.

More alarming than the look of the room was the absence of the wall-sized sea map that had displayed the routes of the magic realms across the world, with its little ships sailing to and fro. All that remained were the corners where it looked like someone had ripped it off the wall in a hurry. In its place was a concrete-block wall, painted a hideous shade of Philadelphia green. Also missing was the Chinese Ming floor vase and the papyrus scrolls tied with leather rawhide strips.

"It might as well be the audiovisual closet," mumbled Will.

"Look," whispered Peter to Cassandra, "the door to the backstage is ajar."

"Do you still have Miss Tweaks's key ring?"

"Yeah, it's right here," answered Peter, tapping his backpack's outer zip pocket.

Mademoiselle Sowbierre seemed quite pleased with the room and it was obvious that it was now her special place, not theirs. She started by assigning them seats, with Peter and Cassandra placed directly in front of her desk. She had Cassandra fill out a seating chart so she could memorize everyone's name by where they sat. Next, she handed each student a brightly colored folder, having written their names on them herself in a large, very artistic, purple script. In the folders were language worksheets.

"I want jou to complete zese every day, zen zere will be a writing lesson on ze white board. When you have completed zis work, jou may read at your desk until lunch. No one leaves zis room until I have zaid you may leave."

After class, the students huddled at their table in the cafeteria. They were much more subdued than usual after the revelations of the morning and the apparent *Power* their substitute wielded.

"She could at least be consistent with the fake accent,"

said Will. "One minute it's so bad you can hardly understand her, then she forgets to use it altogether."

"Did you see the stuff she put out on her desk—a metal drinking flask, the purple-and-black tapestry, the incense burner, and the dish of dried herbs and flower petals? She didn't even try to hide it," remarked Gabrielle.

"I noticed that too. Maybe it's because she's from Europe. They are very open about magic over there," offered Virginia.

"Cool, maybe she'll teach us some continental magic. I read it can be very powerful," said Gabrielle.

"I thought you didn't like her. You said she was a phony," remarked Caitlyn M.

"I don't like her—and she's definitely a phony, but if we can learn something from her, so much the better," said Gabrielle.

"I sense that she's dangerous. In fact, I'm sure of it," said Cassie with an involuntary shudder.

Peter remained quiet as the others talked. He had a very bad feeling about what was to come, and sensed they were in danger. Later that day in Mr. Morgan's geography class, he had a chance to pull Will aside. "Are you able to use your *seeing Powers* to get a sense of what Sowbear is doing here?"

"Not yet, but I'm working on it. It's like there's a concrete-block wall and I can't see through it."

"Keep working on it," said Peter.

As the week wore on, the students got to see Mademoiselle's idea of teaching, and it wasn't good. She was obsessed with studying the oldest books from the library. The students could never make out exactly what she was reading, and they weren't sure where she got them because the oldest books had disappeared weeks ago. When she wasn't engrossed in the musty pages of the old texts, she studied fashion magazines just about as intently. She also often wrote letters in her calligraphy-style handwriting, on fancy paper with purple ink. All of this went on while her students completed endless busy work.

Their writing topics were mind numbingly boring, and each day she increased the number of words required for their essays. The first day was five hundred words about their bedroom. The next day it was seven hundred and fifty words about their house, then one thousand words describing their family members. When Cody, speaking for all the boys in the class, asked if he could write about sports or cars or anything else, the substitute promised them she would include those topics in later assignments—but she didn't. They found their hands cramping from so much writing, and their fingers tended to stay in the position of holding a pen for hours after they'd stopped writing.

The amazing thing was that although they never saw Mademoiselle Sowbierre lift a red pencil in front of them, all their work was returned to them the next day corrected and graded; clearly someone was reading it. After a week, and despite the labeled seating chart Cassandra prepared for her, the only two students whose names she remembered were Cassandra and Peter McBee. The morning homeroom period they loved with Miss Tweaks had become an endless torture session, of which it was hard to tell which was worse, the never-ending writing or the absolute boredom of the topics and pointless exercises. The students could hardly wait for Maggie O'Day's lunches. Over green ghoul salad and bloody fingers, Gabrielle was comparing homeroom to their criss-cross-applesauce days. "I've written my fingers down to stubs. It's like being locked in place during criss-cross-applesauce, but with a pen in your hand that you can't put down. And, to make matters worse, she never gives me a grade higher than 65% on anything I turn in."

"The drama students have it just as bad, or maybe worse," added Madelyn, who had a friend in the theater class. "She made them sit out in the hallway and read scripts of old plays that were done years ago. They can't stop. They just keep reading the mindless nonsense while she ransacks everything she can find backstage behind the curtains."

"I heard she's into Miss Tweaks's trunks and costumes and snooping around everywhere she can find," said Paige.

It was bad enough to have the substitute in their classroom; it was worse to think about her being in Miss Tweaks's enchanted theater and poking around in her things. One bleak morning some of the students stated that they had finished their essays for the day and asked if they could please go to the library. To their surprise, Mademoiselle Sowbierre agreed. It was wonderful to be back in the library, and the class made the most of their time.

When they returned from the library an hour later, a disturbing scene awaited them. The desks in the classroom had been moved to make an even wider aisle down the center of the room. Candles were burning in a half circle around the base of the cheval mirror and Mademoiselle Sowbierre was strutting around in front of it like a movie star. She was decked out in a long, sequined scarf.

Several students gasped and said, "It's Miss Tweaks's Twilight Scarf."

She was so pleased with herself that she didn't notice the students returning and gawking at her with absolute horror.

"Take that OFF!" shouted Gabrielle.

With that, Mademoiselle Sowbierre turned on the class with a look so vicious, the students stepped backwards and some visibly shook. Gabrielle too inhaled sharply with the onslaught.

"You nasty little creatures will sit down and not move until I release you!" she said in a deep, raspy voice, with no accent at all. Next, she pointed her finger at Gabrielle and muttered something in a foreign language they didn't recognize. Before they knew what hit them, all were seated rigidly at their desks, only able to move from the waist up. Gabrielle was seated the same way, but she had tape across her mouth. The strutting in front of the mirror continued. Mademoiselle Sowbierre admired herself in the Twilight Scarf, draped around her long neck and trailing out behind her, as she paraded back and forth, looking at herself in the mirror from every angle.

As soon as the teacher wasn't looking, Gabrielle removed the tape from her mouth and looked over at Cassandra. Cassandra gave her a look of "Be cool and don't do anything," while Peter looked around the classroom to make sure everyone was okay. At this point, a strange thing happened. The tops of their desks, ever-so-slightly, jostled a little, then hovered open just a tiny bit. Will looked carefully at his desktop, then whispered to the rest of the class, "Go ahead. It's okay to lift them." Hidden inside the book storage compartment of each desk was one of Miss Tweaks's posey flower pens. As the students picked them up, they were able to move their legs again, and one by one they slipped out of the classroom in time for the lunch bell. They soon discovered that as long as they had the posey flower pen with them (which was more than a little embarrassing for the boys), Mademoiselle Sowbierre couldn't control their movements—not that they were in a hurry to test her.

From that day forward, while her students labored over their senseless, never-ending essays, Mademoiselle Sowbierre wore the Twilight Scarf and spent most of every morning admiring herself and talking to her image in the cheval mirror. Her students noticed that the scarf seemed to be making her neck thinner and longer.

"Something's going on with her neck," said Cody one morning. "It looks like when my grandmother plucks the feathers off the turkey neck on feast day."

"Yeah," said Gabrielle, "the more she wraps that scarf around, the longer, skinnier, and more fragile her neck looks ... like you could snap it off."

Peter and Cassandra were more curious about where she found the scarf in the first place. Cassandra had carefully hidden it away just as Miss Tweaks requested, and Peter had locked everything up.

"She must have broken the locks on the doors and trunks," said Peter.

"Or she used a spell to open them," said Cassie.

One morning while the students furiously scribbled out their essays, Cassandra stopped to shake out her cramped hand. Three notes—from what sounded like a xylophone—eerily filled the classroom and echoed off the walls. Their teacher was so busy with her preening and mirror watching that she either ignored the sound or did not hear it. The eerie notes repeated a few times over the next hour, and the substitute ignored them, if she heard them at all. At the final sound off, Mademoiselle Sowbierre's metal drinking flask suddenly levitated before slamming to the desk, spilling its blood-red contents on the desk surface. Being closest to the spill, Cassandra ran to sop up the mess with the black-and-purple tapestry.

The teacher was momentarily released from her trance, and she ran to the front of the room where Cassandra was dabbing at the spill. Peter saw a strange look come over Cassandra's face as she started to wipe up the liquid and then stopped. Mademoiselle Sowbierre's smoky-blue shadowed eyes opened wide as she looked in terrified surprise at the liquid on the desk. "OUT!" she screamed at the class, who didn't stick around to see what she might do next and dashed for the door.

At lunch, the classmates guessed at the composition of the liquid. Some suggested wine. Cody thought it might have been slow gin or even a bloody mary—it seemed Cody knew a good bit about alcoholic drinks. They went on to joyously speculate that drinking alcohol at school would cost the substitute her job and they could be rid of her.

Cassandra confided to Peter when they were away from the others. "The spill was a message, written in the red liquid. It was like the sunshine messages Aunt Miranda gets on the kitchen table. Peter—I saw what it said!"

"What was it?"

"The message was 'Do your job! Her living will be our undoing.' That's exactly what it said."

Treasures of Plunder Bay

Peter looked very grim. "Do you think she's supposed to finish off Miss Tweaks? I thought they kidnapped her so Sowbear could take her job and get into the school, but this is something worse. It isn't about stealing valuables from the school anymore, because everything important is already gone and the whisperers aren't around. Remember, Miss Tweaks told me right before she disappeared that she had defeated someone in the theater the night before, and they wanted revenge."

"No, Peter, I think they got rid of her so they could do what they came here to do—kill somebody."

"Cassie, this is really serious. It's time to tell the aunts everything we know."

Back at Cape Peril cottage, the twins let the aunts know they had something very troubling to fill them in on. Aunt Miranda brewed a pot of Delicious Details tea (a favorite with the Cape Crown Quilting Bee Club ladies) and Aunt Penelope called Jacques to let him know she couldn't be on call for the fire department as scheduled that night. As the twins started into their story, a powerful, unexpected storm suddenly swept in—a nor'easter—that hit Plunder Bay so intensely, it was said by the fishermen that it was the worst they had seen in decades. Miranda looked pleased as the storm raged outside the cottage that evening. In the aftermath, the local schools were closed for two weeks—a stroke of good fortune.

Their first morning home from school, Aunt Miranda produced a book from her conservatory called *Gaelic Secrets and McBee Family Traditions*. "Based on what you told us, and since schools are closed for who knows how long with this storm, we're going to work on your *protection*

Powers."

"You know that book of spells that I bought at the Smuggler's Bazaar? Well I was never able to successfully cast any of the spells," said Cassie.

Aunt Miranda laughed and said most often the mistake people made was with their pronunciation. "Your Aunt Penelope has the same problem," she said.

While she was talking, Peter couldn't help but remember Miss Tweaks telling him that last day to learn everything his aunts could teach him.

"We'll start with a spell I rarely use, but it's effective." Miranda placed one of her favorite teapots on the kitchen table. Next, she folded her hands and, leaning slightly forward, said in Scots Gaelic, *"Falaichte."* Blue gave a loud guffaw as the little china teapot disappeared into thin air. "Fine, maybe I use it more often to keep Seadog out of the garbage, and you away from my berry pies," she said to the bird. "These spells worked for dairymaids in the Scottish Highlands for generations, or we wouldn't be here. I don't speak the language, but I listened enough to my grandparents to understand a few words and hopefully get them right."

"So do you have to fold your hands like that?" asked Cassie, pointing at Miranda's still folded hands, "Or wiggle your nose, or twist your tongue, or something to make it work?"

"You're talking about a casting tell. I don't think I have a casting tell, but some people do. I know Reynelda cannot cast a spell without her glasses. They're like a wand for her," said Aunt Miranda.

"That's what happened the day she was nabbed," said Peter. "She left them on top of her book and so couldn't protect herself when they snatched her, and wherever she is now we can't get them back to her."

"All we can do now is try to protect ourselves. We'll practice this, and there are others I will teach you, like *Cuir Stad*, which is to stop or suspend and *Falbh a-mach*, to expel or send away."

"*Ttuiteam gun èirigh*," squawked the parrot, and Aunt Miranda ordered him to stop.

"What did he say?" asked Peter.

Aunt Miranda scowled at the bird. "Just more of that language he picked up from those soulless thugs he hangs around."

As aunt Miranda skimmed through the book, she came across a page that featured an interesting-looking old banner. It was the shape of a shield with a yellow-gold background and a small ship in the center, featuring three oars and rigging.

"Look," she said to Penelope. "It's a picture of the Kingdom of the Isles banner. 'I've never really noticed it before. It says here it was the colors flown by the *Merry Gale*, a cog that sailed from medieval times up to the seventeenth century—a small, two-masted craft with a square stern."

"That's looks like what Inspector Martinez found wrapped up with the old sea charts, right?"

"The *Merry Gale*?" asked Peter, picking up on their comments. "That's one of the ships that was sailing on the big sea chart hanging behind Miss Tweaks's desk."

"Who is Inspector Martinez?" asked Cassie.

The aunts gave each other sideways looks, and most unexpectedly, Blue squawked, "Walk the plank!"

That was adequate distraction for Aunt Miranda to

change the subject and announce they'd covered enough territory on their first day of lessons, and she closed the book.

The morning spell-casting sessions continued every day. During afternoons in the playroom, Cassandra worked on her magic lessons as Peter became obsessed with his Govi watch. Soon, he had mastered just the right touch to get it open with the help of Miss Tweaks's grandfather's book of instructions for fixing clocks. It appeared in his desk the day after the posey pens were discovered.

"Cassie, you know the book Miss Tweaks left in the cafeteria that awful day?

"Yes, *The History of the Great Realms Before Panopoly*. It's part of a series of old books that used to be in the library."

"What's it about? Does it say anything about time?" he asked.

Cassandra leafed through the pages until she found a passage about time and the ancient realms. "Not much here, Peter. It just says every realm kept its own calendar, depending on its age. Days and months were calculated by the sun and phases of the moon, which made trade possible. The lunar cycle was the universally recognized time across all realms—that's all it says."

"That makes sense. If you are going to be crosstemporing between the realms to conduct trade, you'd have to have some kind of universal time and calendar system."

"You know, this book kind of looks like the ones that Sowbear was studying so intently when she first arrived," said Cassie.

"You're right. Let's make sure she doesn't get her hands on this one. We'll keep it here at the cottage."

Treasures of Plunder Bay

One night while cleaning up after dinner with Cassandra and Peter, Aunt Penelope divulged Miranda's casting tell. "You know—your Aunt Miranda does have a tell, even if she won't admit it. It's that folded-hand thing. I've been watching her."

"HA! That's funny and very subtle, said Peter.

"And Peter, I know what yours is too," said Aunt Penelope. "Cassie, have you figured it out?"

"No, what is it?" asked Cassie, surprised that she hadn't noticed it.

Peter looked amused and waited to see if Aunt Penelope had it right.

"Peter almost imperceptibly tugs on his left ear when he wants his own way. He's done it since he was a baby."

"Now that you mention it, that's right!" exclaimed Cassandra.

Peter laughed. "But please, keep it to yourselves."

"I have one too," said Aunt Penelope. "Watch this," she said, straightening and squaring her shoulders.

"Does it really help you cast a spell?"

"I'm pretty sure it does."

"It definitely does," added Peter.

"What about me, Aunt Penelope? Do I have a tell?"

"None that I can see so far—but give it time."

After two weeks of freezing cold and drifting snow, the twins finished their first round of magic spell and casting training, and the aunts felt confident that they could protect themselves well enough to go back to school. Upon arriving in their classroom, they found Mademoiselle Sowbierre more sullen and seemingly angrier than she had been before the weather-induced break. Her metal flask had been replaced by a thick black candle, and she was dressed in her own over-the-top designer clothes again. The Twilight Scarf was nowhere to be seen. She now wore a unique pair of earrings, in which only the left earring contained an unusual gemstone. She barely greeted her students as she passed out their work folders and pointed to their essay writing assignment on the whiteboard. When Daniel questioned her about the corrections on his paper, she didn't answer.

Instead of studying the old books from the library, or looking through her fashion magazines, she spent much of their class time scribbling furiously on pieces of fancy parchment paper in her favorite purple ink. When she completed a handwritten parchment paper note, she lit the black candle and held the note above the flame. A small puff of purple smoke emitted from the parchment paper, leaving the sheet blank so that the message could not be discovered. She wrote many notes and a few times she jiggled her left earring, cupped her hand over it, and nodded as though it was talking to her. By the time most of the students had finished their assignments, Mademoiselle had left the room.

"Hope she went down to visit the rats," joked Cody.

"She couldn't have been more witchy if she had a wart on her nose and a pointed hat," said Gabrielle.

"Shush. She's backstage listening to us," said Peter, ending all further conversation until lunch.

Whether it was having two weeks off to reenergize, or having time to focus on practicing their magic, Mademoiselle Sowbierre's students were feeling more empowered than they had since the loss of Miss Tweaks. That day at lunch, they decided to push back just a little by killing their substitute with kindness. Everyone except Peter and Cassandra devised a gift to bring to her throughout the course of the next week. Gabrielle brought her some homemade applesauce that had the strange effect of making her want to sit cross-legged on the floor. Caitlyn B. brought her a bright red, polished apple— courtesy of her stepmother. Madelyn arrived with a young dream vine, planted in a purple papier-mâché pot that she made in art. Virginia provided a special blend of lavender and belladonna potpourri, which for some reason caused Mademoiselle Sowbierre to fall asleep at her desk one morning. Cody brought her some very, very, aromatic cheese, and managed to leave crumbs of it all the way up the steps from the basement to her desk. (No one knew whether the giant rats found it or not.) And so it went all week, with all the students offering gifts. Mademoiselle Sowbierre seemed confused by the gestures of kindness and unsure of how to interpret the students' motives. Cassandra and Peter watched her carefully, knowing she was capable of more than they could probably imagine.

X Marks The Spot

I t had been a tough winter for lobstering. After the nor'easter, the gale winds and fog made leaving the harbor at Plunder Bay impossible. The light at Cape Peril lighthouse was always on now, but there had been no further visits from Captain McMullen or any other authority. Word around the village was that Plunder Bay School would stay open the rest of the year, but by next fall all of them would be bussed to Cape Crown. Perhaps the worst thing about that winter was that there had been no sign of Miss Tweaks. She had not returned home, nor had she contacted any of her friends. They all feared the worst.

Cassandra started the morning by arguing with Gabrielle, who claimed she had mastered a spell to change the grades on her upcoming report card. Cassandra thought it was a bad idea and told her so. That made Gabrielle furious, and she accused her friend of manipulating grades herself because she and Peter were making A's in Mademoiselle Sowbierre's language arts and history, while nearly everyone else in the class was failing.

As if to prove Gabrielle right, Mademoiselle Sowbierre came in ruffling through her stack of daily assignments and grumbling, "Zhat idiot cannot count, I'm short four packeezts." She handed a packet of worksheets to Cassandra. "Go up to ze copy room on ze third floor and make four more of zhese. If anyone gives jou an argument, tell zhem I zent you and they can take it up with me. When jou get back, pass zhem out. If any of jou finish before I get back, jou may go to ze library and get a book."

With that, Mademoiselle Sowbierre stomped out of the room.

"She's really got the accent going today," said Will.

Cody took Will's cue. "And Cazzie, when juo geet back, flush ze copies down ze toyolet."

Cassandra stood for a few minutes after the teacher left, listening to her classmates' wisecracks, then headed for the door. Gabrielle shot her a disdainful look that said, "Teacher's pet," and at the moment, she couldn't argue with the optics of it.

Cassandra went straight to the copy room and was glad to see that there was no one else around. When she lifted the cover to start copying the first page of the packet, she found an odd-looking sheet of paper already on the copier. One edge was ragged, and she knew immediately that it was a page ripped from an old book. The paper was thick, the ink faded, but it looked like a hand-drawn map. She slipped the page to the bottom of her stack, placed her first page face down on the copier, and pushed the button. When nothing happened, Cassandra looked at the tray and saw it was out of paper. *Too bad*, she thought. It wasn't like she was in any rush to get back to class. As she headed for the door to go down to the office and tell them the copier was out of paper, she ran into Walker Matthews.

"Making copies ... teacher's little helper, are you?"

"Why are you here?" Cassandra snapped back.

"Just came to get Mr. Morgan's coffee cup."

"And what does that make you?" Cassandra fired back, pushing past him and heading down the stairs.

On her way down to the office, Cassandra thought she'd kill a little time and stopped at the girl's bathroom on the second floor, beside the art lab. There were usually a lot of the older girls in there, mixing paint or washing out brushes and talking about grown-up stuff that was going on at the school. Today, unfortunately, the place was empty. Just as she got back to the stairs, she saw the secretary half a flight above her, laden down with reams of paper. Instead of going down to the office, Cassandra followed the secretary back up to the third-floor copy room. When she went in, the art teacher was there, and Walker Matthews was gone.

"Oh good, just in time with the paper," said Mrs. Simpson to the secretary.

"Cassandra, what do you need?" asked the secretary.

"Mademoiselle Sowbierre sent me up here to make four copies."

"Then you can go first," said Mrs. Simpson.

"I'm in no hurry," said Cassandra.

"Mademoiselle Sowbierre will get you if you take too long," joked the secretary, wiggling her fingers at them.

"I'll survive," replied the teacher. She and the secretary were still chatting when Cassandra finished making the copies and left.

When Cassandra left the copy room with the old map tucked between the worksheets her heart was pounding so hard she could hear it. She was determined to show Peter what she had found on the copy machine. She knew it was something important that had been ripped from one of the old library books. She thought it might even be what Mademoiselle Sowbierre had been searching for all those mornings that she pored through the old books at her desk.

"How do I get it out of here so that Peter and I can figure

out what it is?" she whispered to herself as she raced down the steps to the first floor. She knew when it was discovered missing there'd be a price to pay, and she didn't dare get caught with it—Peter either for that matter. On the first floor, she stopped to clear her mind and catch her breath. That's when she noticed that she was standing right in front of Bradley Boggins's locker, which was next to Peter's. Bradley was out for two weeks recovering from having his tonsils out. If she slipped it into his locker it would go undetected until she and Peter could retrieve it. She looked around and saw no one, so she folded the drawing in half and shoved it through the vent in the locker door, the same way she and Gabrielle sometimes left notes for each other.

Something was going on at lunch that day. There were a lot of people coming and going from the office. Several teachers, who should have been in class, stopped by the kitchen for coffee. Mr. Amadan came in looking worried, and whispered something to Maggie O'Day, who laughed out loud and told him to clean up his own mess. Fourth period, Cassandra was taking a test in Mr. Morgan's room when someone brought a note to his door. After reading it, Mr. Morgan announced, "Great! Put down your pencils and turn your test papers over. Some brain surgeon downstairs has lost their very important paper." Then in an imitation of a TV policeman he said, "Open your backpacks and put them on the desk in front of you, and empty the contents of your pockets on the desk. If you can't afford a lawyer, one will be appointed to blow your defense. You are all guilty until proven innocent."

Almost everybody laughed, but Cassandra felt sick. Gabrielle, seeing her friend looking distressed mouthed silently, "Are you okay?" Cassandra nodded and smiled back, happy their morning disagreement was forgotten.

Fifth period, another note came around, and Mr. Lee, the algebra teacher, told them it was locker inspection time, and they'd get a chance to breathe some of that fresh air out in the hall. Everyone in the whole school reported to their locker and waited for one of the teachers to watch them open it while they went through the contents. Cassandra felt pretty calm by now, and her locker was neat compared to everybody else's. First-floor lockers were done fast, but things must have been slower upstairs. Finally, they were told to go to their last class of the day and to take the combination locks from their lockers home with them. Cassandra felt relieved until seventh period, when she was called to the office over the speaker. Her heart began to race wildly and for a moment she thought she would faint. Peter, while not in the same seventh period class, heard her name called and his teacher just nodded when he left the classroom.

A lot of people were in the office when Peter caught up with Cassie. They were all talking at once and it seemed to be mass confusion.

Mr. Amadan addressed Cassandra. "Are you the girl who was making copies for Mademoiselle Sowbierre this morning?"

Before Cassandra could answer, the secretary chimed in. "I told you she came in *after* I got there. Mrs. Simpson was already set up to use the machine."

"Did you pick up a paper from the worktable or the floor?" continued the principal.

"No," said Cassie, thinking that was not really a lie.

"There was nothing in the machine. I told you that a

dozen times," insisted Mrs. Simpson.

"Mademoiselle Sowbierre, are you sure this girl didn't have that paper mixed in with the ones she brought to you?"

"Jou dare to ask me zhat! I passed all ze papers out, zere was nozing zere. If ze idiot who made zose packets in ze first place could count to twelve, I would not be zitting here," she said. She leaned back in Mr. Amadan's chair and crossed her long, boot-clad legs on top of his desk.

That was when the principal threw up his hands in frustration. "Get out. Get out, all of you!" Cassandra and Peter were the first ones through the door.

At bus time while everyone was taking their locks off and cleaning out anything they didn't want pilfered, Cassandra spotted Bradley's older brother trying to take off Bradley's lock. "He texted me his combination, but I can't open it," said George.

"I think I know it," said Peter. He bent down so he was eye level with the metal lock. Cassandra heard her brother whisper, *"Fosgailte,"* which she knew was Scots Gaelic for "release." Peter give his left ear a subtle tug. When the lock popped open, he handed it to George, but left the door closed until Bradley's brother was far down the hall.

"Is this yours?" said Peter, handing her the folded paper.

As the twins rushed through the door that afternoon, Aunt Miranda asked, "How was school?"

"Homework!" they said in unison, and hurried up the stairs before Aunt Penelope was even through the door after them.

"I wonder what they're up to now," she said, looking at Ms. Mew.

Once inside the playroom, Peter exploded. "What did you *find* and how did you do it?"

"I think it's a map of something from that set of really old books from the library." She stretched out on the blue rug and gently unfolded the page.

"It's definitely been torn from a very old book," said Peter.

"Anyone who knew the old books in the library would know they can't be copied. It's some kind of *protection* enchantment."

"Any idea of which old book it came from?" asked Peter.

"I didn't get a chance to look around for the old book in the copy room. It was lucky that I got the map stashed before Walker Matthews showed up."

"Not a good thing that he saw you in there alone. Wonder what he was doing in there?" Peter traced the line on the map with his index finger and decided it looked like a rough sketch of a coastline, with a little river attached to a house or building.

"There are a couple of written words, if you can make them out, and maybe that blue 'X' means buried treasure. Your guess is as good as mine. I just don't know," said Cassie.

The map was still a mystery when they were called to dinner. In twenty minutes, they had finished eating and returned to do their homework with a borrowed magnifying glass. When they entered the playroom, Peter addressed the round window. "Show me a chart of the coastline around Plunder Bay to Cape Peril."

The window complied, and a chart of the coastline appeared. Peter studied it carefully and a look of recognition came across his face.

"The coastline part resembles the shoreline east of the

village, and right here you can make out the words, 'Low Tide.' Maybe this blue 'X' is supposed to be a marker, and I think this square thing represents the old trading post, as it would have been when it was built."

"Right," said Cassie, "and that's the old wing of the school now."

"I've got it!" exclaimed Peter excitedly. "This is an old map of how to get to the trading post from the water—at low tide. What looks like a river must be a tunnel. I even think I know that marker—it's the big blue rock that nearly got me knifed by Bobby Briggs a few months back. We can go check it out when the weather clears up, but we've got to be careful. Somebody searched long and hard for this map, and then wanted it badly enough to go to a lot of trouble to get it back."

The next morning, everyone at school had their own idea about the reason for the locker search. A lot of kids claimed to know someone had taken a copy of Mr. Boggins's physics final. Others seemed certain it was the principal's credit card account information. There was speculation about love letters, and some were certain it was information about the disappearance of Miss Tweaks. Cassandra's greatest fear was that Walker Matthews would tell that he'd seen her in the copy room by herself when he came in to get Mr. Morgan's coffee cup. To add to the mystery of it all, Mademoiselle Sowbierre didn't show up for class that morning, leaving her students to read in the library until the lunch bell sounded.

When they were alone, Cassandra asked Gabrielle, "Do you want me to take a look at some of your graded essays to see why they're rated so low? Maybe there's a way to fix them."

"Thanks. It baffles me what I'm doing wrong, and nearly everyone else too, for that matter."

"Wait, look at this," exclaimed Cassie. "Mine, like Peter's, are graded in Sowbear's handwriting with purple ink."

"And mine ... like everyone else in the class, are graded in red by someone with different handwriting," said Gabrielle. "You don't have to be a detective to see that someone else is grading everyone's work but yours and Peter's."

"I can't believe I didn't pick up on this sooner," said Cassie.

And, after Mademoiselle Sowbierre's speech in the front office, it was apparent someone else was putting her worksheet lesson packets together. Gabrielle suggested it might be the secretary, then both agreed she was too lazy to do her own work, let alone Sowbear's. The secretary was well known for being a terrible gossip, a rumor monger, acting more important than she was, and stirring trouble. Maggie O'Day had threatened more than once to cook her in a stew.

To add to the confusion, there were visitors in the school. Two fleshy men in khaki pants and sweater vests were parading around like they owned the place. Rumor had it that they were to be the principal and vice principal at the new Cape Crown School, where most of the Plunder Bay students would be next year. What seemed odd about the visit was that Principal Amadan was not guiding the tour. Instead, Mademoiselle Sowbierre was entertaining them. She had one of the drama students bring down a tray with tea and treats and set it up on the library counter. Joking and laughing, she seemed quite comfortable with the two visitors—almost as if she knew them.

Treasures of Plunder Bay

When the lunch bell rang, her homeroom students piled out behind her entourage, who were headed back to the main building. Just at the point where Peter and Will had tried to tackle the whisperer, one of the men stood aside to let the students pass. Later, Peter compared it to déjà vu, as if the same man, in the same corner, were wearing the same shoes that had stepped on Cody.

Death Trap

That foggy Friday, the day started weird and got worse. Aunt Penelope got an early fire-rescue call, which turned out to be bogus, and by the time she got back to Cape Peril cottage, Cassandra and Peter were already late for school. There was no one in the front office to report to, so the twins made a brief stop at their lockers and headed to homeroom. That room was also empty.

Within a few minutes, Mademoiselle Sowbierre rushed into the classroom and grabbed a green suede moto jacket from the back of her chair. "Jou two are late, and everyone has gone to ze gym for a bus zafety meeting. I am entertaining in ze library, zen will continue ze touring. Go now to ze theater costume room and ztraighten up a bit for me. Jou know ze room."

"Okay," said Cassandra, wondering how Mademoiselle Sowbierre knew about them being in the costume room before. As soon as she left, the twins climbed the four steps, walked across the stage, and found the door to the costume room ajar. When Cassandra flipped on the light, they saw the place was in shambles. All the costume trunks were thrown open, some had been dumped out on the floor. Clothes were strewn everywhere. Boxes of jewelry had been spilled and the stage makeup from the big tray was everywhere.

"Someone sure did a number on this place," Peter said, but Cassandra was already too busy to reply. She seemed to be everywhere at once, setting trunks upright, folding

191

clothes, and stacking them away.

"What's the hurry?"

"I'm looking for the Twilight Scarf. All the same things that were here before are here now, except for Miss Tweaks's Twilight Scarf."

At that point, Peter joined the search. Apart from getting distracted by weapon props that were authentic eighteenth- and nineteenth-century swords, crossbows, and daggers, they found no trace of the scarf. Both were too engrossed in the contents of the costume room to notice the room growing dimmer and the closing of the door, but when the heavy latch clicked shut, they dropped what they were doing and ran to open it. When the handle would not budge, Cassandra tried calling out to anyone on the other side of the door. When that didn't work, she doubled up her fists and pounded.

"Give it up," her brother said. "This was no accident. Someone meant to lock us in here."

"Do you still have the keys?"

"They're in my backpack, back in the classroom."

"How about the spell you used to open Bradley's locker?"

Peter whispered, *"Fosgailte,"* and tugged his left ear. This resulted in static and a blue arc springing from the knob to Peter's hand, giving him a shock. Standing further back, he tried again with exactly the same outcome. The twins tried casting the "open" spell in unison, and both got shocked, twice as severe as Peter's shock. The smell of singed hair hung in the air and the light began to flicker.

"We're trapped," said Peter grimly. "And no one is coming to help us because no one knows we're here."

"I'll focus my *finding Power* on another way out," said Cassie, turning her attention back to the room. "This room is a mirror of our classroom, and it has two doors, so over here should be another opening."

Their first impulse was to knock on the walls, listening for a hollow sound. The room began to grow darker as the lights continued to dim. In earnest they moved trunks, searching for a trap door in the floor. In desperation, Cassandra remembered the "reveal" spell from her Smuggler's Bazaar casting book and tried repeating it with every tell she knew. Peter joined in, and from the now misty darkness, a doorknob appeared. Peter grabbed hold and tugged with all his strength. The door gave way suddenly, sending them tumbling backward onto a trunk. The room went dark, except for the pale-yellow glow of Cassandra's ring. After dusting themselves off, they approached the open doorway. It was completely dark on the other side.

"I'll see where this door leads, must be a hallway behind the theater," said Peter. He stepped through the door, out into the darkness.

Cassandra heard a thud, followed by an expletive from her brother. "Are you okay? What can you see?" she called down, taking it for granted that he was still alive and not badly hurt.

"Nothing. It's pitch black and wet, and it stinks. Can you get me back up?"

With nothing but the glow from her ring, Cassandra began knotting costumes together to make a kind of rope. Twice she lowered her creation to Peter, but it didn't reach. When he finally said he felt it brush against his face, Cassandra added enough fabric to tie it around the doorknob, securing it in place on her end. After several failed attempts, Peter gave up, saying he could not get any footing on the slippery wall. There was even some discussion about Cassandra dropping down to join him, but she was reluctant to be in the basement, or wherever, with Cody's rats.

"At least there's air down here, even a strong draft," he called up. "If your ring's still glowing, I could see better. I might figure out which way to go. At this point I'd rather face the rats than be stuck here."

"Me too. Hold the rope steady. I'm coming down. Worst comes to worst, I've got on rubber-soled boots, and with some light I can climb back up."

As soon as Cassandra landed in the slushy mud beside her brother, the light on her finger grew bright enough to see their dim surroundings.

"I think there is only one way out—down this long, dark, sloping tunnel," said Cassie.

"It's where the air is coming from. Don't fall, it's a mess down here," said Peter.

Holding Cassandra's ring out in front of them, the two made their way down the tunnel. It had a gradual slope, and about four meters in they were wading in water up to their ankles. Peter stopped. "We have to go back!"

"Are you crazy? Go back where?"

"Up that screwy rope, back to the room."

"Then what, stay locked in there until we die of old age?"

"No," said Peter, "just until about four this afternoon. The tide is coming in. This is seawater, and we're in the smugglers' tunnel!"

"The one from the map I found?"

"The exact tunnel from the map you found."

Without another word they turned, and headed back quickly through the tunnel. Cassandra grabbed onto the costume rope but as she pulled, she felt it slipping loose, and at her first try to hang on and brace her feet against the wall, the whole contraption landed on her head.

"Whoever locked the door ... untied the knot. What do we do now?"

"Maybe we can make it out the other end, but we have to hurry. It kind of depends on how long the tunnel is."

They were running now, and Peter reached in his pocket for his watch. He flipped it open, hoping he could make it work to slow time, but even though it would sometimes tick, he had not mastered the skill of moving the hands in any direction. Without much hope, he blew on its companion—the shepherd's whistle—before hanging both around his neck.

Cassandra and Peter were too scared, too busy, and too cold to talk. The water had reached to their knees, and the force of the tide was pushing them backwards, inhibiting their forward progress. An eerie sound from out of the darkness echoed off the tunnel walls.

For a short time, the weight of their soggy shoes and clothes helped to hold them down and keep some footing. The light from Cassandra's ring was shining brightly, and even though she tried to hold it out in front of them, her hand would sometimes slip below the water which had reached chest height. The ring's glow flashed onto the stone walls on either side and illuminated the water. They could see their feet, but there was nothing to grab hold of. Peter tried to push his sister from behind, but he could barely touch the bottom and she was starting to bob up and down. A few meters more, and both were swimming, struggling to keep their eyes open as the seawater splashed against the tunnel walls, closing in the space above their heads. Peter swam ahead and tried to pull his sister forward, the pocket of air above was closing fast, and the exhausted swimmers bounced against the ceiling.

"Imagine we are safe," Cassandra spluttered, and in return, her brother squeezed her hand tightly.

"Daylight ahead!" Peter gasped.

They each took a last gulp of air, and as the water surged over their heads, they propelled themselves forward—under the water, toward the light. With a desperate push upward, they bobbed to the surface of the water inside a small grotto. The seaworn rocks were not hard to climb, and they scrambled high enough to escape the tide as the gulls circled just outside the opening.

"Are we okay here?" asked Cassie, gasping for air.

"I hope so. I've been here before—at high tide, but sometimes it's higher than others—depends," said Peter breathing heavily.

"I really wasn't in the mood to go swimming today!" said Cassie.

"No, me either."

They were both shivering and Cassandra's teeth were chattering. They had climbed to the highest rock inside the grotto, knowing it was best to stay out of the wind. After wringing what water they could out of Cassandra's big sweater and Peter's sweatshirt, they huddled together, trying to stay warm under the soggy clothes. The haunting sound they had heard in the tunnel continued, and they realized it was the foghorn from the lighthouse. Every few minutes, one of them would give their shepherd's whistle a blow. Waiting for the tide to turn, and the beach to reappear so they could walk out, seemed their only option at this point.

C. S. Leonard

A few freezing minutes later, Cassandra thought she heard a dog barking. Then Peter heard it too, and thought it sounded like Seadog. He blew again on the shepherd's whistle, and Cassandra called the dog by name. A moment later, the sandy dirt above the grotto began to hail down, and Seadog splashed into the water and scrambled up beside them. A great deal of face licking, hugging, and tail wagging followed. Seadog continued barking as he snuggled in beside them. He was wet, but he was warm, and finally they weren't alone.

When the rescue boat from the fire department pulled up a short time later and threw a rope to them, it was the dog who caught it in his teeth. Climbing aboard was shaky business for the exhausted twins. Blankets and a little sip of brandy were administered by Aunt Penelope and, once home, Aunt Miranda had remedies of her own. Thankfully, there were not too many questions yet, because it was the next morning before either swimmer felt truly warm again.

On their way down to breakfast, Peter and Cassandra knew they would be in for an interrogation by the aunts. They settled around the kitchen table to fill the aunts in on how they had come to be swimming out of the smugglers' tunnel. Aunt Miranda had heard tales of the tunnel and explained that ill-gotten pirate loot, wooden boxes, and barrels had been floated up to the trading post at high tide and were retrieved at the bottom of the steps, which over the years must have washed away—a fact the twins had sadly discovered the day before. It was an easier and more secretive way to move the looted treasure than hauling it through the village. As far as the aunts knew, the tunnel's location had been unknown for decades. At this, Blue screeched from his perch, "X Marks the Spot."

Aunt Miranda brought the subject back to who could have locked Cassandra and Peter in the costume room and why neither of them could break the spell. In particular, the blue arcs caught her interest. She had spoken with Maggie O'Day, who told her there were no black vans or strangers in the school except for the two men, presumed to be the new principals, who Mademoiselle Sowbierre was entertaining in the library.

"She—or they if she told them—would have been the only ones who knew we were at the school, and in the costume room," said Cassie.

"She could have been overheard by someone when she gave you the instructions," said Aunt Penelope.

"I don't know," said Peter, "but someone seriously tried to kill us. It was no accident."

"But they couldn't have known you would find the tunnel, and as the high tide was coming in, to boot," said Aunt Miranda.

"Don't forget," said Cassandra, "They untied the makeshift rope, trapping us in the tunnel. That could have sealed our doom."

"The question is ... who and why!" said Peter. He slammed his fist on the table hard enough to rattle the teacups in their saucers. This prompted Blue to fly down and perch on his left shoulder.

"Well, it will take more to kill us than that," said Cassie.

The Naughty Puffin Inn

A nother six kilometers up the Coast Road, past the lane to the lighthouse, the Naughty Puffin Inn sat on a bluff overlooking the sea. Of late, the enchanting old inn had fallen into disrepair, which was a shame, because it was built from salvaged ship timbers with authentic trappings like hanging lanterns, wide plank decking, and portholes. The tables and chairs were handmade from whiskey and molasses barrels and wooden shipping crates. Especially on stormy nights, when the old timbers creaked with the wind, and the swaying lanterns cast shadows on the decking, diners had the sensation of being out at sea. In its prime, the Inn Special was always the catch of the day, and the dusty bottles of wine from the cellar were mellow and mysterious.

In the last few years, however, things were quite different. The new owner, Bobby Briggs, boasted of ten guest rooms, a gourmet seafood restaurant, and a full bar—all of which was a gross exaggeration. In truth, it had four small rooms with shared baths, and a bunkroom in the garret. What food they served was terrible because no decent, local cook would work for him, and the bar was rough and noisy. Wine glasses had been switched out for shot glasses and pitchers of cheap, watery beer. Now, peanuts, pickled eggs, and dry pizza were the catch of most days, but despite its fall from grace, the inn had been unusually busy all winter.

Proprietor Briggs's long-term guests wiled away the cold

nights watching the sports channel on a tacky flat-screen TV behind the bar, or engaged in the proprietor's long-running poker game. In fact, it was rumored that Briggs had won the inn in a crooked card game three years before, which surprised no one in the community whose ancestors had died at the hands of wreckers centuries ago. On that particular foggy Saturday night in early April, all that had been usual was about to change.

Bobby Briggs watched as two young, hulking strangers in blueberries—the old navy fatigues—came in and took the small table by the door. They didn't come up to the bar for their drinks, so he put his bar towel over his shoulder and went to take their orders. When they told him they would wait for the rest of their crew to arrive, he saw the potential for big bucks and told the three tables of regulars to triple up at one table.

The next group of strangers through the door were a mixed bag of different ages—some looked military but others not. A bald fellow with huge, muscular, tattooed forearms ordered tankards of ale for his men, and when the owner said he only had mugs and pitchers, his customer insisted on a pitcher for each of them. When the seven pitchers were delivered, the bald man laid out a stack of one-hundred-dollar bills on the table and ordered Briggs to keep the beer coming. Curious about the group, Briggs glanced out into the fog to see what they were driving, he half expected to see motorcycles. He wondered if this was the meeting of a biker gang—a danger he'd been warned about—but no vehicles were in sight. There was definitely something of the sea about his guests, but he knew most of the local fishermen, and these men were complete strangers.

As the throng grew, the noise level went up. People came and went from the parking lot and there was no way to keep up. Soon, his kegs were running low, and he knew enough about his business to understand that it was not a good idea to run out of liquor with a large drunken crowd. He thought it fortuitous when someone called for rum, and he brought out all he had in stock. He was so busy making money he couldn't keep track of what was owed. Pipe and cigar smoke made the big room hazy, and from a dark corner table, a harmonica began a rousing sea shanty, then another. Feet stomped on the planking, deep voices sang along, and a fellow with one gold loop earring danced a jig. While delivering a bottle of rum to a table, Bobby Briggs overhead one of the men say, "We've seen some fair weather and some heavy weather, mates, spilled blood on the decking boards, and nearly sunk with gold, but when the captain calls, there's not a one of us that don't come, you may lay to that!"

As Briggs was walking away, he heard the men sitting around the table pound their fists, shouting, "AYE, AYE!"

While the newcomers seemed a jolly enough group, it was obvious the by-now regulars, who had been staying there for months, did not appreciate the invasion of their privacy. They were arrogant, intimidating bullies who had long ago driven out the few locals who came to drink beer, play cards, and gossip about the strange events at the old school. They came and went at all hours, lurking around in big, black coats with their hoods pulled up. They kept themselves to themselves, always whispering and giving any other customers the evil eye. Their lodging bills went unpaid for months, and any effort by Briggs to make them pay up or leave, ended with nasty threats. There was something very dark and sinister about them, and Bobby Briggs knew a good amount about dark and sinister.

The man who was the leader of the group was called Deilman. The others took their direction from him. Deilman crossed the room and stopped at the corner table, where he stared down menacingly at a man with a bandaged right ear who was playing the harmonica. The musician ignored him, and the music continued to resonate. With a swift movement, he slapped the little instrument away. "Enough!"

The room grew quiet and all eyes focused on the corner table. A tall, burly, red-bearded man in a blousy white shirt stepped out of the shadows. For those who knew the history of Plunder Bay, and had paid attention to the statue standing in the park, the man was unmistakable. The captain had a gratified look about him that implied he had been waiting for the opportunity to confront the dark group—and that desire was about to be fulfilled. He caught the harmonica in midair with one large-knuckled fist, and leveled his gaze squarely at Deilman.

Deilman addressed the room, now so still and quiet only the wind and creaking ship's timbers could be heard. "Who's in charge here?"

The man with the tattooed forearms growled from his table near the door, "Take your pick—and state your case. You see, we're all freebooters here."

The word *freebooters* told Bobby Briggs everything he needed to know, and more. These raucous new patrons were pirates, and living or dead, they were not a force to be reckoned with. He also knew that his long-term guests were *Powers* wielders. He was dreadfully afraid of both, and took the opportunity to back slowly behind the bar.

In a smooth, deep-baritone voice, the red-bearded man tossed the harmonica back to its musician and said, "Jacks, you play on," without breaking his gaze on Deilman.

Deilman was unphased and stepped forward calmly, pointing with his chin toward the door, and looking the man straight in the eye with such menace that even his fellow thugs looked nervous. "Leave now—ALL of you."

The music started up again, now mellow and sad. The Naughty Puffin Inn began to creak and then rock on imaginary waves. The group of dark strangers struggled to keep their footing on the rolling floor. The seamen weren't phased, and watched to see what would happen next. Deilman, not to be outdone, gave a backhanded wave with his arms, resulting in the outside door blowing open. Instead of sucking the guests out as he intended, salty sea spray splashed across the floor, and then the door slammed shut and the dead bolt dropped with a thud.

Deilman was surprised, but he wasn't giving up. With the next wave of his hand, he upended the tables. Shattered glass flew everywhere, then fell to float in jagged chunks in the seawater sloshing across the floor. Smirking, he faced the crew triumphantly with a look that said there was more where that came from.

"Heave to!" ordered the captain, and the room suddenly pitched hard to port at about a sixty-degree angle, washing the broken glass and debris behind the bar. The swinging lanterns overhead flared brightly, casting monstrous shadows around the room just as ghostly phantoms filled the corners and stretched out across the room to right the tables, one by one with heavy thuds.

Deilman moved away to join his companions whispering at the poker table. Something was passed hand to hand,

and a second later, two vanished from sight in a puff of soot. Just as fast, these two were snatched up by the two young men in navy fatigues, doused with beer and set down hard at a back table. The time had come for the whisperers to start talking.

Deilman, in one last attempt to gain the upper hand, broke a bottle of rum across the edge of a barrel table, and sent it flying menacingly toward the captain's face. It shattered in thin air before reaching its target. At that, the harmonica stopped for a moment, then began a dirge. Bobby Briggs, owner of the Naughty Puffin Inn, headed through the kitchen to the back door. The gas lanterns dimmed, and the captain calmly ordered, to no one in particular, "Contain him." With this, a gleaming cutlass with an impressive, bejeweled handle, appeared at Deilman's throat. The sharp, curved blade ever so slightly drew blood that trickled into the collar of his expensive Shetland wool sweater.

Bobby Briggs, on his way out the back door, didn't fare much better. He was met by an old acquaintance—the one-armed seaman with his blade.

"I ... I ... had no idea who they were ... I swear it," said Bobby. "It was just ... business. I'll be glad to rid the place of them, and that gargantuan woman too."

"We'll do with ye what'ere the captain says," said Old Tom. Then, he took a certain gold doubloon from his peacoat pocket, flipped it into the air, and caught it. "I'd bet this here ole' coin has brought me better luck than it has you, but I'm of a mind to give it back."

Seeing the captain had the scene well under control, the bar began to empty out. Many left in the longboats moored at the wharf below. One of the two black vans was parked right outside the door, but being under close watch, the former whisperers dared not bolt for the door which was being guarded by the navy men. All but Deilman—who was still standing, very still—looked incredibly nervous. The hushed conversation at the back table lasted for a long time, with occasional mocking laughter from the red-bearded man who was questioning the two who had tried to disappear. It finally ended when the two sooty fellows stood up and emptied their pockets. The captain gave his orders to those who remained.

"Those two, and the two here, are outliers. Brand them and send them on their way in one black van. Burn the other van. The two with *Powers*—pitiful as they are—will go aboard ship with me."

"Cap'n, what do ye want done with Bobby Boy?" called the one-armed man from just inside the kitchen door.

"Whatever you want, matey," was the reply.

Back in the kitchen, the conversation turned to punishments due. "Well now let's see," proclaimed Old Tom, as much thinking out loud as talking to Briggs. "What would be a fittin' way to deal with a lubber like you, Bobby? I knows ye to be the worst kind o' outlier, and ye've been caught a time or two, judging by them black-spot brands behind your ear. When ye does harm to innocent people, ye has to pay the piper soon or late. Messin' with that little fella on the beach was bad enough. Housin' that bunch o' conjurers and whisperers who scared the kiddies at the school and shanghaied their teacher is just more against ye in the book."

"You might as well use your blade and do me in now. After tonight, I'm done here anyway. My past always catches up with me, as sure as if I'd lit those wreckers' fires on the beach hundreds of years ago," said Briggs, blaming his behavior on his own ancestors' bad blood.

"That's the truth it is, ye're a pitiful man with a bad reputation and a shameful family name. Reckon there's not a Briggs alive that shouldn't be hanged for the murder 'n' pillagin' done o'er two hundred years. But then spillin' your blood here would do a shame to this good kitchen. I'd think a hangin' from the yardarms would do best, if I can get you aboard tonight."

"Don't send me out to sea with them! I know what happens there. I've done some really bad stuff. I've lied a lot, cheated some, and stolen when I had to, but I don't need to die. I promise to do better."

"'Course there's them that did as bad and hold their heads up high and walk the streets," said old Tom, taking off his cap and running his knife across his stubbled chin.

After thinking about things for a while, he suggested they take a seat out front, have a glass of rum, and parley over what needed to be done. Briggs was all too happy to comply with the suggestion—and stepping over broken glass and checking all the empties—he found a bottle that was still half full. After a couple of shots of rum, the proprietor noticed his captor nodding off, his knife lying on the table, just within his reach; but a dash out the back door seemed the better plan. Though the empty room had long ago stopped rolling on the waves, the floor was sloshy wet and slippery, so he doubted the other could catch him. He stood up slowly and had just made it behind the bar when Old Tom's blade whizzed by his cheek and pinned him by his ear to the door jamb.

"You was just about to tell me the finer details of that card game where ye won this place from that drunk fool

Lockhart," said the old man, retrieving his knife.

"Nothing to tell. I had four of a kind and he had two pair," said the other with a quivering voice, as blood trickled down his neck.

"There was a lot o' money on the table?"

"I worked my uncle's boat all season. It was a good year and a fair share."

"And how many kings was in that deck?"

"I had four in my hand, that's all that counts."

"Them's ill-gotten gains, Bobby Boy. Did he give ye the deed or an IOU?"

"His IOU was enough to get the deed switched over. He was a man of his word and never gave me any trouble."

"Well, we know you're not a man o' your word and I'm the kind to give ye trouble, so I'll buy ye out right here and now, and ye can sign over that deed you've got in the lockbox under the bar."

"How much?" asked Briggs, forgetting this was not the time or place to bargain.

"One solid gold doubloon," said First Mate Tom Johns.

"No deal, old man. This place is the only good thing that's ever happened in my sorry life."

"And ye run her aground, boy. Look here, the place is wrecked, and you're out of stock. Sign it over and let's be done with this. You're almost out of time, and my boat sails with the tide."

And so it was that the Naughty Puffin Inn had a new owner, and her course was forever changed.

Before dawn that Sunday morning, something else happened at the old inn—a story that was never told. A well-known SUV pulled alongside the Naughty Puffin Inn.

Treasures of Plunder Bay

A very large lady in a raincoat stepped out of the passenger side, and a much smaller lady in a red parka and rain boots closed the driver's door without a sound. The lanterns in the bar room were still glowing, but the stairway was dark. In room number three they found what they were looking for. With the thin blanket from the bed, they gently wrapped the prize. It took both of them to support their frail and silent friend downstairs and into the backseat.

It was already daylight when they reached the big house at the harbor's head, but mercifully, the stormy night before had given way to a dense morning fog. The rocking chairs on the Victorian porch were neatly placed with the familiar tea table in between. A lone seagull was perched on the gabled roof, the lamp in the drawing room window was on, and the door unlocked. Inside the house, plants thrived, and everything was warm and neat—the work of caring friends and neighbors who for four long months had not lost hope.

A word was never spoken as the three friends gathered in the kitchen for Miranda's tranquility tea and the lemongrass soup, which she touted as the cure for any illness. It may have been a shock to see Reynelda's pile of sandy blond curls, hanging grey and limp down to her shoulders, and her bright eyes dim and glazed, but no one else would ever know. Maggie O'Day suggested a long warm bath and Miranda went along to add the bubbles, lay out comfy clothes, and turn down the bed. They sat with her until she drifted off to sleep, still without a word or question from any of the three.

"I'll stay at night and you can have day shift," said Maggie. "Looks like she's been half starved and frozen. If it's a curse, I'll figure out which one and send it back on them with a vengeance."

"I think perhaps she has transplaned somewhere to survive," said Miranda.

"If that's the case, we'll go find her and drag her back, but what will we tell folks? They'll soon figure out she's here."

"We will tell the truth, that she was traumatized by an event and is resting to recover. Those who know her will understand and stay away until she's ready."

"What about the nosy ones?"

"They won't make it through the door—I'll see to that right now." Miranda then called up her favorite *Do Not Disturb* spell.

Principal Amadan was the first to test Miranda's spell. When no one answered his persistent ringing of the muted doorbell, he knocked on the glass storm door, only to feel it turn molten hot at his touch. Stupefied, he did not try again, but turned to questioning Ms. O'Day about her friend. Not only did she tell him nothing, she forbid him from coming near her kitchen. After two weeks of silence, Juliet d'Eon joined the triumvirate of secrecy and proved she had many *Powers* beyond *brewing* and making muffins.

Miss Tweaks's glasses, library book, and key ring remained on the playroom table, and although they reminded the aunts about them, no one seemed ready to return them to their rightful owner. Miss Tweaks's students understood their teacher was resting and recovering from being kidnapped by the whisperers, who had since been dealt with by the proper authorities—whoever they were.

The new owner of the Naughty Puffin Inn ordered extensive repairs to be made and hired Charlotte Cloutier, Cody's grandmother, to manage the inn. That was a particular delight to Cody, who moved there with her, to help out. The plan was to have the restaurant opened by the time lobster season ended and the tourists arrived.

Sea Monster In The Bay

The East Side Wharf was a busy place on Saturday mornings. This close to the end of the season, many of the lobster boats brought in their traps a few at a time rather than piling them high and overloading their boats like they did on Dumping Day. The sun was shining, and the bay was calm when Peter walked out to the far end of the wharf and sat down with his back against the piling.

This was one of his favorite places because he could watch the boats coming and going from the harbor entrance, or look up at the cliffs and see the waterfall on the west side of the harbor. He slid on his sunglasses to cut the glare on the water and gazed out into the open sea beyond, feeling relaxed and drowsy.

"Hey there, Peter!" called out the familiar voice of his friend Bradley Boggins, who was paddling by in a bright red canoe with his little sister. "Mom, Dad, and George are working at the shop, and Paige is spending the day with Virginia at her house, so I get to babysit."

"Maybe we can get in some fishing later," said Peter.

"Sounds good," said his friend, paddling away.

A few minutes later, Peter saw something floating—no, swimming—past the wharf. At first he thought it was a log or maybe a capsized haul; but no, it was definitely moving under its own power. It was never easy to explain this first sighting to anyone. All that Peter could be sure of was that the thing he saw was very long, and shiny, with a slight splash of color. Before it passed completely by him, it went from being a meter or two deep, to diving out of sight. Peter shook his head in disbelief and readjusted his sunglasses to shade his vision more. He was sure of only two things, something very big had swum by him very fast, and now he couldn't see it anymore. Anyone but Peter might have called to others around him asking what they had seen, but Peter had long ago learned to keep the unusual to himself. At least he wasn't drowsy anymore. He stood up on the wharf with his eyes keenly focused, scanning the surface of the water near and far.

In less than an hour, it returned. This time it came from the harbor head toward the narrow entrance to the bay that connected to the open sea. It was further away and harder to see, but it was there. At first glance the creature looked like it was all tail, but Peter could see its long body leading it in a straight line, more like a water snake than any fish he'd seen. He tried to think of familiar things to compare in size. It was as long as a tractor trailer, and about as wide as a dinghy boat. He only got a quick glimpse of the spiked tail that glinted in the sunlight.

In that fateful moment, instead of heading out to sea, the creature swung around, swimming directly toward Peter and the East Side Wharf. It began circling, off the end of the wharf, like it was trying to catch its own tail. Peter could see it more clearly now. It was the strangest color. One second it was an iridescent white-silver, like the glow of the full moon on a clear night, the next second it appeared to have shimmery, milky shades of pink, blue, and green. The closer it got, the faster it swam in a circle. As Peter was watching it, Bradley and his sister came paddling back toward the wharf, directly into the path of the thing. They couldn't see it, and it wasn't paying attention to what was around it.

Peter jumped up and down, waving his arms, pointing, and yelling at the top of his lungs, but Bradley only smiled and waved back. Not wanting to see the two swallowed whole, Peter turned this head away and closed his eyes. He heard the terrified screams and felt the wharf shudder. He turned back just in time to see the canoe flying backward through the air, dumping its passengers into the water. He saw the top of a small brown head bobbing on the water and a hand reaching up to grab the air, before both disappeared below.

Without a thought, Peter jumped off the wharf feetfirst, but before he could bob back up to the surface, he was struck by something powerful that knocked him spinning underwater. When he came to the surface, he grabbed a breath and dove back down, trying to open his eyes; he saw feet kicking above him and no one around him in the water. He surfaced to find Bradley clinging to the overturned canoe and his little sister hanging onto him. With a few painful strokes, Peter—shocked and out of breath—was able to join them. His heart was pounding wildly, his whole body was stinging with numbness, and he could taste blood in his mouth. He was vaguely aware of scores of people screaming from his former spot on the wharf. At some point he heard little Alexis mixing baby talk with sobs and he remembered Bradley beside him in a rubber raft. Then he quit fighting his nightmare and passed out.

In the emergency room at the hospital, Aunt Miranda took his hand. "You may feel a little foggy, but we are here with you now, and so are Cassandra and Gabrielle and probably half the village. The hospital staff checked you out and you'll be fine—bruised and a concussion, but nothing you won't recover from soon."

For a long while, Peter was only aware of voices. It seemed like hundreds of people were talking to him and he could not move his mouth to answer. When he was finally able to open his eyes, his aunts were standing above him.

"I wish, Peter, that you would wait a few more months before going swimming again," said Aunt Penelope. "Folks are getting tired of fishing you out of the water."

"I'm sorry," Peter heard his own voice say, but it sounded far away. "Bradley and his sister?"

"They're all right too. In fact, they're already out in the hall with their parents, waiting to go home as soon as they are sure *you're* all right," said Aunt Miranda.

"Can you get me out of here? I just want to go home."

"We'll go as soon as the doctor releases you," said Aunt Penelope. "But in the meantime, I want to warn you ... everybody wants to know what you saw out there on the wharf. I don't think now is a good time to talk to anyone, but that's up to you."

Peter sat up in bed, rubbing the side of his face and grimacing. "That thing sure walloped me good."

"What was it, Peter, do you know?" asked Aunt Miranda.

"I'm pretty sure it was a sea monster," said Peter, amused by the thought.

"If you think we ask a lot of questions and put you on the spot, just wait and see what happens now. There are coastguardsmen trying to get to you before the newspaper reporters and photographers."

Cassandra and Gabrielle came around the corner at that point. "Peter, you're alive!" said Gabrielle, in her most dramatic voice.

"You okay?" asked Cassie softly.

"Yeah, yeah, but I guess I'm in trouble again."

"I'd say more like famous than in trouble. Did you actually see that thing they're all calling a sea monster?"

"Yeah—it was unbelievable."

"There's a guy out in the lobby with a sketchpad drawing sea monsters based on eyewitness accounts, so at least you're not the only ridiculous person in the village. I even heard the Coast Guard chased it all afternoon with boats and helicopters," said his sister.

"They didn't hurt it, did they?" asked Peter. "It was so cool, Cassie. I wish you could have seen it."

"Bradley said it was slimy and green with big teeth, and it tried to eat the three of you," said Gabrielle.

"What? Bradley never even saw it! He was looking at me and he paddled right up onto its back. That flipped the canoe in the air backwards and they went in the water."

The doctor and the harbormaster came in and the doctor checked Peter over again and said he could go home, but he needed to rest. Jacques suggested they might want to leave by a back entrance to avoid the crowd in the hall.

"It's your call, Peter," said Aunt Miranda, sensing that Peter wanted to share in the excitement of the moment.

"Let's go out the front. I won't say much. But I would like to see the drawings that guy has done."

"Then let's go," said Aunt Penelope.

In the short distance from his room to the exit, Peter must have had his picture taken a hundred times. A lady with a TV camera on her shoulder said, "Did you see anything unusual out there in the water today?"

"Yes," said Peter, but at that moment Bradley and Alexis appeared and Alexis threw her arms around one of his legs and everybody cried, "Ahhhh."

Peter was so embarrassed he could have died. Then a familiar-looking Coast Guard officer stood in front of Peter and announced flatly to the crowd, "This is an official inquiry into a boating accident, nothing more. If there is any more information, I will call a press conference."

"You bet you will," threatened the lady with the camera.

They all made a mad dash for the back door, where the McBee SUV was parked.

By the next day, Peter was sorry that he didn't get to talk to the man with the sketchpad and give his description of the creature. That was because Will came to visit him at Cape Peril cottage and brought him a T-shirt that read, "The Sea Monster of Plunder Bay," emblazoned with a drawing of the monster. It was vivid chartreuse, with large, sharp, blood-stained teeth, and it was holding a little girl in its mouth. Peter thought the shirt was an insult to sea monsters everywhere.

"I guess Adam Boggins and his brother-in-law stayed up all night making a screen print and turning out these shirts. They're based on Bradley's description of the monster, and accurate or not, they're selling like crazy," Will told him.

"Leave it to Mr. Boggins to turn anything into a buck— even the near-death of his kids."

"Whatever it was out there, and whatever happened, has really caused quite a stir. I guess the Coast Guard looked everywhere for it. Dozens of people saw it and no two people had the same description. My parents have been called over from the park to ride around on the cutter and try to come up with some scientific explanation of what people saw."

"I saw it up close and personal, and it didn't look anything like the picture on this T-shirt."

"What did you see, Peter? I don't mean to pry, but I'm truly curious to know if there's something floating around out there that's going to eat the population or ruin the fishing."

"I saw a great big silver thing swimming at a pretty fast pace. It had a really long tail with a small, spiked end. It could dive deep and fast."

"So what propelled it through the water?"

"Maybe some kind of side fins that I didn't see. Could be that's what hit me underwater."

"Then it might have been a manta ray, if the propulsion came from both sides and not the tail."

"And there was a big thud. I think it was trying to avoid the canoe and ran into the wharf."

"You said it was swimming in a circle? That might mean that it was trapping its prey. Dolphins do that to trap fish before eating them. I'm sorry, man, I sound more like the son of biologists than somebody visiting an injured friend."

Aunt Miranda arrived with cinnamon buns and hot tea. That changed the conversation, and she explained to Will it would probably be a week or so before Peter would be able to return to school.

"We'll miss you, buddy, but in the meantime rest up, because things are happening around the village. It may never be the same."

Treasures of Plunder Bay

Cassandra stayed home with Peter on Monday, and they spent the day doing their own drawings and writing down any details Peter could remember about the sea monster in the bay.

"Peter, the more you describe the sea monster, the more it reminds me of my ring. I know that sounds crazy, but look at it," said Cassie. She removed the ring from her pinky finger and handed it to Peter.

Holding it up for close examination, Peter concurred. "Yeah, I see what you mean. The tail of the sea monster was like the side of your ring that has the crescent moon on it. And its skin, or scales, or whatever it has, were the same colors that are in this little stone. Even the head looked a little like the shape of the star on the other side of your ring."

"Do you think they're somehow related?" asked Cassie.

"It's possible. What did that lady in the jewelry shop tell you about seawater?"

"She said to keep it in a saucer of seawater, in the full light of the moon. She said that would make it glow."

"Well, after our swim in the smugglers' tunnel, it definitely got a soaking in seawater," said Peter.

"And, as I recall, that night was the peak of the full moon," added Cassie.

"We need to do some research. Maybe we can find something in that old book we still have."

"I'll see what I can find," said Cassie, "Wouldn't it be amazing if my ring conjured the sea monster?"

"Hmm ... that could have a lot of implications," said Peter.

The local radio news said that officials were looking into

the capsizing of a small boat inside the harbor at Plunder Bay. The occupants of this canoe, and a bystander who dove into the water to assist, had all been treated and released from the local hospital. Several eyewitnesses reported that they had seen a large animal in the water at the time, but no information had been released by the Coast Guard. The radio station was conducting a contest to name the bay monster.

On Tuesday, Captain McMullen made an appointment to return to Cape Peril cottage. Aunt Penelope was handling all the phone calls, and there had been a lot. It was one of the few times she was glad they still had their old wall phone in the kitchen and her cell wasn't being bombarded. Aunt Miranda requested that if the Coast Guard were to talk with Peter, they be accompanied by the harbormaster. Cassandra went to school that Tuesday, mostly to catch up on everything that was being said so she could report back to Peter.

The interview took place over tea and cookies in the cottage kitchen. Peter told Captain McMullen about the length and breadth of what he had seen that day in the water. He made the point that what he saw was neither green nor slimy but more translucent, a word that he and Cassandra had agreed upon which did not really describe its color.

Peter was careful not to name what he saw as a creature or a monster, or even an animal. That was because he was afraid it might be hunted down and killed. During the interview, Blue sat on his kitchen perch and occasionally interrupted Peter with loud squawks and the occasional curse word.

Treasures of Plunder Bay

The harbormaster wanted to know whether Peter had hit the object or if it had hit him after he dove into the water. Peter said he thought he had hit the object and bounced back, but he couldn't be sure. Captain McMullen asked to see Peter's bruises and brush burns, and surmised they had been caused by something scaly, not smooth like a sea mammal. There were a number of questions about teeth, but Peter had not seen any teeth, nor did he remember hearing any sound it might have made.

Jacques d'Eon said that they had carefully examined the wharf, which had been struck by something heavy, but it had only minor damage. He asked Peter if it were possible that what he had seen in the water might have been a large inanimate object like a floating tree, or debris from an old shipwreck. Peter responded that he thought that was a possibility. In fact, that was his first guess. When Captain McMullen asked him what made him change his mind, Blue piped up with a series of loud squawks, so Peter never really answered the question. Before they left, the Coast Guard captain found himself once more apologizing to Miranda McBee, when what he really wanted to do was ask her out to dinner.

When they were gone, Aunt Miranda chided her nephew and the interrupting parrot for not being more forthcoming with information. She believed that the fewer facts the Coast Guard had, the more credence people would give to wild imaginings. Apparently, Captain McMullen, the harbormaster, Blue, and the twins felt the opposite to be true, and were working on a cover up.

"How do you hide a sea monster in a busy, high-traffic bay?" Miranda asked herself. Blue squawked, "Run a rig, Run a rig".

When Cassandra got home that night, she was a wealth of information. The latest story going around school was that Peter had jumped into the water with a knife in his teeth and attacked the sea monster just before it swallowed Alexis. She thought that version had come from Bradley. But Cody was spreading the tale—and the knife part did sound more like Cody than Bradley.

"Where was I supposed to have gotten the knife?"

"From your tackle box. Cody even gave a detailed description of what the knife looked like."

"He ought to be able to describe it. He borrowed it last summer and never returned it—maybe we can sell it and split the cash."

"Oh, and one of the lobstermen, Conner Cartwright, reported having seen something a week earlier that resembled the monster, but it was no bigger than a seal. That started the rumor that the sea monster was a mother whale who had returned to the bay looking for her lost baby."

The local radio station that was running the contest reported that they had received hundreds of suggestions for names—the most popular being Shelly and Plundra. Cassandra went on to tell Peter what his aunts already knew too well—the village was wild with sea monster fanatics. There were tourists with binoculars and cameras scurrying up and down the windy beach. There were trucks from the cable channels, and even a magazine crew staying aboard their yacht, which was anchored down at the marina—and they were offering to buy any legitimate photos of the beast. There were so many people in the village that Gabrielle's mother was getting ready to open the muffin shop a month early. Mr. and Mrs. Boggins had already opened their shop and were selling sea monster shirts, little plastic toy monsters, and anything else people would buy.

The man who had done the sketches was selling his drawings for as much as one hundred dollars each. If any person who said they saw the monster autographed the sketch, they got twenty dollars. The fastest-selling sketch was based on the description they had gotten from Bradley. Mr. Boggins's brother-in-law—who probably had seen nothing—was raking in cash, autographing everything. Bradley and Alexis were supposed to have signed a deal to sell their story to a clickbait website for a bundle of money. The kids and teachers at school wanted to know when Peter would be well enough to come back. And Ms. O'Day was naming a special dish in his honor.

After dinner one night, Cassandra and Peter found themselves alone in the kitchen with Aunt Penelope. "Are you going to open the shop early?" asked Peter.

"Probably not."

"Everyone else is cashing in on the sea monster story. Why not the McBees?" asked Peter.

"I don't know exactly, but something about all this doesn't feel right to me. I can't explain it. You've had a lot of calls for interviews, but I hadn't told you yet. Do you think I was wrong?"

"No, I don't want to be rich or famous, unless of course we need some of that money. It doesn't feel right to me, either," said Peter.

"Miranda feels certain that all the strange things that have happened—like the sea monster, and the two of you nearly drowning in the smugglers' tunnel—are related.

When you were babies, we were warned that you might face great danger, though neither of us knew what kind of danger."

"Was it Inspector Martinez who warned you?" asked Cassandra.

"Yes. He said the circumstances when he found you in the wrecked ship were suspicious."

"Like what?" asked Peter.

"I don't know, really. The faint scent of gun smoke, and the fact that no other living soul was anywhere to be found, dead or alive," explained Penelope.

"What does Aunt Miranda think about the sea monster?" asked Cassie.

"She believes it to be a magical creature, not seen in centuries, and that it portends of great hardships for people of *Powers*. When there were great magical realms throughout the world, things like sea monsters and dragons were weapons of war. Supposedly, such creatures were destroyed at the Battle of Panopoly when the biggest magical realms collapsed, and people of *Powers* went deep into hiding."

"I found some interesting information in the old book from the library that Miss Tweaks left behind that day. It says that after the Battle of Panoply, those responsible were punished by being confined to their ships—to sail the seas forever, never permitted to touch down on land, anywhere," said Cassie.

"What they did must have been pretty bad for that severe of a punishment," said Peter.

"I don't know that much about the evildoers, but having *Powers* is both a blessing and a curse. And although both of you seem to have extraordinary gifts, you would need years of training and experience to stay safe."

"I feel certain the sea monster did not come here to hurt us. I even think maybe it would help protect us if it's still around," said Cassie.

Countdown
To Death

A lthough the voices in the tunnel echoed, making them sound distorted, they could be understood by Cassandra and Peter.

"All the magical conduits from the school are gone. Those idiot outliers brought them out through this tunnel, then lost them. Stupid and dangerous as it was, this completes the last of my orders to help Number One get the ring. I sail tomorrow."

"Without the others?"

"What others? Deilman and Hicks, who had greater *Powers* than Gorgona's Number One, seem to have disappeared into thin air. The outliers, all four them, took out of here like bats out of Hades, and no one's heard from them. If they'd hired competent outliers, things might have turned out differently, but Number One was calling the shots and encouraged them to take anything they could carry away, only to have that stuff disappear from the van before they got it back to the inn. Then they got caught up in that tale about gold coins, the supposed treasure Boggins—that weirdo teacher—was guarding."

"This despicable place—it's a cesspool, a pitiful little excuse for a lost realm without a sorcerer or a guard to protect it. It's a place where children with real *Powers* run amuck, casting spells, and playing at magic. It was one of them that released the moon dragon. Is it any wonder why the great ones despise children and even deny their own?"

Treasures of Plunder Bay

"There must be hundreds of places like this. Why were we sent here, to this one?"

"Her greatness thought it was important, and she wanted to test the *Powers* of her favorite new alpha apprentice."

"Hush. She'll hear you."

"Gorgona's not listening—she's got bigger problems to deal with. Now that the moon dragon is free, and she doesn't control it, we'll be facing another war like Panopoly. But Gorgona can handle it. There are only two or three great realms left, controlled by ancients who survived the last war. Even a Sorcerer can't live much beyond five hundred years. When they're gone, *our* apprentice class will be the new crop of Sorcerers, the ones with all the *Power* and wealth."

Cassandra and Peter had used the full moon and warm spring night to slip out of the cottage and climb down the cliffside toward the beach. They hoped to catch sight of the sea monster at low tide. When they reached the spot just above the grotto where Seadog had found them weeks ago, they heard the voices in the tunnel. They stayed perfectly silent among the rocks above, careful not to shake lose any dirt or pebbles. Now, both were determined to get a glimpse of these two, the one who spoke with an English accent, and the other with a deep, softer voice.

Looking up, Cassandra saw a bad omen, a red ring around the moon. "Blood on the moon," she whispered, pointing up.

Peter put his finger to his lips to shush her, and at that moment they heard footsteps running through the tunnel, followed by shouts. The twins watched in stunned silence as something emerged from the tunnel, right below them, into the moonlight. It was the sea monster with its long, scaly body, and pointy tail. It moved quickly across the rocky beach, then disappeared soundlessly into the water.

"That's it," said Peter. "No wonder they couldn't find it. It's been hiding in the tunnel. It can traverse dry land and navigate the sea!"

"What happened to the two guys? Did it eat them?"

"Who cares? We got to see it! That's what counts."

As if in answer to Cassandra's question, the next thing to emerge were two limping men, each trying to hold the other upright. Both were tall, one with a husky build and the other slim. The heavier of the two men had light-colored hair, pulled back into a ponytail. The slender man had very short, brown hair and looked like his clothes had been shredded. Moonlight caught the reflection of glistening droplets of blood between scraps of his trousers. They staggered and stumbled over the rocks, falling, and cursing. Their faces were turned downward as they headed a short distance down the beach and climbed aboard a jet ski, then whisked away toward the village marina on the opposite side of the bay.

"I wonder who they were?" said Cassie.

"At least we got to see the sea monster. She was bigger the last time I saw her. Probably hasn't had a decent meal all week," said Peter.

Carefully climbing hand over hand back up the rocky cliff to the lighthouse, Cassandra asked her brother, "What about all the things those men said tonight? You know, about lost realms and sorcerers. Miss Tweaks mentioned those things last fall in our lessons with her. I think if we could talk with her, she could make sense of what we heard."

"I'm not sure she's ready for visitors yet. I guess we could ask Aunt Miranda, but without telling her too much of what went on tonight. The last thing I want is to hear that silver bell and be grounded at home all summer."

In the week that followed, there were no more credible sightings of the monster. The harbor remained full of boats large and small, most of them with sonar equipment searching the bay. Captain McMullen, via the Coast Guard, and the Department of Natural Resources—with the help of Will's parents—did their best to keep a handle on the water traffic. But the beaches and quay were a different matter. There were two interesting specials on the educational channel but nothing official about the sea monster. The name Plundra had won the radio station's contest and had been added to Mr. Boggins's T-shirts.

Just as Peter was obsessed with making his watch slow time, Cassandra was equally caught up in the idea that she and Peter may have been the two kids who set the sea monster free. Every night after school she hurried to the playroom and resorted to her only source of magical information. When she asked the big round window to show her a lost realm, it popped up with the Serengeti, as it had done before. When she was more specific and asked to see the people of the lost realm, it showed her a charming little village with happy African people going about their daily lives— shopping, farming, and going to school. When she asked to see the sorcerer of the magic realm, she got static—and for the guardians of the realm, all the window would give her was a large herd of stampeding antelope that she could not identify.

After dinner that night, Cassandra asked to see a second lost realm. The window obliged, showing her a coastal town with Runic writing on the signs. Here too the people seemed quite normal, with no one zooming around on brooms or waving wands. When she asked to see the sorcerer, she got a brief glimpse of a large bed, in a darkened room, before static returned. The most interesting thing about this request was when she asked for the guardians of that realm; the window showed her a fleet of Viking ships.

Since the window was being cooperative, if not explanatory, she rushed in after her shower and asked to see a moon dragon. What popped up in front of her made her catch her breath in disbelief. She saw an enlarged image of her little silver ring. It had a crescent moon on one side and a star on the other. In the center of the star was a small white stone, dancing with bright pink and blue floating colors, like the fires of an opal. Then, remembering the overheard conversation in the smugglers' tunnel, Cassie asked the window, "Who controls the moon dragon?"

What Cassandra saw next both terrified and thrilled her. Staring back at her from the window was her own image.

Before they got to class on Monday, the announcements called for all the students to report to the theater for an assembly. It was the first time in months that the doors had been unlocked. The students were cheerful and noisy, glad for the change in routine—regardless of what kind of an assembly it would be. Before they were all seated, the rarely seen Mr. Amadan stepped up to the podium and tinkered with the microphone, which this time blared at twice its normal volume. He commended the students for their cooperative behavior and reminded them they had a month of classes yet to go. He was going over the testing schedules for the coming weeks and prattling on about leaving soon, but that he would return for a closing ceremony to be held for Plunder Cove School.

"O-M-G," said Gabrielle, clapping her hands over her ears. "He's the principal and he doesn't even know the name of the school."

Peter was keeping a close eye on Mademoiselle Sowbierre, who looked to be in a darker mood than usual. She was sitting in the row in front of her students, next to Mr. Morgan. Mr. Morgan looked like he would rather be anywhere than next to her. She tried leaning over to talk to him a few times, resulting in him leaning away to the opposite side of his seat. This resulted in the boys sitting right behind him to chuckle and make a few comments under their breath. Mr. Morgan shot them a *shut up!* look out of the corner of his eye.

When they were dismissed, Mademoiselle Sowbierre's students headed down the back stairs from the stage to their homeroom. Their teacher lagged behind to talk with Principal Amadan. The students, arriving ahead of their teacher, came face-to-face with a new addition to their homeroom. A large, antique brass hourglass was standing on the corner of Mademoiselle Sowbierre's desk, right in front of Peter's seat. It was about the size of a large camping lantern, and the red sand inside glowed eerily while it was falling, as if in slow motion. Cassandra and Peter knew exactly what it was.

"It looks like the one from the Dark Arts Emporium," whispered Cassie to Peter.

"Where did this come from, and who put it here?" asked Gabrielle to no one in particular.

Even Cody took notice. "What an awful-looking thing."

As they stood staring at it, Will, in an unnatural-sounding voice, began to speak. "When the last grain of sand through the hourglass flies, time runs out and someone dies."

Everyone turned to look at him.

"Geez, Will, you're kidding, right?" said Jason.

Will shook himself out of the trance. "Sorry, I *see* these things out of the blue. Usually I can control them," he said in a worried tone.

"This thing is creepy!" exclaimed Madelyn, grabbing the hourglass and turning it over.

When she did, the red sand stopped falling but did not reverse its course. More might have been said, but at that moment the substitute arrived, glared at the students, and told them to sit down. She seemed as surprised by the hourglass as her students had been. Like Madelyn, she tried inverting its course, but to no avail. In fact, it fell with a gush when set right again, making up for the granules that had not fallen when it was inverted. After studying it for a few minutes, she took the thing and put it on the floor behind her desk. Without being seen by anyone, the hourglass reappeared in its same place. Seeming determined to rid herself of this unwanted gift, she buried it under papers in the trash. A short time later it was back again, right in front of Peter.

As he slid into his seat, directly in front of the hourglass, Peter estimated there couldn't be much time left.

"Zat assembly was a stupid waste of school time. Jou could have got more out of staying in class."

"You looked like you were having a good time with Mr. Morgan," Cody unwisely blurted out.

Treasures of Plunder Bay

At this, Mademoiselle Sowbierre's face contorted with rage. She focused her gaze on Cody, and for a moment everyone held their breath, wondering what was coming next. Dropping her accent, she turned on him. "You impertinent brat—GET OUT—you're expelled!"

Cody looked stunned and got up slowly, hoping she would change her mind. Then he headed out the door with his eyes downcast.

Mademoiselle Sowbierre gave them an essay assignment of one thousand words on their favorite piece of jewelry. The class moaned out loud, and Cassandra and Peter gave each other a sideways look that said: *don't mention your ring* and *don't mention your Govi watch*. Mademoiselle Sowbierre sat rigidly at her desk, looking like she was plotting the end of the world, as she read over a stack of old letters tied with purple ribbon. She kept checking her cell phone, and sent out two dispatches by way of the black candle. Halfway through the morning, she rummaged through her desk and came up with the same screwdriver the boys had used to put the sign on the classroom door. She looked at Will and asked him to take it and see if he could get the cheval mirror off its stand.

"Not me. Cody's the handyman. Besides, that mirror is school property. I don't intend to get in trouble for messing with it," he said, looking her straight in the eyes.

The whole class could see Mademoiselle Sowbierre's anger rising again, and they secretly reached for their posey pens. In a fit of rage, she looked at the screwdriver, now sitting on the top of her desk, and with a swoosh of her hand, sent it flying across the room straight for the mirror. The students in the back row threw up their arms to protect themselves from flying glass, but there was no sound—nothing happened. The students turned in their seats to see the screwdriver was entangled in the dream vine. From the time Madelyn had given it to Mademoiselle Sowbierre, it had grown considerably and had tentacles meandering out in all directions. From the odd way the screwdriver dangled in the vine, Cassandra thought perhaps the plant had reached out and caught it. No one was more surprised than Mademoiselle. She got up and walked back to the mirror. The closer she got, the more troubled she became. When directly in front of the mirror, she stared intently at her image, then drew back in horror like she had seen a ghost. The whole class heard her gasp, then she turned and rushed to the front of the classroom and up the steps to the back of the stage, and did not return.

"She's wigged out completely this time," stated Gabrielle.

"What do you think freaked her out so badly when she looked in the mirror?" asked Virginia.

Cry of the Banshee

That same afternoon, Cassandra found herself back in the copy room on the third floor to get a packet of construction paper for art. Out of sheer curiosity, she lifted the cover on the copy machine and was almost disappointed to find it empty. She had never understood why Walker Mathews had not told anyone he had seen her there, but in a weird coincidence, the door flung open and Walker stomped in. He seemed surprised to see her, mumbled a hello, and started lifting the lids off several big cartons. The search seemed to make him angry, and in a short while he gave up looking and left. Cassandra couldn't resist the urge to nose around a bit. Beneath the teachers' worktable she found a box marked "Copy Paper" with a big purple X. When she lifted the lid, she saw a dozen sharpened red pencils and a pile of ungraded student assignments. She recognized them immediately as the ones from Sowbear's morning class—her class.

"I told you they were here. Did you even look?" said the secretary, pushing Walker into the room ahead of her.

Cassandra hurried to fill her arms with construction paper, mumbled something about art class, and hurried out just as the secretary announced, "See, it's right under your nose. Pull it out and carry it downstairs."

This was the kind of tantalizing mystery that Cassandra McBee was not about to leave unsolved. Between classes she shared her findings with Gabrielle, who made a point to stop by the main office where she spotted the box on the floor next to Cody, who was still waiting. After leaving the office, she stopped by the cafeteria to alert Ms. O'Day about Cody, then hurried to her next class.

A short time later, Maggie O'Day left her kitchen and stormed into the front office with a submarine sandwich for Cody and a showdown with the departing Mr. Amadan.

"Why are you in here instead of in your kitchen?" the principal demanded, returning from the front door where he had deposited a suitcase and two bags.

"Why has this student been sitting in the office without any lunch for over three hours?" she barked back.

"That's for me to know and you not to question," he said in a most unpleasant tone as he donned his raincoat and grabbed an umbrella.

Physically blocking his escape through the narrow office door, she restated her case, "Why is this boy sitting here? Since you are in a great hurry to leave, let's settle the matter now, just in case we never meet again."

"Mademoiselle Sowbierre wants him expelled," pipped the secretary, like a seagull.

"Tell her she can't do that without a hearing. It's against school policy."

"Go tell her yourself, and while you're at it, take that bloody box back to her," he said with a mocking grin and a slight bow, as a familiar black van pulled up outside.

Maggie O'Day left the office with Cody and the box.

Mr. Amadan left the school much as he had arrived, through the double front doors, in a wild windstorm. He deposited his belongings in the back of the van and had just fastened his seat belt when he discovered that the cloaked figure driving was someone he had never seen before—a brawny stranger with muscular, tattooed forearms.

And so it was that months of bad grades were explained, and Gabrielle could prove that all the assignments, with the exception of Cassandra's and Peter's, had been graded by the galactically stupid Mr. Amadan.

When Peter and Cassandra arrived with their Aunt Miranda at the big Victorian house at the head of the harbor, Juliet d'Eon greeted them and whispered, "She's in a great mood. Just play it cool. Don't press her too hard about anything."

They found their favorite teacher looking quite her normal self, sitting in a rocking chair by the window where she could watch the boats. "We brought you something you lost a while back," said Peter, handing her the book and glasses she had left in the cafeteria the day she had called out to Mr. Boggins and had been spirited away by the two men in the black coats.

"Oh! Thank you so much, Peter. I've been half blind since that day—and I must return this book, it's months overdue," She slipped the glasses into her curly hair and looked relieved to have them back. "As I often tell Adam Boggins, anything taken from the school by someone who is not the rightful owner, will find its way back."

"We've missed you," said Cassie. "School just hasn't been the same since you left."

"I'm so sorry to have worried everyone. I don't know if they've told you, but I had a wonderful vacation in Madagascar. The islands are quiet and peaceful, the climate delightful, and the native cuisine is simple but tasty, with all the fresh fruit imaginable."

C. S. Leonard

"A lot of things have happened at school since you left. There were some nasty people hanging around the school, but they're gone for good now—and Principal Amadan left today."

"Poor Glenn, he was such a fool. But tell me about the sea monster in the bay."

"I think it's a moon dragon that was accidentally set free," said Cassie, watching carefully for Miss Tweaks's response.

"I see. You believe it to be the moon dragon, known to be a powerful guardian throughout history. We were going to go into a lot of magical history this year, but ..."

"Our substitute was not much of a teacher," said Peter.

"Oh really ... she bragged to me herself that she has mastered the seven *Powers* and is an apprentice in training," said Miss Tweaks.

"You talked to her? When? Where?" asked Peter.

"We spoke once or twice—I don't exactly remember where, maybe in the theater or in Madagascar. She had a terrible fake accent."

"If the great realms disappeared after Panopoly, what happened to all the people with *Powers*?" Cassandra asked, not wanting to push Miss Tweaks too hard, too fast.

"Most of us believe they broke up into smaller communities and have stayed hidden ever since. That's what we refer to as the lost realms. If the two of you are interested, there is an old series of books on the subject. One in particular called *The Guardians of the Ancient Realms* is helpful. You can find it by looking in the black card catalog next to the little clock behind the library counter."

"I'd love to do some research in that book!" said Cassandra.

"It's one of the old books on the top shelf of the third

stack back from the reading bay, at right angles to the credenza, and not far from the bust of Euripides. Nice looking man, Euripides was. I know young people don't do much reading in the summer, especially with so much happening on the quay, but I think you would find it interesting. Which reminds me, have you had any luck fixing your watch? I think I left you my grandfather's information?"

"You did, and thanks. It's been helpful. It will open and tick, but I haven't gotten it to the point where it will tell time. I'm not giving up, though," replied Peter.

"That's marvelous. You know, my grandfather loved clocks, collected them from all over the world. His favorite was the big clock in the library that hovers under the skylight. I suppose that's my favorite too. And what about the other kids from class? How are they doing?"

"Gabrielle is into casting spells, and she's really good at it—but her *brewing* needs work. I'm pretty sure Madelyn has mastered *creating*. You were right about Will, his strongest *Power* is *seeing*, but he fights it. Jason can build anything from a drawing or diagram—that's *realizing*, isn't it?" reported Cassandra.

She might have gone deeper into things, but at that point Juliet, Aunt Miranda, and Aunt Penelope came in from the kitchen with tea and cookies.

As they turned up the Coast Road, Cassandra and Peter had a lot of questions. "Was she really in Madagascar or was she transplaning?" asked Peter.

"And why wasn't she able to escape from her captors?" added Cassie.

"We have another stop to make tonight, an important

one," said Aunt Miranda, totally ignoring their questions.

To the twins' surprise, they passed the drive into Cape Peril cottage, and ten minutes later turned into the Naughty Puffin Inn. They had not gotten through the door when they were greeted by a smiling Cody. He explained that Ms. O'Day had driven him there after school because his grandmother was working.

"We're moving here next week," Cody explained. "The Inn has a new owner—Grandmother is going to run the place and I'm going to help her."

"With a lot of help from my friends too," said Charlotte Cloutier, emerging from the stairwell lugging a bucket and mop. "But first I need to know what's going on at school. I thought after that rowdy bunch of sailors ran off the whisperers, things at the school would calm down. Now I hear that awful substitute tried to expel Cody!"

"Yeah, Mademoiselle Sowbierre overreacted to something Cody said and blew up at him," explained Cassandra.

"Fortunately, Adam Boggins is going to switch Cody to another language arts class for the last month of school, and I've warned Cody to stay clear of her," announced Maggie O'Day, coming out of the kitchen with a kettle of Mulligan Stew and a freshly baked Plundra Pie.

"So Charlotte, you're going to run the inn for the new owner. That's really exciting news. Who is he?" questioned Miranda.

"A merchant seaman named Mr. Johns. He bought it the very same night that they had all the trouble here."

"I heard about that," said Penelope.

"There are several versions of what happened that night. Bobby Briggs said a gang of strangers came in and attacked his guests, then took some out to sea and sent the rest packing. He told me one of them threatened to gut him with a big knife if he didn't sign over the inn," Charlotte rolled her eyes as she told Bobby Briggs version of the story.

"Of course, we all know Bobby Briggs stretches the truth to suit himself—runs in the family," said Maggie O'Day.

"Now, Mr. Johns has quite a different story. He said words were exchanged between some of his crew and a group of ruffians who had been hiding out here. There apparently was a bit of a ruckus, things got smashed up, and Bobby declared he was done with the place. Mr. Johns said he would buy it, they agreed on a price, and it was sold. I'm just happy to have steady work," said Charlotte.

"Work is the right word," said Maggie. "This place looks like it got caught in a gale. Broken glass everywhere, and the place has needed repairs for years. Then there's the expense of restocking the food and liquor."

"That's where I'm lucky. Mr. Johns has hired some of the off-season fisherman to do the carpentry, paint, and revamp the restaurant and guest rooms. He said Cody and I are welcome to live in the garret apartment. It's quite nice up there compared to where we live now. He even has connections with a wine merchant, and plans to restock the cellars with nice wine."

"And I'll help you get the restaurant up and running as soon as school is out, and Juliet is going to do the baking," said Maggie.

"I'll throw in the seafood seasoning for free, and your guests can be taste testers for my teas," exclaimed Miranda excitedly.

"We can sell them here, and maybe put together a little

gift shop with seashell art and driftwood pieces, and your quilts, Grandma," offered Cody. Tourists love that kind of stuff."

"Just skip the ugly sea monster T-shirts," interjected Peter, and everybody laughed.

On the way back to Cape Peril cottage, the aunts discussed how things were finally settling down for the residents of Plunder Bay. Even the sea monster was turning out to be a good thing—good for business anyway.

Peter was not so sure he agreed. "Who is Mr. Johns—do we know him?"

"From what Jacques told me, I think his full name is Tom Johns, and he's a seaman who comes and goes from Plunder Bay. He's missing his left arm and doesn't seem like anyone you'd want to tangle with if you were up to no good," said Aunt Penelope.

"He often walks the beach at night. Keeps an eye on things from what I've heard," said Aunt Miranda.

"Oh, yeah, I know who he is now. We've met. And what's the back story with this Bobby Briggs?" asked Peter. He remembered the name from his unpleasant episode with the man who was intent on finding the blue boulder on the beach.

"Well, let me think," said Miranda. "Bobby Briggs would be Walker Matthews's uncle, and his sister was your kindergarten teacher. The Briggs descend from wreckers who built fires on the beach below Cape Peril cliff to lure ships onto the reef and loot their cargo. They're the main reason that Captain Benjamin built the lighthouse, to save lives and put their kind out of business."

It was late as they approached the cottage. A heavy fog

had settled in, and it was the lighthouse that guided them to the lane. Peter couldn't get the image of the hourglass out of his mind as he thought about recent events. Was it intended for him or Cassie, he wondered. He thought about the message Cassie had seen written in the red liquid on Sowbear's desk. "Do your job," it had read. He was still deep in thought when the three of them reached the front door and a horrible sound shattered the stillness of the night.

"*Sheeeeee*," was the bone-chilling cry that lingered in the air and froze them to the spots where they were standing. No one said a word or asked a question. They all just stood there, staring into the dark, wondering and waiting. Seadog scratched at the inside of the door and whined, but didn't bark.

"Maybe it's hurt, or lost. Should we go out and find it?" Cassandra finally asked.

"That won't be necessary. It's found us," said Aunt Miranda, pushing them inside.

Last Warning

Mademoiselle Sowbierre developed a kind of ritual. As soon as her students were gathered, she would pick up the hourglass she had upended the day before, set it right, and it would instantly dump a night's worth of red sand to the bottom. For some reason this twisted little game seemed to amuse her. Peter felt sure this performance was intended especially for him, because immediately afterward, she would lock eyes with him and then dismiss the whole class to the library for the rest of the morning.

On Friday, theirs were the only two sets of eyes fixed intently on the hourglass. The black candle was lit, and Mademoiselle Sowbierre was scribbling notes in purple ink. Peter took his watch from his pocket, fumbled with it, then held it to his ear to listen to it tick.

There was a sudden tremor that shook the room, followed by a soft boom like a faraway jet breaking the sound barrier. The watch stopped ticking, and everything around him looked like he was seeing it from inside a beaker of clear water. No one was moving; no one was talking. The purple note above the candle stayed suspended in the air. A grain of falling red sand had stopped midway in its course. Peter was ecstatic—he had finally used the Govi watch to slow time.

Before he could contemplate the consequences of his victory, his watch began to tick again, but slowly. He counted to himself: *one thousand one, one thousand two, one thousand three, one thousand four*. It was ticking every other second. There was movement in the room around him, and the purple note drifted to the floor and landed at Cassandra's feet. No one seemed aware that anything unusual had happened, but he saw his sister scoot the note under her desk with her foot and then reach down to pick it up. Mademoiselle Sowbierre was scribbling her next note, and his classmates were fidgeting in their seats, anxiously awaiting their release upstairs to the library. The only thing that hadn't started up again was the grain of red sand trapped in its downward motion.

After what seemed like several minutes, Mademoiselle Sowbierre glanced up and saw what had happened inside the hourglass. For a moment she seemed confused, like she was looking around for answers, then she understood. Peter had achieved a monumental task using powerful magic—magic she had never mastered. Her eyes met Peter's and he couldn't help but grin. Enraged, she jumped up from her desk, sending her chair crashing to the floor. Peter stood up too and that got everyone's attention. In a fit of rage, she sent the hourglass flying through the air, and it shattered on the floor at Peter's feet—pouring out its contents and forming a blood-red puddle on the floor between them. Neither moved, nor broke their stare.

"Library time!" announced Cassandra, standing up and gathering her books.

"Hey man, let's go," said Will, stepping forward and tapping Peter on the shoulder.

A short time later, Will and Peter joined the rest of their class in the back bay of the library.

"That was so intense. Who blinked first?" asked Gabrielle.

"Cassie, you spoiled all the fun. I really wanted to see what happened next," said Caitlyn B.

"It's still school, and she's a teacher," Cassandra answered. "What good was there in Peter getting into the same kind of trouble as Cody?"

"My money was on Peter. I've seen him win that kind of staring contest before," said Gabrielle. "Anyway, she's leaving after this week, so it wouldn't have mattered," said Paige.

"What do you mean she's leaving?" Peter asked. "There's another month of school."

"She asked my brother George if he would help her tomorrow morning to load her stuff into a van she's renting today. Of course, he said he couldn't because he had to work at the shop, but trust me, she's leaving town."

"Too bad she expelled Cody. He could have done it," Will said.

"It's already been a long morning. I can't wait for lunch and this week to be over," said Madelyn, settling into one of the big armchairs and opening her book.

Cassandra used the lull in the conversation to drag Gabrielle into the stacks. "I've got something I need you to look at." She produced the scribbled purple note. "For some reason, it didn't go up in a puff of smoke. It landed on the floor and I pushed it under my desk. I think it's written in Italian. It starts out, 'Amore mio,' so I guess it's a love letter, but that's all I can understand."

After studying it for a long time, Gabrielle came up with her best guess, based on the similarities between Italian and French. "She's asking someone, her boyfriend, to meet her at the marina at ten o'clock tomorrow night and load her belongings onto his yacht. She's worried he won't get there before someone, who is very angry with her, gets there first. It's not an exact translation, but I think it's pretty close."

"I will be so happy when she's gone," said Cassandra.

"I wonder if she'll steal the costume trunks from the theater—she's been so into that stuff all year," said Gabrielle.

"Maybe we should alert Mr. Boggins."

"Since she talked to George, he would have told his father. Everyone likes Mr. Boggins, but sometimes I wonder if he's really on our side."

Peter was still counting seconds. Everything that had happened that morning had him psyched. Time was still in slow motion, and he seemed to be the only one who knew. When he checked the time against Will's cell phone, everything seemed normal. He also had no idea how far ranging this time anomaly reached. Perhaps the rest of the school had finished lunch and gone to afternoon classes in the other part of the building. Since he wasn't sure what he had done to make the watch slow time, he had no idea how to end it. For something he had worked so long to make happen, he now questioned how best to use it. After what seemed like an eternity, the lunch bell solved his dilemma—without so much as a tremor the time anomaly ended.

The slow-motion event had left the lunchroom in turmoil. The kids seemed confused about whether or not they had eaten and went back for seconds. The potato buoys were cold in the middle, the salads were wilted, and the butter patties too liquid to spread, which had Ms. O'Day in an uproar. That afternoon in math class, Miss Lemley drifted off while they were doing problems, and in art, Mrs. Simpson kept dumping and refilling her thermos, leaving for the teacher's workroom every few minutes. Their bus driver drove ridiculously fast like he was behind schedule, and the twins were happy they were going no further than the village.

The quay was crowded with tourists a full month before the season normally started. Because all of the other shops on the quay were open, the aunts opened McBee Maritime Spice & Tea Trading Company early. The muffin shop was humming, and Juliet had added three more outside tables. There was no mistake—this was all about the sea monster in the bay. It was strange that many of the locals who had actually been on the wharf that day of the sighting didn't have much to say, and acted embarrassed when questioned by strangers. There were others who worked very hard to keep the story going. Almost every day there were sightings of a tail or fin, something green and slimy that came to the surface when lobstermen pulled their traps, or something that followed a fishing boat back to the harbor.

In every vacant spot, there was either a camera tripod or an artist's easel, much to the dismay of the gulls. The market for chartreuse sea monster T-shirts had grown to include sweatpants and hoodies, largely because it was still nippy by the water. There were little kiosks set up and even a handcart or two selling everything imaginable—and there was no shortage of customers. Occasionally, someone would point Peter out as being the hero of that day, so he was not surprised to see a lanky stranger raising his hand to wave, taking long strides in his direction. Despite Peter's best effort to avoid him, the man caught up with him before he could slip into his aunts' shop.

"Peter, I've been looking for you everywhere." Seeing Peter's befuddled expression, the man went on, "It's me, Josiah, from the Smuggler's Bazaar last fall. Remember?"

"Oh ... yeah, Brother Josiah. I didn't recognize you without the monk's robe."

"It's just Josiah. I'm not really a monk, but I figured you already knew that."

"No, I didn't. I thought you were researching a book on a brotherhood of monks—was that whole story a part of the disguise?" asked Peter, suspiciously.

"I can tell you got your watch working," he said, ignoring the question. "Look, we need to talk."

So Josiah was aware of the time warp, thought Peter. He wasn't so sure they needed to talk, considering the many strange things that had been happening since the Bazaar, and all of the unusual—if not downright dangerous—people who he and Cassandra had encountered since the Bazaar.

Accurately assessing the look on Peter's face, Josiah added, "I'm not your enemy, Peter."

"Let me guess. Next you're going to tell me I can trust you, right? Sorry, I'm just not big into strangers at the moment."

"Okay, I get it. Since last fall you've had some trouble and you've learned not to trust people, but let's have a sit down, somewhere quiet. I think I can help you make sense of some of what is going on."

"Really? Why's that? Doing research for another book?"

"It's me who should be peeved at you after what you did this morning—at 10:25 a.m., to be precise. It was very bad timing. Took me an hour and a half to dock a Beneteau forty-six-footer."

"If it's the watch you're after, I don't have it with me," Peter lied.

"I don't want your watch, and I don't care how you made it work. I'm here to show you how to use it correctly ... and responsibly."

With those words, Peter decided to at least hear what Josiah had to say, so he headed for the only empty table outside the muffin shop. Seeing Cassandra and Gabrielle laughing and chatting with another girl, he changed directions, and the two of them headed for the far end of the wharf, away from the shops.

Cassandra caught sight of them walking down the wharf and paused for a moment in her banter with her friends. "Who is that? There's something familiar about him," she said.

This caught Gabrielle's attention, and that of the third girl who had joined them. Gabrielle quickly responded, "I've never seen him before."

Their new acquaintance, however—a young woman in her early twenties who'd introduced herself as Maeve Campbell, from County Mayo, Ireland—did know him. "That's Josiah, and that's his yacht over there, anchored in the marina," she said pointing at a sleek, white sailboat in the farthest slip at the marina.

"That's his yacht?" exclaimed Gabrielle.

"Yeah—he sailed up with some other people all the way from the Caribbean. Just made it here this afternoon. I'm joining them when it's time to leave."

Maeve had carrot-colored hair that fell to her waist. She spoke with the cutest Irish brogue accent. Their conversation had started when she noticed Gabrielle subtly casting a spell to stop napkins from scattering all over the quay. She said she knew a bit of magic too, and with a fast brush of her thumb over her lips, she closed all the umbrellas against the stiffening evening breeze. As the crowded quay cleared out, they joined her at her table and discovered she was traveling on business for her family's security company. She had spent two years at a private girls' school in Great Britain, before deciding to opt out of a university education.

"I love what I'm doing now. I'm free to travel and meet others like me," she explained.

"Did you learn your *Powers* where you went to school?" asked Gabrielle.

"No, it was a dull school of non-magic people, and the girls could be downright mean. I mastered what skills I have from my dear grandpapa, who tutored me."

"So is your security company in Plunder Bay because of our sea monster?" Cassandra inquired.

"What we really do is not so much security as early warning systems."

"Oh, like for tornadoes and tsunamis?" asked Gabrielle.

"Umm ... kind of," replied Maeve.

"Then you're not here to put up a siren to warn us when the sea monster is around?" asked Cassandra.

"No, definitely not," said Maeve.

She taught them a few more spells, like twisting someone's tongue so their words came out ridiculously, and how to tie someone's hair or beard in tight knots. Though Cassandra couldn't cast it, her favorite of Maeve's spells was filling the air with butterflies.

"But seriously, girls, enjoy your magic and practicing your *Powers,* but be careful. I'm not that much older than you, but I have made some dreadful enemies who would rather see me dead than face competition to their own ambitions."

It was at this point that Gabrielle knew she had met Maeve before. "I remember you! We met at the Smuggler's Bazaar ... in the Dark Arts Emporium."

Maeve nodded. "Yes, we did."

"What? Where did you meet? Dark Arts?" said Gabrielle.

Cassandra avoided Gabrielle's questions and shot her a look that meant *later*. "We've had our trouble with outliers here in Plunder Bay this year," Cassandra said to Maeve.

"I'm not talking about outliers—they're dangerous enough. The ones to steer clear of are those apprenticed to dark sorcerers. Avoid them at all costs, and do not challenge or tangle with them for any reason."

Now, far enough away that they couldn't be overheard, Josiah continued the conversation with Peter. "You and your twin sister caused quite a stir at the Bazaar. At first, I thought it was accidental, but now I'm not so sure."

"What are you talking about?" asked Peter.

"You manage to find magical objects that have been lost for a hundred years or more. And on your first time through."

"What can I say? Cassandra has amazing *finding* abilities."

"That, or you are in league with a powerful sorcerer," said Josiah, watching Peter's face closely.

"Nah—we're just a couple of kids with *Powers*, running amuck," responded Peter glibly.

A strange look came across Josiah's face. "Interesting choice of words. So, let's just say that's true. Maybe buying the watch was a fluke, but getting it to slow time is another matter completely. How long ago did you figure it out?"

"Not long," said Peter, studying Josiah's thin, angular, young face and close-cropped hair. He really did look just like what Peter thought a monk would look like, passive but tough—maybe more Shaolin than Gregorian. "How'd you get here? You said something about docking a boat. Is it yours?"

"I'm borrowing it," responded Josiah dismissively.

"So what do I need to know about using the watch, Josiah?"

"You have extraordinary *Powers*, Peter, or you could not have done what you did today. I don't know if you thought about it or not, but when you slow time, you need to have a valid reason and know the people and the place that you will affect."

"Go on," said Peter, not particularly in the mood to be lectured.

"Things in the real world are very closely timed. Planes and trains run on schedules, and don't need to be running into one another. The unsuspecting person in slow time soon becomes exhausted, dazed, and confused, which often exposes them to danger. Prolonging life or postponing death was the one thing Govi feared the most. I told you the truth last October—the watch was given to the monks to extend the time they had for charitable works. When it was misused by evildoers—and it was— there were consequences. This kind of *Power* calls for artful awareness and intelligent reasoning."

"I get it. You made your point. So how do I define the right time and place?" asked Peter.

"I've read there's a brief moment before it starts, to name the place. For example, in the lunchroom instead of the entire bay, or in the movie theater as opposed to a whole city. And of course, it returns to normal when a preset timer sounds, like the chiming of a clock or even a reminder on your cell phone."

"If you screw up or there's an emergency, can you change back early?" asked Peter.

"I honestly don't know."

It was now dark enough for the gulls to go to sleep in safety, bouncing on the waves. As Josiah turned to head back toward the shops, he left Peter with a sobering message. "The dark ones know about your time *conjuring*. There's a price on your head, and they mean to kill you before you grow more powerful and become a threat to them."

"What about Cassandra? Is she in the same kind of danger?"

"She set the dreaded moon dragon free, and rules it, so what do you think, Peter?"

"So are you here to *protect* us?"

"Peter, I can *brew* a decent sleeping potion, which is what I call cocktails. I use my limited *enchanting* skills in lecture halls and podcasts. And, I can sail a pretty big boat. I'm an academic, a student, a teacher, and an amateur sailor. *Seeing* and *realizing*, not *protecting*, are my natural *Powers*. I'm only here to teach and forewarn." He turned and strode down the wharf, leaving Peter to process what he'd just been told.

Juliet and the aunts were locking their shop doors. The adults were too tired to talk, Peter was morbidly quiet, and Cassandra was more thoughtful than usual. Only Gabrielle chatted happily about their new Irish friend, and the fun things she had taught them. The evening air was clear but windy, and the moon was in its last night of waning. "*Sheee*," came a cry that filled the dark night's sky and bounced across the water. "*Sheeee*," it came again seconds later, as birds fluttered in the treetops and porch lights flashed on. "*Sheeeee*," it repeated, sounding longer, louder and more melancholy with each howl.

"I'm going home and locking the doors," said Gabrielle.

"Not a bad idea for all of us," advised Juliet.

"You knew what it was last night, and you said it had found us. So why is it making that noise?" Cassandra demanded of her Aunt Miranda.

"It's a banshee, an ancient creature that sends out warning calls of bad news."

"The bad news is someone's been targeted to die," said Peter.

"I just hope no one panics and calls the fire department. I'm bushed," said Penelope.

"How are you not bothered by any of this?" demanded Peter.

At that moment, the Cape Peril light, high on its bluff at the east end of the bay blinked on, the wind died down, and the fog came rolling in.

"See, kids, we'll be fine," said Juliet, as she and Gabrielle headed toward home.

"What did she mean by that? 'We'll be fine?'" said Peter, still pressing the issue on the drive home.

"She feels safe here, and her *Powers* are stronger than her fears."

"What if the danger the banshee is warning about has more *Powers* then she does?" asked Peter.

"Then Miranda will convene her charmed circle." Aunt Penelope laughed.

"That didn't work for poor Miss Tweaks," Cassandra threw in, taking Peter's side in the discussion.

"You are both right. We need to do a better job of keeping each other safe," said Miranda, and before they made it through the door, another "*Sheeee*" rang out.

The Last Day of School

T he next morning heavy thunderstorms blew in from the southwest. The mysterious fog was still thick and the aunts headed to the quay to open for Saturday shoppers. Peter and Cassandra stayed in the playroom and talked about the warnings they had received—hers from Maeve and his from Josiah. Peter explained to his sister what had happened with his watch, and Cassandra told him about Mademoiselle Sowbierre's note to an unnamed love, and her travel arrangements. Other than the mysterious loss of their parents, both agreed that their current round of trouble had started with the Smuggler's Bazaar. They spent an hour or more trying to remember all the characters they had met there and who the people were that were watching them on that last day at the Creaky Spar.

"Josiah was watching us at the Bazaar. We saw him speaking with the woman from the jewelry shop who sold me the moon dragon ring," said Cassie.

"And we saw that man with the red beard and tri-corner hat like mine talking with the kid from the junk cart who sold me the Govi watch," added Peter.

"Just how many people do you think were monitoring us and what we bought?" asked Cassie.

"Apparently a lot more than we realized, and some of them were keeping us from harm's way. Remember the woman who ushered us out of the Dark Arts Emporium?"

"Yes, the one with the blue cloak, that's Maeve, who gave the warning to Gabrielle and me."

"I don't think Josiah sitting at our table that day was a coincidence," said Peter.

"Probably not. And how strange that he and Maeve are here now."

"They're like everybody else. They came to see the sea monster."

They laid out Peter's watch, the light whips, and the scrimshaw whale, as well as Cassandra's book of spells, and her black-light flashlight. Cassandra even came up with the soot ball the whisperer had dropped, but Peter told her it was all used up.

"I'm not sure there's anything here we can use to defend ourselves," he said, then opened his watch and read the instructions on the box of light whips.

"They were right, you know, those two creeps who got torn up in the tunnel by my moon dragon. They said Plunder Bay was a pitiful excuse for a lost realm, with no sorcerer or guard to protect it, where kids with *Powers* run around casting spells and playing at magic."

"Your moon dragon? You are laying claim to it?"

"If it got released from my ring, and therefore I control it —then it's my moon dragon. And, she's a *She* not an *It*. Her name is Plundra."

Things were not going well for Mademoiselle Sowbierre in the old wing of the school. Because she had been late arriving, the van she reserved had been rented out to someone else, and she ended up with a compact sedan. She could find no one around the village or the school to help her load the theater costume trunks she wanted. Even the cheval mirror was so entwined in dream vines now, she could not budge it more than a few centimeters. With no shortage of expletives that would have made Blue blush, she crammed all the theater clothes she could carry into two large suitcases. She spent extra time on her hair and makeup, dressed herself in black leather pants, a red silk blouse, the snow leopard bolero jacket, and topped it all off with the Twilight Scarf. She wanted to look good. After taking a few minutes to admire her image in the mirror, she wrestled the two incredibly heavy suitcases into the ridiculously small car, maneuvered her large body into the driver's seat, and dashed off to keep her rendezvous.

Even though it was Saturday, the fog and stormy weather had kept customers away, so the aunts closed the shop at four o'clock and came home for dinner. Instead of hiding under the table waiting for tidbits from Cassandra's plate, Seadog stayed in the hallway with his back against the door. Blue sat on his perch with his head tucked under his wing like he had gone to bed early, and Miss Mew didn't touch her dinner.

"Wonder what's going on with them?" said Penelope.

As the aunts were putting away the dishes that Peter and Cassandra had dried, Aunt Penelope's fire-rescue pager went off, and Miranda's cell phone rang.

"The school's on fire!" screamed Aunt Miranda. "Reynelda can see the flames from her house."

"Maybe the fire boats can reach it. We'd better go. They'll need all the help they can get."

Peter and Cassandra jumped up from the table and went to get their jackets.

"No!" shouted the aunts in unison, and Miranda added,

C. S. Leonard

"You must not leave this house for any reason. Promise?"

Before the twins could promise, both aunts were gone. They stood at the open door and heard the screaming fire trucks from Soulac go by. The phone in the kitchen rang incessantly, but neither went to answer it. They ran upstairs to Peter's bedroom window on the north side of the house, but all they could see from his window was fog.

"Maybe the window in the playroom will give us a better view," said Cassie.

What they saw there only made things worse. The old Plunder Bay School could still be recognized, but with bright yellow flames leaping through the roof and bursting from the windows. There was a scramble of flashing lights as rescue vehicles jockeyed for position to aim their hoses at the burning building and siphon water from the bay. Above the flames, clouds of black smoke mingled with the fog, shut out the last daylight.

"I can't watch anymore," said a tearful Cassandra, heading back downstairs to the kitchen. She had reached the landing when she saw Seadog with his hackles up, and heard his low growl. There were headlights coming very slowly down the lane, and she called up to Peter.

From just inside the door, they watched as a very tall figure, in tight-fitting black leather pants, knee-high laced-up boots, and a black-and-white fur bolero jacket rose from the small car and walked toward the cottage.

"Cassandra and Peter, I know you're in there; come out so we can talk," came a deep, resonating voice like someone speaking from the bottom of a hollow well.

When neither twin responded, the hydrangea bush in front of the cottage burst into a ball of fire. They waited in silence, and a minute later, the forsythia shrubs on both sides of the cottage were burning.

"Come out or burn alive in there," threatened their attacker. "I've done the school. A house or two makes little difference to me now."

They knew their adversary, and they knew the lack of her fake French accent meant she was out for blood. Peter took his sister's hand and squeezed it, as he had done that day in the tunnel, and whispered, "Playroom."

They had reached the top of the stairs and turned to call the dog, when they heard the scream of the banshee. The horrid noise came from a small figure standing on their porch. The small woman was putting the fires out as fast as the other lit them, by summoning little rainclouds over each of the burning bushes. As the small visitor stepped out into the drive, a wall of water descended like a shield between the two dueling intruders and Cape Peril cottage. Keeping a lot of distance between them, they circled around one another. After a few minutes of this hostile dance, the fire starter shot a shard of white lightning at her opponent. From the playroom window, the twins could see it all. With the first white flash, Peter and Cassandra recognized the bright blue cloak of the lady who had rescued them at the Bazaar, and who warned Cassie the day before. For each white strike directed at her, Maeve returned one of her own, in glittering red bursts which were more intense, but did not travel as far or last as long.

Anything struck by the lightning shards disintegrated immediately—the gate into the kitchen garden, two small pine trees, and even the front porch step. When the tall one's car collapsed upon its axles, the fire starter rushed the banshee, using both huge hands to lob crossed beams of lightning. That brought Sowbierre into range of a direct red strike, and she doubled over in pain, bringing a temporary halt to the battle. Once recovered, Sowbierre rose in stature, and with a twirl of her wrist, sent out a blast of wind laced with blinking white sparks like fireflies in the summer garden. The hot blast was so strong it sent the debris from the forest floor flying through the air, causing the lady in blue to shield her eyes.

In return, a strong north wind blew in. It brought with it sleet and snow that created a blinding whiteout on the scene. Small ice devils with red eyes marched out of the forest to claw and bite at the fire starter's feet and ankles, but were soon sent rolling away like tumbleweeds in the wind. The hot wind hissed, and the north wind howled, as Peter and Cassandra stood there mesmerized. Of course, the twins were rooting for the lady in blue and would have done anything they could to help, but for now she seemed to be holding her own against her much taller adversary. There was a lull in the battle as the two combatants stood facing off against each other, with their hands resting on their knees and both gasping for breath, like they were out of wind.

Then Sowbierre stood up and raised both hands in a sign of surrender, she walked past the destroyed vehicle, and strode a short distance down the lane. Maeve relaxed a little, but before going too far—Sowbierre turned abruptly and cast a golden lasso of light that caught the lady in blue around her neck. Pulling it tighter and tighter, Sowbierre walked the golden-light rope back, laughing wickedly. She pounced upon her strangled victim—already on the ground—and began kicking her viciously.

Peter was out the door in a flash, then stopped at the east side of the cottage. "You want me? Here I am. Come get me!" He began walking backwards along the east side of the cottage.

"Hello, Peter," said the dark one in the same deep, echoing voice. She looked Peter straight in the eye, challenging him, she wanted a confrontation. Peter saw the Twilight Scarf, looped artfully around her long, thin neck.

"Hey, you know that snow leopard jacket is as fake as you are." He wanted her to follow him and drop the rope that was strangling Maeve.

Cassandra had followed right behind Peter and was standing just off the front porch. Once Sowbierre had turned the corner, in pursuit of Peter, she bent down beside the lady in blue. She loosened the gold lasso around her neck and checked to see if she was breathing. For a moment, she was torn between helping their brave defender or running to face the enemy with Peter. She realized there was a way to do both. Reaching into her jeans pocket, she grabbed the soot ball she had meant to throw away and gave it a hard squeeze. Disguised by soot and darkness, Cassandra half carried and half dragged her limp friend into the gazebo. She could see that Peter was keeping Sowbierre focused away from her and that he knew she was there. She grabbed the biggest fallen tree branch she could find. She crept up behind Sowbierre and delivered a powerful whack across Mademoiselle's head.

Sowbierre stumbled, but she didn't fall. She turned on Cassandra with feral green-black eyes, full of rage—but she couldn't see her. While she searched around the dark grounds for her attacker, Cassandra was gathering every big rock she could find and piling them in the gazebo. Peter took the moment of distraction to ready his light whips, and when Sowbierre came back toward him, he cast out thin coils of blue light that also made a popping sound.

Sowbierre stood with her hands on her hips and laughed at him. "You're a joke, a little boy with toys. You're as stupid as Deilman and Hicks."

"And how did that work out for them? I'd be careful if I were you," Peter warned, sounding braver than he felt.

Hearing or sensing movement in the gazebo, she turned and sent the little wooden building in motion, first with slow jerks, then spinning clockwise with increasing speed. It tossed the limp body of the banshee around the floor and left Cassandra visible.

"Cassandra, so glad you've joined us," she said, rubbing the back of her head. "I think I'll kill you first—slowly and painfully—while your brother watches." And with that, she cast a low ring of fire that encircled the twirling gazebo.

Scared, but not yet out of ideas, Peter took a running leap over the flames, grabbed hold of the railing, and joined the others in the moving structure. He fumbled in his pocket for his Govi watch, hoping he might stop time long enough for them to escape or slow it down enough for help to arrive. It wasn't there, he had left it on the table in the playroom, along with his shepherd's whistle. Cassie read the look on his face and knew they were in trouble.

"Cassie, use *your* shepherd's whistle!" he said.

"I left it in the playroom," she replied. With that sad fact, they felt all hope slip away.

Under the circumstances, the twins would have thought Mademoiselle would be elated, watching and enjoying her victory and their demise. Instead, she appeared to be afraid. She rose above the ground, and glided in the opposite direction around the gazebo, with the beautiful long scarf unwrapping itself several loops and wafting out behind her. The light from the ring of fire surrounding them showed her face, ugly and contorted—and just as she often did in class, she began talking to people who weren't there.

"I am *Number One*! No one has more power!" she called out as she circled. "All I had to do was get the ring, and I could have done it on my own, without their meddling." Sounding more desperate with each pass, she continued. "The librarian caught me off guard in the theater that night, but I dealt with her!"

The wooden wind chimes in the spinning gazebo rang out melodically like nothing was wrong. The ring of flames around them grew higher and hotter as Maeve stirred back to life, trying to sit up. Peter was astounded to see Blue on his perch, watching Sowbierre fly by with only a slight ruffling of his feathers.

"I would have taken the moon dragon ring from her dead finger, but she found the tunnel opening before the tide could drown them," she confessed into the night air. "She is a very skilled *finder*, very valuable. I can give her to you now in exchange," Sowbierre proposed, widening her circles of flight to avoid the hot flames.

The only response to her bargain plea was a long roll of distant thunder.

"One mistake—I only made one mistake. Why Gorgona, why must I die now in this infernal place?" she screeched.

It was at this point that a most peculiar thing occurred. The trailing Twilight Scarf tangled around a limb of the big grey birch tree. Holding her tightly by her long, thin neck, it swung Mademoiselle Sowbierre—the Number One apprentice to a very dark sorceress—far out over the cliffs, to the waves breaking on the jagged rocks below.

The spinning gazebo slowed and stopped, and a gentle spring shower poured down to dampen the fire. The light in the lighthouse tower came to life, and the occupants of the gazebo staggered back indoors.

Maeve was a little worse for wear, but had certainly proven she could do more than close umbrellas. The aunts were shocked to see Peter pouring tea for a stranger in the kitchen when they arrived home very late that night.

"This is Maeve Campbell, and she was dying for a cup of tea," said Peter, hoping to lighten everybody's mood.

"Whose wrecked car is in the driveway, and what happened to the front porch step?" asked Aunt Penelope, collapsing onto a kitchen chair, smelling of smoke and ashes.

"Pretty much the same thing that happened to the school. Is there anything left of it?" asked Cassie.

"Nothing. Everyone is devastated, and we worked so hard to put it out. It's heartbreaking,"

"How is Miss Tweaks taking it? Losing the school might be the end of her," said Peter.

"Oh, she's quite relieved," said Aunt Miranda. "The fire didn't touch the historic stone wing, just the newer cinderblock portions. The fire marshal inspected the inside and said there's not even a broken pane of glass in the library ceiling. I guess Reynelda scored a hit with that last protection spell—even though it cost her dearly."

"They do know it was arson, don't they?" asked Peter.

"Oh yes, they know because she started the fire in a dozen different places, with no effort to conceal what she was doing," said Aunt Penelope, as she dragged her tired body toward the stairs.

"Then everyone knows it was Mademoiselle Sowbierre?" asked Cassie and Peter in unison.

"Apparently you two do," said a surprised Aunt Penelope, returning to the kitchen. "Why did you say it was Sowbierre?"

"Why did you say the arsonist was a 'she'?" returned Peter.

"Because Adam Boggins and his brother-in-law said when they left the school shortly before the fire started, she was the only one still in the building. Now it's your turn, you two."

Peter remained quiet, probably because he had no idea where to begin, and it was Cassandra who spoke up. "Sowbierre was here tonight and made it clear that she burned the school. She also revealed, in a strange sort of confession, that she did a lot of other bad stuff."

"Where is she now?" asked Aunt Miranda calmly.

She's dead," said Cassie, realizing immediately how strange it sounded.

Maeve squirmed in her chair a little and decided to let the twins handle the explanations.

"She's dead? How did she die?" she asked, glancing up at Blue.

"Well, she came here after you left and said she was going to burn Peter and me alive in the cottage, then she had a fight with Maeve and flew around the gazebo wearing Miss Tweaks's Twilight Scarf—until it got caught in the birch tree and slingshotted her over the cliff," explained Cassandra, without stopping to take a breath.

"It was an accident," said Peter solemnly.

"With that," said Penelope, "I think I'll go take a shower and head to bed."

"Yeah, me too," declared Peter before anyone could ask any more questions.

Cassandra offered Maeve the spare room for the night, and they headed up after Peter.

"I think I'll just have some quiet time alone," said Miranda, putting on the kettle.

Unnoticed in the dark and terror of the night, the great moon dragon rose from the rocky shore when the tide rolled out, then spread its nearly invisible, translucent, silver wings and flew out over the sea.

Bye-bye Bandicoots

Maeve Campbell ate a hearty breakfast, exclaiming how much better it was than breakfast made in the galley kitchen on the yacht. "Josiah will be in a panic wondering where I am. We're friends, and often work together at bazaars or on special assignments of magical importance. I hate to rush away, but it's probably best that I do, before too many people start asking questions."

"Is that your wrecked car out in the driveway?" asked Miranda.

"No, it was hers, and we shouldn't leave it there like that. Since I broke it, I guess I'll have to be the one who fixes it. Mechanical things are a specialty of mine, kind of a hobby."

Peter gulped the last of his orange juice and hurried out behind Maeve to watch what she was doing. Looking through the wreckage, they found two nearly empty large suitcases and a fake snakeskin purse, which both decided should remain in the back seat of the car. Then, Peter watched intently as the lady in blue took a small wooden wand from her cloak pocket, tapped the front and back of the vehicle, and before his eyes, it was not only repaired, but the motor was idling.

"It's a rush job, but it will have to do for the time being," she said. She climbed behind the wheel, adjusted the seat and mirrors, and fastened the seatbelt.

Cassandra and Aunt Miranda rushed out to exchange email addresses and wave goodbye.

"Wish we had reminded her to fix the garden gate," said Cassie, which really meant she would have liked to spend more time with their new friend.

"The most important thing right now is to get your Aunt Penelope out of bed and for the McBees to try to get our stories straight."

"Swab the decks!" Blue was screeching when they got back to the kitchen, and Miranda agreed that was probably the first thing they needed to do. She sent Peter and Cassandra outside to clean up what they could of last night's disastrous battle. The old gazebo was scorched but didn't look that bad. Peter walked out to the edge of the cliff where the Twilight Scarf still dangled from the big birch tree. He stood there for a long time, looking down as if he expected to see Sowbierre's body splayed out on the rocks below, but it wasn't. Cassandra joined him, and together they tried to free the tangled scarf. It was not until Blue came to help that they could retrieve it. Cassandra gently folded the long, dazzling piece of cloth.

"Actually, this saved our lives," she said to her brother. "I guess you could say Mademoiselle finally picked out just the right outfit.

"Apparently, she was marked for death by Gorgona as soon as the moon dragon came to life," said Peter. "Remember the message on her desk, *Her living, will be our undoing*? After that, the hourglass was marking time for her—and she knew it."

The twins were happy to learn that they had been inside all last evening watching the live streaming coverage of the fire. If they had a visit from the arsonist, they did not know it. The poor hydrangea bush was a mess, but the forsythia looked good after Penelope wacked it with the shears. The porch step and the garden gate were missing entirely, so there would be need for explanation there.

As it turned out, it was not necessary for any McBee to lie or answer questions. The authorities, with the exception of the young fire marshal, handled the absence of Mademoiselle Sowbierre in the same slipshod way they had dealt with the matter of Miss Tweaks. If there was no body, there was no crime, except for the small matter of the landmark school being burned to the ground, and that was the fire marshal's problem to investigate.

By afternoon, it was time for the McBees, like everyone else in Plunder Bay, to go see the smoking ruins of the old school. All but the theater and library were rubble. All of the Plunder Bay residents fought back tears. The fire chief walked among them, apologizing for not being able to save more of the building. Some of the older people were telling stories of the happy days they had spent there. Others were angry, tossing around theories about how the fire had started and who the guilty party was.

Peter and Cassandra joined Will and Gabrielle, who were trying to picture where the cafeteria used to be. They pondered among themselves as to what the loss of the school would mean for the village. They had already accepted the reality that they would be going to school somewhere else next year, but that did not make the scene less devastating. They vowed to stay close with their friends, and Gabrielle brought up the idea of starting some kind of club so they could keep their magic lessons going over the summer.

"I hope Cody's rats made it out alive," said Peter.

"You mean the bandicoots?" said Will.

"The what?" said the other three together.

"Yeah, I found out a long time ago they were a breed of marsupial, an endangered species, omnivores from Australia—not giant ferocious rats with glowing eyes. Whatever the poor things were doing down in the school cellar, I never figured out. Someone was feeding them scraps and stuff the grocery stores throw out. Poor buggers."

"And you didn't tell anybody?"

"I told my parents what they were, but I don't think they believed me, and I was afraid it'd cause more bad publicity for the school. Probably doesn't matter now."

The harbormaster joined his niece and her friends to report what information he had gathered. The fire at the school was not an accident and had most likely been set by an unstable woman, a substitute teacher at the school who was terrified by the sea monster stories and had recently been jilted by some guy she was in love with.

"So, did they arrest Mademoiselle Sowbierre?" asked Gabrielle.

"They found her beat-up rental down at the wharf, with a few personal items the police are holding. Best guess is she left by sea during the commotion last night, or even started the fire to cover her tracks. I was too busy last night to see what boats were coming and going."

"Maybe the Ministry of Education paid her to do it after Amadan tried and failed to destroy the school?" said Will.

The harbormaster laughed. "You sound like Maggie O'Day."

On their way down to the shops on the quay, the friends stepped aside to let a truck go by. It was a vehicle they had never seen before because it had been tarped all winter. It

Treasures of Plunder Bay

was an old box truck, hand-painted in a myriad of cheerful colors. Behind the wheel was Mr. Boggins's brother-in-law with his wife and kids. As it turned left on the Coast Road, the three could plainly see, in faded colors painted on the side of the truck, three snarling rats and a sign that read:

Come One, Come All!
See The Amazing Giant Rats
Live From The Sewers Of Paris!
Admission: Adults $10 - Children $5.50

C. S. Leonard created the McBee Magic series incorporating her insights and understanding of young readers after a career teaching middle school and high school literature, creative writing, and theater. Woven into her storytelling are vivid characters and rich scenes inspired by her personal experiences teaching and working with young people. Her love of all things nautical and magical—combined with a passion for bringing captivating stories to readers—makes the McBee Magic series an enthralling reading experience!

Connect Online

DaegbrecanPublishing.com

 @Daegbrecan

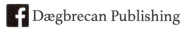 Dægbrecan Publishing

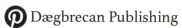 Dægbrecan Publishing

CPSIA information can be obtained
at www.ICGtesting.com
Printed in the USA
BVHW032242120222
628890BV00008B/87/J

9 781955 810128